ROSIE CHAMBERS loves writing uplifting, feel-good stories set in sun-filled locations around the world. Her stories are filled with fun, friendship and foodie treats, which Rosie hopes will bring a smile to her readers' faces. She's always in the market for quirky stationery and is never happier than with a pen in one hand and a cup of tea in the other. *A Year of Chasing Love* is her debut novel.

A Year of Chasing Love

ROSIE CHAMBERS

ONE PLACE. MANY STORIES

This novel is entirely a work of fiction. The names, characters
and incidents portrayed in it are the work of the author's
imagination. Any resemblance to actual persons, living or
dead, events or localities is entirely coincidental.

HQ
An imprint of HarperCollins*Publishers* Ltd
1 London Bridge Street
London SE1 9GF

This edition 2020

First published in Great Britain by
HQ, an imprint of HarperCollins*Publishers* Ltd 2020

ISBN: 978-0-00-836476-2

MIX
Paper from
responsible sources
FSC® C007454

This book is produced from independently certified FSC™ paper
to ensure responsible forest management.

For more information visit: www.harpercollins.co.uk/green

Printed and bound in Great Britain by
CPI Group (UK) Ltd, Croydon, CR0 4YY

To all those who choose love.

Prologue

'There's a guy in reception asking to see you, Olivia.'

'Did you ask him to make an appointment?'

'I did, but he said he'd wait for as long as it took for you to see him.'

Olivia sighed. As a divorce lawyer she often had clients calling into the office, hoping to see her straight away, desperate for someone to listen to their story. Usually she didn't mind, and if she didn't have a prior engagement, she'd try her best to accommodate them in her crammed-to-bursting diary. After all, she knew how hard it was to take those first steps to visit a solicitor, never mind rustling up the courage to divulge the most heart-breaking details of your failed marriage to a complete stranger.

'Okay, no problem. I'll squeeze him in before I see Mrs Coulson at eleven thirty.'

'Shall I show him up to your office?'

'No, no, it's okay. I need a coffee so I'll come downstairs with you. You never know, I might be able to persuade him to make an appointment.'

Olivia pinned a professional smile on her face and followed Katrina down the corridor, giggling at the clickety-clack of their stilettos on the polished wood flooring. Little did she know that

1

would be the last time she would laugh for a long time, because as soon as she stepped into the reception area, a crumple-faced man leapt out of his seat, reached into the pocket of his grubby raincoat, and extracted a large manila envelope which, incongruously, he then waved in the air. The glee reflected in his hard, ball-bearing eyes was the absolute antithesis of the bewildered confusion that was racing through her veins.

'Mrs Fitzgerald?'

'Yes?' Very few people outside her circle of friends knew her married name. Alarm bells started to ring, and she exchanged a quick glance with Katrina who was staring at the man with patent dislike. 'What can I do for you, Mr …?'

In order to elongate the drama, the man took a few moments to survey the elegant, marble-walled foyer of Edwards & Co, Solicitors and Commissioners for Oaths – already devoid of its Christmas decorations despite twelfth night being the following day – deriving obvious pleasure from the perplexed expressions on the faces of his audience. A tickle of recognition began to agitate at the edges of Olivia's memory; the dishevelled attire, the ill-disguised porcine proportions, the whiff of stale nicotine. Where had she seen him before?

'Just leave the papers and get out!' snapped Katrina, the first of her colleagues to step forward to break the freeze-frame image.

Without further ado, the envelope was thrust into Olivia's hands and the process server ambled towards the smoked-glass elevator, a grin on his face and an air of satisfaction following in his wake. As the doors slid shut behind him, the burble of conversation magnified. No one needed a Private Detective badge to work out that what had just transpired had come as a complete shock to Olivia.

'Come on,' said Katrina. 'I think some privacy is—'

'Hey, I know that guy!' announced Miles, a fellow divorce lawyer and Olivia's least favourite colleague. 'That was Jack Leyland, Ralph Carlton's personal lackey – does all his dirty work for him. What was he doing here, though? I thought we instructed that ballet-shoed princess, Heidi Fowler, to deliver all our court documents, not that piranha. Although, I've always said that Jack does have his uses. Are we changing our approach at last?'

Ralph Carlton was renowned throughout the legal profession as the go-to rottweiler in the field of matrimonial litigation, which could only mean one thing. Olivia's stomach gave a pain-filled lurch and a curl of nausea began its assiduous journey around her chest.

Oh God, surely not!

'No, Miles, we ...' she muttered, desperately trying to reconnect her brain to its modem.

'Because I have to tell you, all this conciliatory, non-confrontational malarkey is starting to scratch at my balls. We need to get a lot tougher in our negotiations, especially after that article about you being London's Top Divorce Lawyer appeared in the local rag. Ridiculous accolade, if you ask me – just because you've achieved the questionable milestone of having handled five hundred divorces doesn't mean that—'

'Shut up, Miles. Haven't you got secretaries to harass?' said Katrina mildly, taking charge of the situation and guiding Olivia out of the reception and back down the corridor to her corner office.

By now, panic was beginning to ricochet around Olivia's body, her throat had contracted around what felt like a prickly pear, and she felt light-headed. She collapsed onto the overstuffed leather sofa she used to interview the more emotional clients who sought her advice and slowly slid the paperwork out of the envelope as if it contained a poisoned pen letter – the effect it caused was almost as bad.

Because London's Top Divorce Lawyer had just been served with her very own divorce petition.

Chapter 1

'I didn't think he'd do it, Kat.'

Olivia sunk into the 'sympathy couch' and met her friend's eyes, her fingers trembling on the rectangular missive of tragedy. The shock of the public ambush had begun to thaw but the horror remained, settling just below where her heart hammered out a symphony of sorrow against her ribcage. Nausea lingered at the back of her throat, constricting the flow of oxygen, and the threat of tears blurred her vision.

'I know, Liv, I know,' murmured Katrina, patting her hand and offering her a tissue.

Olivia accepted, dabbed the corners of her eyes and started to peruse the documents.

'Oh, my God, no! I don't believe it.'

'What?'

'Nathan's cited Unreasonable Behaviour! Listen to this! *The Respondent is a workaholic, often spending in excess of eighteen hours a day at her office, refusing to accept, and dismissing the importance of, her responsibilities to their relationship. Many holidays and weekends away have been cancelled or cut short due to the tenacity with which the Respondent pursues her career.*'

'Oh, Liv, I'm so sorry ...'

'And what about this: *The Respondent has persistently neglected the Petitioner and their extended family and friends despite numerous attempts by the Petitioner to rectify their growing estrangement.* And this: *Since the inception of their partnership, the Petitioner has made clear to the Respondent his desire to start a family but* … Oh my God, no, no, no, no …'

The anguish churning through her veins threatened to overwhelm her as she continued to read the painful litany of accusations, and the stark truth of what lay at the crux of their problems was revealed.

'*But the Respondent refuses to contemplate the proposal, continually deflecting the Petitioner's heartfelt pleas to participate in a rational and intelligent conversation, citing the importance of her career over the creation of a family.*'

Olivia raised her eyes to meet Katrina's and the sympathy scrawled across her friend's face almost caused her to crumble completely. She swallowed down hard, inhaled a steadying breath and made an attempt to corral her rampaging emotions. She had to admit she was acutely aware of Nathan's desire to start a family. At his lavish fortieth birthday party at The Dorchester just before Christmas, she'd witnessed for herself the hunger in his heart as he had hugged each one of Katrina and Will's three young children in turn when they presented him with a selection of home-made birthday cards covered in dried pasta and sequins. But reading about his rejected yearning for fatherhood as a ground for her 'unreasonable behaviour' in bold, black typescript, well, it shocked her to the core.

'Look, Liv, these things always sound worse when they're written down.'

'We always say that to our clients, don't we? Well, let me tell you now, for the record, those words are no consolation. I promise that from now on, I won't be caught trotting out that old chestnut again.'

'And you know what? I'm absolutely certain this is all Ralph

Carlton's doing – he's the ultimate exploiter of human misery! No wonder you had no advance warning – it's his trademark.'

Olivia thought of the undisguised triumph in the process server's eyes. The knowledge that he would, at that very moment, be scurrying back to his employer to recount every painful detail, caused her cheeks to flood with warmth. Then, her mind switched to the headlines that had been splashed across the local newspaper the previous month. The story had also been picked up by the *Law Society Gazette*, as part of their end-of-year round-up of news, which had ensured maximum publicity for the article celebrating the debatable accomplishment of her five hundredth divorce.

She had squirmed at the label the tabloid had bestowed on her – *'London's Top Divorce Lawyer'*. She knew the dubious badge of honour would rile many of her peers but especially Ralph Carlton who had grabbed that self-styled accolade for himself years before. In fact, she wouldn't put it past him to casually leak the little gem that that same 'Top Divorce Lawyer' had joined the exclusive club no one wanted a golden pass for. She knew any gossip would spread like red wine on a cream carpet, and even if Ralph didn't breach the code of ethics on client confidentiality, she had no difficulty in remembering Miles's fascinated attention in the foyer and he was one of the biggest gossips she knew.

'Liv, everyone knows Ralph Carlton is a rabid vulture who feasts on the bones of broken relationships. I can totally picture him now, grinning away on his dung-splattered perch as he drafted those awful allegations. Nathan would never say any of those things.'

'But, sadly, not one of them is untrue. I *do* neglect Nathan, and our family and friends! I *do* work all waking hours here at my desk – my personal life is just one of the casualties I left in my wake when I chose the marbled entrance hall of Edwards & Co twelve years ago. I *do* cancel our date nights and I *do* miss important landmark birthdays. Remember Nathan's mother's sixtieth?'

Olivia grimaced with shame as she recalled the expression of displeasure on her mother-in-law's over-powdered face when she'd dashed into The Music Room at The Ritz an hour after the word 'Surprise!' had been hollered.

'Yes, maybe, but Nathan works just as hard as you do. *And* he's away from home more often than you are.'

Loyalty drew an indignant expression on Katrina's olive-toned features, but no amount of heartfelt empathy could distract Olivia now that she was on a roll of rigorous self-analysis and recrimination.

'*And* remember those VIP, rarer-than-gold-dust tickets Nathan landed for the opening night of *Waitress* at the Adelphi Theatre last year? How I'd been banging on about going to see the show for ages? But it was Hollie who ended up going as his "plus-one" – his wife's best friend instead of his neglectful wife! And I've lost count of how many "must-have" restaurant reservations we've cancelled.'

'But, Liv—'

'*And* the one about the missed holidays is true. In the seven years since our honeymoon, we've managed a weekend trip to Blackpool to watch Rachel and Denise dance at the Winter Gardens, and a flying visit to Edinburgh to see his brother, Dan, get married. But, if I recall correctly, even on that occasion I insisted we caught the first flight back to London so we could be at our desks at the crack of dawn on Monday morning. In fact—' she loathed the squirm of guilt that wriggled through her abdomen '—I have to confess that I actually popped into the office on the way back from Heathrow.'

'Olivia—'

'*And* Nathan has tried to talk to me about starting a family. That one's true, too. It's just I'm not ready to give up on my career for a pile of dirty laundry and cracked nipples. Miles would almost certainly muscle in on my caseload and he'd ruin everything I've been building these last few years with his attitude of bulldog rather than guide dog! I can't give it all up to swan off and have a family. I just can't!'

'Life doesn't end when you have kids, you know.' Katrina smiled, sweeping her long mahogany hair over her shoulder, her eyes softening at the mention of children.

But Olivia had all the evidence of the impact of motherhood right in front of her eyes. Katrina possessed a first-class honours degree in law from Durham University, Olivia's own college where *she* had only managed a 2:1. In fact, if Olivia were brutally honest with herself – and what better time than now – she would have to admit that Katrina was a better lawyer than she was. Nevertheless, her friend was content with her position as paralegal at Edwards & Co in return for flexible, part-time hours so she could put her expanding family's needs first. *'Date nights, not late nights'* was Katrina's mantra.

'Nathan is ambitious, too,' insisted Katrina, coming to sit next to Olivia on the couch. 'Wasn't he in Paris for a month before his birthday, and isn't he about to start a six-month secondment to Singapore next week?'

Olivia acknowledged the veracity of Katrina's argument but didn't mention the qualifying mitigation that Nathan had pleaded with her to fly over to Paris for a pre-Christmas weekend whilst he was there, all expenses paid. The 'City of Romance' held a special place in both their hearts as the French capital was where they'd honeymooned, and yet despite this, Olivia had been unable to drag herself away from her precious clients, or her volunteer work at the local homeless shelter at their busiest time of the year.

However, she knew it was her refusal to contemplate a sabbatical from work to travel with him to Singapore that had provided Nathan with the impetus to end their marriage – the first step of which she held in her ice-cold hands. She cringed as she recalled the disappointment and hurt that she'd seen etched on his handsome features as he had begged her to start the new year by seizing the opportunity to mend their flagging relationship.

'How can he expect me to ditch my career and go chasing after him halfway around the world?' she pleaded, twirling a strand of her toffee-coloured hair absent-mindedly around her fingertip, but she could see from Katrina's hesitancy that her chosen line of advocacy was weak.

'He only wanted you to take a couple of weeks off, help him to settle in, spend some quality time together – not resign your partnership at Edwards & Co.'

'But my clients depend on me!'

'Your clients would've managed without you, Liv. Miles might be a pain in the butt and profess a different approach to marriage breakdown than you, but he's a good enough lawyer.'

'But I loathe the way Miles and Ralph Carlton do business, racking up the acrimony with twisted truths and spurious allegations.' She brandished the envelope in her hand as evidence. 'Inciting the parties to fight over their pepper pots and garden gnomes so that their legal fees are exorbitant and the money cascades into the lawyers' coffers.'

Olivia knew that the majority of her clients were involuntary refugees from the countless matrimonial conflicts waging across London and the Home Counties. They chose to consult her because she took an interest in their emotional wellbeing as well as the paperwork. She listened to their grievances, smoothed over the thorny issues of contact with the children and dividing the joint assets, offered pragmatic solutions as well as the astute application of legal principles. An involuntary smile twitched her lips as she recalled the ridiculously childish correspondence she had been forced to discuss only yesterday with Martha Grainger, the CEO of an ethical jewellery company, when Ralph's client, Martha's ex-husband, had demanded shared access to their allotment of chickens.

Would she and Nathan descend into the quagmire of such pettiness?

Her emotions crashed again. It was the new year, a time for looking forward and making resolutions, and she was getting divorced! All the sadness, the verbal spats, the possessiveness, the obstructiveness and the squabbling that she dealt with on a daily basis would be lurking for her own indulgence as the dissolution of her marriage travelled through the divorce court.

Then an added horror poked its nose above the parapet. Was Nathan involved with someone else? She shoved that pernicious thought deep into the crevices of her mind. If Nathan was anything at all, he was an honest and straightforward guy, favouring the communication of difficult issues in a balanced, non-confrontational way, but he had been pushing against an immoveable concrete barrier the previous year when wanting to talk seriously about their future. Whenever they were at home together in their pristine apartment overlooking the River Thames, she was usually so exhausted that any conversation beyond what was for dinner was too taxing to contemplate. No, she knew Nathan would not be dating anyone else.

There would be no vitriol or salacious accusations for the Fitzgeralds. Whilst she was mortified at the way the divorce papers had been delivered, and revolted at his choice of legal representative, after the initial shock and disbelief had dissipated, she had to admit the commencement of the divorce process had not come as a surprise. If there was ever a good time to end a marriage, then this was it: a new year, a fresh start, *and* whilst Nathan was away in Singapore – leaving her alone in London to sort out their apartment without the added awkwardness of living together under the same roof.

A mantle of loneliness draped its folds around her body and settled heavily across her shoulders. The delivery of that simple brown envelope meant her destiny was now shrouded in a veil of ambiguity.

'You're due loads of leave, Liv. Why don't you take a trip to see your parents in Yorkshire?'

'I can't go to Yorkshire, Kat.'

Olivia pushed herself out of the depths of the sofa, straightened her charcoal-grey pencil skirt and strode over to her desk. She shoved the offending documents into her bottom drawer and turned to look out of the window. From the twelfth floor, the view over the angular rooftops of the City of London was awe-inspiring but one which she seldom noticed, much less appreciated. A shaft of early January sunshine had the audacity to bathe the room with its wintry light, and she managed a brittle smile at the irony – surely there should be a cacophonous thunderstorm raging and rain lashing against the windowpanes?

Except this wasn't a nightmare, or a horror film; it was reality and she had to deal with it.

'I suppose I'd better inform Henry of my impending single-hood.'

Chapter 2

'I'm extremely saddened to hear your news, Olivia. Nathan is not only an intelligent and competent corporate lawyer but a decent, considerate man. Jean and I were delighted when we heard he was being promoted to Lead Counsel at Delmatrix Pharmaceuticals at their Singapore office. You youngsters today have so many opportunities.'

Olivia squirmed a little under the steely pewter gaze of Henry Edwards, the senior partner of Edwards & Co, feeling dwarfed by the gravity of the situation she found herself in, and the wing-backed leather chair facing his gargantuan desk that wouldn't have looked out of place in a Gentleman's Club. However, after being his business partner for almost ten years, she knew whatever pearls of wisdom he was about to dispense, they would be judiciously selected and carefully delivered.

'Olivia, it's time I spoke frankly with you. Jean and I are worried about your health. It's apparent to even the most casual of onlookers that you're not sleeping well. And when did you last enjoy a decent meal – and I do *not* mean those psychedelic cocktails that you, Hollie and Matteo devour with such gusto? You need to take a break from the legal grindstone, especially after this life-changing event.'

'Henry, I—'

'No, please, just listen.'

Henry ran his arthritic fingers through his thick, ash-coloured hair, for the first time displaying a hint of reticence, clearly somewhat uncomfortable with treading the line between showing concern for his younger partner's obsessive work patterns and invading her privacy.

'I know you're not going to like me saying this, but I miss the spirited, rosy-cheeked woman of twenty-nine I met ten years ago; eager, ambitious, brimming with energy and enthusiasm for the law. It hurts me to see how much that young lawyer has transformed into the frazzled, exhausted, stressed-out person who sits before me now and I truly regret not noticing sooner.'

'Henry, I'm not—'

'Please, Olivia, hear me out. For the first time, Jean and I have made a few New Year's resolutions and if all goes according to plan, this time next year we'll be boarding a luxury liner for a round-the-world cruise. Life is short, and every day becomes more precious as the age of seventy is waiting in the wings to ambush us. Jean deserves the indulgence of her long-held dream, and to that end I've reserved a Princess Grill Stateroom on the *Queen Elizabeth*.'

Olivia smiled. She was delighted that Jean had got her own way at last. She knew the division of labour in the Edwards marriage was considered old-fashioned; Jean, giving up her career as a midwife to devote her gentle-but-firm skills to steering their two beloved daughters through life's challenges – both of whom had chosen to follow their mother's footsteps into medicine – whilst Henry performed the role of breadwinner and doting father. She was about to congratulate him on his decision, but Henry had already launched into the next part of his submission.

'I struggled to recall the precise nature of the clause in our partnership agreement pertaining to the taking of sabbaticals, so I took the liberty of checking. After ten years of service, all

Edwards & Co partners, including you, Olivia my dear, qualify for a ten-month sabbatical at half their monthly drawings.'

'I qualify? I thought it was you and Jean who were planning to take the world by storm?'

The switch in focus caused a twist of anxiety to whip through Olivia's veins and she dug her fingernails into her palms to prevent herself from reaching up to fiddle with an escaped tendril of hair to alleviate the unease that had settled in her gut. What was going on? She didn't have to wait long to find out.

'Take a break, Olivia. Spend some time away from the crazy, soul-destroying world of divorce and relationship breakdown, of clients squabbling over meaningless possessions, of financial skulduggery and underhand espionage. Do you know, I even heard the other day that a lawyer had plundered the depths of decency by removing the dustbin from a spouse's back garden? I mean, what is the legal profession coming to? How you and Katrina remain sane is a constant worry to Lewis, James and I.'

Henry expelled a sigh filled with incredulity, and not a little relief, that his chosen legal specialism was commercial property litigation and tax management and not the cut-and-thrust of verbal jousting prevalent in the field of matrimonial litigation. However, his words had sent Olivia's thoughts reeling and it took her a few seconds to catch up, her throat dry when she spoke.

'Henry, I really can't take time off at the moment ...'

'I'm not saying you won't be missed, or that we don't appreciate how valuable your contribution is to our practice. You listen to your clients, Olivia, really listen. You empathise with their circumstances, and somehow you manage to instil in them the belief that their case is your only priority. Indeed, since you joined us, the Family Law department has flourished beyond anything we could have hoped to achieve. Clients, particularly women, have flocked to your office, but the fact that divorce has become so increasingly popular dismays me. Why don't couples stay together nowadays? No, you don't have to answer that!'

Henry settled back into his captain's chair, steepled his fingers and tapped them on his lower lip, eyeing Olivia carefully.

'But I can also see that the pressure of an ever-expanding caseload has sapped your energy and dulled that initial sparkle. And now, it seems, it has destroyed your marriage. Is it contagious, this incessant search for the elusive prize of contentment?'

'I love what I do, Henry …'

'Only too obvious, Olivia my dear, as I understand you already struggle to delegate even the most straightforward of cases to Miles, even though he is a very competent practitioner.'

Olivia clenched her jaw in a futile attempt to prevent Henry from reading the doubt she knew was written boldly across her expression. She had never been first in line when they were handing out acting accolades – learning how to hide her emotions was still a work-in-progress, and it was one of the few essential skills required to be a first-rate lawyer that she had trouble mastering.

'Oh, I know that you and Miles have conflicting views on how you conduct your cases, but I also know that he is eager to prove himself, to carve out his own niche in the department – the law had always possessed a vociferous appetite for the naïve but ambitious young lawyer seeking to make his mark – and I'm not entirely unsympathetic to his desire to change the firm's approach to our matrimonial cases.'

Like many lawyers, Olivia relished sharpening her advocacy and negotiation skills against her legal adversaries, but never to the detriment of her clients' interests. It had always been her aim to assist her clients in a more holistic way, by offering accurate legal advice coupled with a dose of therapy, a cordial attitude to negotiations and a conciliatory approach. Of course, she was going to be better briefed than most on the up-to-date case law in her field because her long-time friend Rachel Denton, who had recently gained a Professorship in Family Law at UCL, made sure of that.

'I can't take a sabbatical, Henry, if that's what you are suggesting. My clients rely on me to be here for them and I can't let them down.'

'They can easily transfer their matters to Miles, and I dare say that Lewis will do his bit.'

Olivia's mind immediately flicked to her fellow partner Lewis Jackson's office, where the windowsill was piled high with carelessly discarded bottles of single malt whisky – gifts from grateful clients as tokens of appreciation for the personal injury compensation he had won on their behalf. Even James Carter, who handled their criminal defence work, had been known to receive a bottle or two of Cognac, although its provenance probably didn't bear close scrutiny. On the other hand, Olivia's office sported a plethora of flower-bedecked cards from clients whose shattered lives she had been a reluctant but necessary part of, and whom could not bring themselves to *thank* her for her involvement in such an interlude of pain.

'Katrina will be a more than competent adviser, too. And what an opportune time to take a break having passed that dubious milestone that I saw reported in December's issue of the *Law Society Gazette*.'

Olivia gulped as her predicament rushed at her like a runaway express train and an involuntary shudder ran the length of her spine as she realised her own marriage would now be joining that running total of five hundred marriage dissolutions. And Henry was wrong – if ever there was a time to take a break from the treadmill of corporate life, this was most certainly *not* it! She needed the distraction.

'But, Henry, I really can't contemplate ...'

She heard him inhale a long breath, splaying his liver-spotted hands across his desk blotter, clearly preparing himself for what he had to deliver next and her heart crashed against her ribcage, causing spasms of trepidation to ricochet around her body.

'It's a timely solution, Olivia. This is a difficult subject for me to discuss, but the firm's income has tumbled considerably over the last year or so. All this ruddy uncertainty has bitten us all hard. To be honest, a 50 per cent reduction in your drawings would ease the burden on our Office Account expenditure.'

Olivia didn't know what she had expected Henry to say, but it wasn't that. Trepidation swiftly morphed into full-blown panic – if she'd thought her discussion with Henry about her divorce was going to be difficult, this conversation had climbed to a whole new level and she needed to fight her corner.

'Henry, I realise the way I conduct my cases means there are fewer contested trials, and therefore there are not as many lucrative invoices at the end. But even so, the effects of a countrywide economic downturn can't be laid at my office door!'

'Of course not, and I wasn't implying that, far from it. I'm actually very troubled by the breakdown of your marriage, Olivia, and the fact that your intensive work ethic may have in some way contributed to the sad state of affairs. No more ideal a couple have I come across than you and Nathan, and Jean agrees with me. You are so right for one another. If I'd been a betting man, I would have placed a month's salary on you and Nathan being in the lucky half of the UK marriages that don't end in divorce.'

'Me neither, Henry, but it's happened, and I have to deal with it.'

A surge of sorrow spread through Olivia's chest when she saw the genuine sadness reflected in Henry's eyes, but she also saw a steely determination to deliver his next, much more personal bulletin of truth and she wondered what he would think if she jumped out of her seat and ran back to her office.

'I'm sorry, Ms Hamilton, that cool, calm exterior doesn't fool me. I know you're devastated by this turn of events, and who wouldn't be? You crouch in that chair like a starved waif, with sunken eyes and a blanched complexion, not a highly skilled, respected professional. The law is a demanding mistress; many a lawyer has become addicted to the daily buzz delivered by the joust of advocacy, sucked into the euphoria of winning cases, obsessed with that spurt of adrenaline delivered to their veins as they spar with the likes of Ralph Carlton. They're addicted to arguing the toss with their equally eloquent opponents, then adjourning to the pub to drink themselves delirious in order to douse their rampant stress levels.'

Olivia opened her mouth to argue, to tell Henry he was wrong, but, unusually, words failed her and she was relieved when the next part of his soliloquy was more softly delivered.

'I can't force *you* to invoke the sabbatical clause in our partnership agreement, but *I* fully intend to. I hereby give you notice that from the first of January next year, Jean and I will set sail from Southampton bound for Gibraltar; we will send regular postcards for the office noticeboard to remind everyone that there's a great big world out there waiting to be explored! I truly hope that you'll grasp this opportunity to take stock, Olivia, to answer some of life's questions before you celebrate your fortieth birthday in December, so you *must* act now! If you agree to begin your sabbatical on the first of February, ten months—'

'Ten months!'

'Ten months would bring you back into the Edwards & Co fold on the first of December – two weeks before your milestone celebration – hopefully with a healthier, more balanced view of the world, with lessons learned and a readiness to move forward.'

'No way, I can't do it, Henry! What on earth will I do for ten months?'

The mere thought of spending all that time either holed up in her empty flat, alone, untangling her life from Nathan's whilst he was in Singapore, or meandering aimlessly between her parents in Yorkshire and Hollie's parents down in Cornwall sent shivers of dread through her body. Tears smarted at her eyes, but she gritted her teeth because Henry was continuing to press his case.

'Travel. Reconnect with those neglected friends. Write your

autobiography. Take up ballroom dancing with Rachel. Make a start on that "bucket list" you and Katrina are always talking about. Just take some time out to refocus on *you*.'

'Thanks, Henry, and here was I thinking I was indispensable!'

Chapter 3

Olivia sat at her desk, staring out of the window as the last rays of daylight filtered through the gathering clouds. The door to her office was closed; a rare phenomenon caused by Miles's newly acquired pastime of prowling the corridors on the hunt for stray titbits of gossip as his usual sources of information – Katrina and Geraldine, his long-suffering PA – had remained tight-lipped over Olivia's future plans.

Over the last three weeks, she had felt Nathan's absence from their apartment ever more acutely, despite the fact that even before he'd left for Singapore, they'd been the proverbial ships that pass in the night for months. Both Katrina and Geraldine had been sympathetic to her situation, but singleton Geraldine's insight into the current dating scene had not been as helpful as she had imagined, and Miles's contribution had been even less supportive – spending every day leading up to her impending departure smirking at the absurdity of her situation.

The prolific divorce lawyer had become one of the statistics! Hilarious!

The irony had not escaped her either, even in her pain-infused state, and she was desperate to unload a smidgeon of her distress into the ears of her oldest friend, and to receive her calm, level-headed advice and support.

'But Rachel, seriously, I can't just wallow around watching the Food Channel for the next ten months. Not only will I pile on the weight, but I'll go stir crazy with boredom or self-analysis – and don't you dare suggest I go on a world cruise like Henry did!'

A friend of both hers and Nathan's, Rachel Denton had been an integral part of their close-knit gang at Durham University. But, whilst she and Nathan had marched off to put the legal principles they'd learned into practice, Rachel had continued the academic life of research, publishing papers, writing articles for specialist journals, as well as inspiring the next influx of eager, fresh-faced students. Then, last summer, her professional dream had materialised in the guise of a professorship, and she was currently engrossed in a project analysing the causes of marital breakdown in the twenty-first century, a subject she was passionate about, apart from the Dean's refusal to allow her the funds to engage the services of a research assistant.

'Well, the answer to your conundrum is to *not* sit around and stew at home. Why don't you get the apartment valued, put it on the market, then jet off on a well-deserved holiday? I hear the Maldives are glorious at this time of year!'

Olivia smiled as she imagined Rachel ensconced in her cluttered study, flicking the end of her biro at her dangling earrings. Her friend was famous amongst her students for her vast array of hand-made earrings and Olivia had never known her to wear the same pair twice. She knew Rachel adored her life as an academic despite the tongue-in-cheek accusations of Anne, her now-frail mother, who called her daughter a 'nosy parker'. Rachel, on the other hand, categorised her craving for digging into the personal lives of strangers as 'an essential personality trait for all academics'. Whatever the label, Anne had been so proud when her only child had become the first girl in the family to attend university and achieve a first to boot.

Apart from her extensive academic duties, a close second in Rachel's hit parade of obsessions – and on which subject she could wax lyrical until Olivia pleaded for mercy – was ballroom dancing. She was fond of reminding her friends, acquaintances and anyone else who would listen, that her passion for the Tango, Waltz and Cha-cha-cha pre-dated the current onslaught of all things *Strictly*, and she was the proud owner of a wardrobe full of sequin and gem-encrusted costumes that would make the 'Ladyboys of Bangkok' salivate.

And as for the shoes!

Olivia recalled Rachel's admission that she had even, on one occasion, slept with a particularly special pair of glitter-heeled pumps – brand new, sparkling and not yet sullied by any contact with the pavement or dance floor – next to her on a silk pillow all of their own. She knew that to Rachel these sartorial creations were objects of great beauty, crafted by the hands of artisans. For all her quirkiness, or maybe because of it, Olivia loved Rachel; she was a down-to-earth, straight-talking Lancashire lass – there was no 'War of the Roses' between them.

'Why don't you come with me and Denise to Brighton on Saturday night?' offered Rachel, the deep concern for her work-aholic, neglectful friend and blinkered spouse, but all-round decent human being, evident in her voice. 'You should see the dress I've splashed out on for the Salsa competition on Sunday. It wouldn't look out of place on a dance floor in Copacabana Beach!'

'Kind, but not really my thing, Rach.'

A shudder shot down Olivia's spine as her imagination conjured up an image of herself in one of Rachel's skimpy bejew-elled outfits, her pale, stick-thin legs on public display. In reality though, her main objection was that she was so unfit there was no way she could manage ten minutes of the strenuous dance routines Rachel, Denise and their friends got involved with on the amateur ballroom dance circuit, let alone three hours.

'Hey, hang on. I might just have a great idea!'

'What sort of an idea?'

'Yes, of course, it's perfect!'

'What's *perfect*?'

Oh, God, she didn't think she could stomach another of Rachel's infamous 'great ideas'!

'So, am I right in thinking that sitting at home for the next few months, missing Nathan and mulling over what life has flung in your path, is not an appetising prospect?'

'What do *you* think?'

'Oh, I agree with you. I know you better than you know yourself, darling. "Driven" is a kind way of describing your manic work ethic.'

Olivia thought back to the last time she had set eyes on her friend. Not for a prearranged glass of her favourite prosecco rosé or a warm cinnamon latte at the local trendy café, but at a chance meeting in the local deli at eleven o'clock at night as they both searched for something to keep mind and body together – fast Italian food to replenish the soul, neither of them cared what it was. Whilst Rachel regularly frequented the university's canteen to eat and augment her social life, ensuring a pleasantly rounded physique with calf muscles that even Bradley Wiggins would be proud of, her own waistline had not fared so well from her frenetic lifestyle.

Although Rachel would never have uttered such sacrilegious comments, Olivia knew her friend considered her to be unattractively slender and had tried to suggest lunch, an evening out, offered tickets to myriad dance exhibitions and, of course, Olivia had agreed to go, but had subsequently ended up cancelling or simply forgot. She had stopped counting the times she'd stood Rachel up. Their friendship over the last year had been sustained via Nathan or short, to-the-point email bulletins and the occasional random meeting at the deli.

'And you're not against taking a holiday, *per se*?'

'No, but who would I go with? It's February! Hollie and Matteo are saving their annual leave for the Easter holidays next month – Hollie is traipsing down to Cornwall to look after her parents' restaurant so that they can take their annual break from the hungry hordes of Newquay, and Matteo and Hollie's brother Elliot are jetting off for a week in the clubs of Ibiza before Elliot takes up his job as head chef, can't remember where, but it's definitely somewhere exotic.'

Hollie's twin brother, Elliot, was Matteo's childhood best friend. He'd been ecstatic about landing a prestigious position on his own merits and not because his parents owned a Michelin-starred restaurant. All four of them had celebrated long and hard one Saturday night at their local wine bar so the precise details of his new venture were a little fuzzy in Olivia's mind.

'What if I had a solution?'

'You mean if we went together? Don't you have research to do over the Easter break and getting your students ready for their exams?' said Olivia, scavenging at the edges of her brain for plausible and persuasive protestations.

'Exactly, I do. Not to mention an Argentinian Tango to perfect. Dennie would never forgive me if I went swanning off for a jolly when we could be rehearsing. No, but I do need someone to help me with my project. I can't hope to be as thorough as I'd like to be without help and who better than a "Top Divorce Lawyer"? Ms Olivia "five-hundred-divorces-under-my-belt" Hamilton. *You* can be my research assistant! Only, Liv, I can't pay you anything.'

'Sorry, Rachel, I'm definitely not going to get involved in any academic projects. I don't think I could stomach any more study.'

Olivia pushed herself out of her seat and went to look out of the window. On the pavements below, swathes of dark-suited commuters, heads bent, bloodshot eyes averted, jostled with their counterparts to save a few precious seconds in their rush to reach the Tube station at the end of the street. Even the tourists utilised their sharp elbows, impatient to capture the best photographic record of the magnificent London architecture that was studiously ignored by its inhabitants. Culture, art, history, they all oozed from the very fabric of the capital, but those who worked in the City had no time to stop and stare.

'I wasn't suggesting any study. What I'm talking about is research – a field trip, if you will.'

'What sort of field trip?' asked Olivia, aware her voice contained a suspicious edge.

'A foreign one.'

'Where to?'

This time her tone held an uptick of interest, and upon hearing the pique of curiosity, Olivia knew Rachel would be preparing to reel in her catch.

'Well, my research is officially entitled *"What causes marriages to break down?"* I'm supposed to be looking at domestic abuse, financial difficulties during the recession, alcohol and drug addiction, the effects of the care system. But what I'd really like to focus on are the factors found in marriages that endure. The positives, if you will, rather than the negatives. An integral part of the project is gathering evidence to support the benefits of a "no fault" system in our divorce process, like they have in Denmark. Yes, almost 50 per cent of marriages *do* end in divorce for all the reasons I've been charged with researching, but, on the other side of the argument, that also means that over 50 per cent succeed and I'd like to find out why.'

'Let me get this straight,' mused Olivia, now that she had patiently listened to the 'State of the universe' according to St Rachel. 'Are you suggesting your heartbroken, "soon-to-be-divorced" friend undertakes a fact-finding mission on your behalf to identify and report back on the elements found in failed marriages? Bit tactless, don't you think?'

'Not why they fail, why they succeed! Haven't you just racked up five hundred divorces at Edwards & Co? Well, I am offering you the opportunity to redress the balance of negativity and misery with a shot in the arm for marital harmony and relationship contentment.'

'I'm sick and tired of people referring to that article!'

'All I'm saying is that you are ideally qualified to ask the right questions. You have time on your hands, and I take it you're entitled to continue drawing your salary whilst you're on sabbatical?'

'Half, but as you know I've never had time to indulge in life's luxuries, so I do have some savings put by. I suppose I can justify a foreign jaunt. But alone?'

'You're a big girl, Liv. I have the utmost confidence in your abilities. In fact, you are the ideal person for the role. Not only are you professionally skilled to undertake the research and write up your findings in a cogent and intelligent manner, you will also, unfortunately, have a unique personal insight of the process.'

'Okay, so where is this wonderful place where marriages last and everyone lives happily ever after? Narnia? Cinderella's Castle at Disneyland?'

'Actually, it's not just one place. Several countries score highly in the enduring relationship league – you'll be surprised by some of the places on our list. New York has one of the lowest divorce rates in the US, would you believe?'

'You want me to go to New York? Okay, the answer's yes! I'd love to!'

In fact, now Olivia thought about it, there was something to be said for escaping the inevitable enquiries of family and friends, colleagues and clients, about her embarrassing personal tragedy. In Manhattan, she could blend seamlessly into the throng of anonymous tourists and citizens, her woes concealed from scrutiny.

'Sorry, not New York, Liv. Malta.'

'Malta?'

'In fact, I've already arranged the meeting with my contact over there. We *were* going to try and do it by Skype but Niko asked for a personal visit as his grandparents would struggle with being interviewed via webcam. They've been married for sixty years and his parents have been married for forty. It'll be fantastic if you could interview both couples. Malta holds the record for having one of the highest marriage rates in the EU coupled with one of the lowest divorce rates. *Something* good must be going on over there in the southern Mediterranean sunshine!'

'Malta's never been on my wish list, I'm afraid. Look, Rachel, I'm really not sure about this. I don't think I should be leaving the country at the moment. I'm not convinced Miles and Lewis can handle my caseload, and there's the apartment to—'

'Did Henry give you his blessing to keep popping back into the office to inspect your colleagues' progress whenever you like?'

A squirm of embarrassment snaked through Olivia's abdomen. 'Well, no, not exactly …'

'What did he say *precisely*?'

'"You're barred from the premises"?'

'So there's no real reason why you can't go to Malta other than your inability to accept that Edwards & Co can function without you?'

'Well, no, but …'

'And we might as well tackle the elephant in the room now. Did you talk to Nathan last night?'

'I tried to call him, but …'

'But?'

'Well, his voicemail was on and I didn't want to leave a message.'

'So you call him again later!'

Olivia began to feel steamrollered. Her breath quickened and her temples felt as though they were being squeezed in a vice-like grip – with friends like Rachel who needed enemies! Of course, she was right; she did need to talk to Nathan, but he was in

Singapore now and it just didn't feel right, winding up their life together over the phone. She'd sent him a short text before he left two weeks ago, telling him she'd received the petition, and would be in touch to discuss it at some point, and she had got a one-word acknowledgement back, which had hurt more than she had expected. She knew he'd been about to board the plane, but how could things have got so bad that they were reduced to communicating via text message?

'And don't you think this trip to Malta will be the perfect distraction? Keeping busy will stop you from descending down the slippery slope into melancholy.'

'I'm not descending into melancholy!'

'Great, that's settled then. You are officially my unofficial research intern. What I'd like you to do is undertake a series of trips to ascertain ...'

'Hey, back up there, Professor Denton, I'm not sure I heard you right. Did you just say *a series of trips*?'

'Yes, marriage breakdown statistics have ballooned all over the world. It's not just a UK phenomenon. Not every country allows divorce, of course. Some, on the other hand, have quite relaxed divorce laws. But as I've said, your brief is to concentrate on the institution of marriage. Much more inspiring, wouldn't you say? I expect the evidence collated by you in Malta to confirm that similar cultural backgrounds factor highly in the longevity of marriage. Then, there's Hawaii.'

'What!' Olivia spluttered. 'I can't just jet off to Hawaii!'

What exactly was happening here? Was this some sort of parallel universe?

'Olivia Hamilton, correct me if I'm wrong, but I recall a very wistful expression on your face two years ago at my mother's seventieth birthday party when you announced you had *always* wanted to visit Hawaii.'

'Well, yes, but I didn't mean now ... and not by myself,' she added softly because she had hoped to one day explore the exotic volcanic islands in the middle of the Pacific Ocean with Nathan by her side. 'A trip to Hawaii is "bucket list" stuff – something to do before you die!'

'But who of us knows when that will be?' Rachel rushed on, excitement exuding from every word and preventing her from detecting the snippet of sadness in Olivia's tone. 'Oh my God! I never dared hope my dream research project would be possible. I'd resigned myself to focusing on the negative factors in divorce required by the university's grant parameters.'

'Look, Rach—'

'And then there's Denmark.'

'Denmark?' squeaked Olivia, her throat hoarse from the rising panic.

'The happiest country in the EU, according to recently published research, yet graced with one of the highest divorce rates. Why is that?'

'But Denmark—'

'And there's Paris: the "City of Romance"—'

'Okay. Stop. Right. There. I am definitely not signing up for a round-the-world trip! No way. No chance.'

'Oh, not all in one go. No. Malta is scheduled for next week, but you can go to Hawaii in May. Denmark is already fixed for October because it's extremely difficult to arrange an interview with Professor Andersen, my counterpart in Copenhagen. And last, but not least, there's Paris in November to finalise your conclusions. You'll need to submit your written report to me by the first of December so I can collate the evidence and have my submissions ready for a Christmas deadline, but you're due to return to Edwards & Co then, anyway. It's perfect timing!'

'Perfect? Perfect?'

All in one dreadful month, she had been shamed in front of her colleagues when served with documents to terminate her marriage, had been informed she was professionally expendable and forced to concede control of her caseload to the questionable practices of Miles and take an involuntary sabbatical, and now, instead of her oldest friend offering a sympathetic shoulder to cry on – accompanied by an offer of remedial cocktails and a late-night curry – she was being cajoled into packing a suitcase and jetting off to Malta. To say she felt overwhelmed was an understatement, and fear of what lay in her future nailed its splinters into her heart. She had one last line of defence to pursue, though.

'What about the soup kitchen?'

'What about it?'

'I can't let them down. Greta is always short of volunteers at this time of the year ...'

'I'm sure they'll manage.'

'No, I can't let her down, and I'm helping one of the guys there with his paperwork and—'

'Okay, what if Dennie and I put in a few shifts whilst you're away?'

'Really, you'd do that?'

'Of course.'

'Well, that's great, thanks.'

'So it's a yes then?'

'Can I have some time to think about it?'

'No. I'll have the Air Malta plane tickets biked over to you. And, Livvie ...' Finally, Olivia heard a softening in Rachel's voice, her Lancashire accent becoming more pronounced. 'I know what a painful blow you've been dealt, but this is exactly what the psychologist ordered.'

Suddenly every ounce of fight seeped from Olivia's bones. She felt as though her nerve endings were anesthetised to any further doses of trauma, her brain temporarily paralysed by the swiftness with which her life had imploded, so she struggled to utter any words beyond 'I suppose so.'

'Good. Now your contact in Malta is Niko Garzia. I worked with him a couple of years ago when he joined our department on secondment from Malta University in Valletta. I'll ask him to meet your plane. And, Liv?'

'Mmm?'

'I truly am sorry that you and Nathan couldn't work things out. As a couple, you were a perfect match.'

Chapter 4

'So, you fly off to Malta next week? Lucky you!' said Hollie, crossing her ankles to make herself comfortable on the overstuffed sofa in Harvey's wine bar, their regular post-work haunt.

'You think?' Olivia counted out her so-called 'luck' on her fingers. 'I've been publicly humiliated by a rat-faced process server announcing to the whole world that my marriage has crumbled, I've been expelled from my office for the next ten months, and then, probably worst of all, I've been arm-wrestled by my oldest friend into becoming her new research assistant. You call that "lucky"?'

Olivia saw a flicker of remorse glide across Hollie's features when she tossed her copper waves from her eyes and she instantly regretted her outburst. Hollie was her best friend, a fellow warrior on the battlefield of legal causes and volunteer at the local soup kitchen, and someone she knew shared her pain as well as her love of cocktails.

'Sorry, Hol, my nerves are like a jangling tambourine at the moment. Look, there's Matteo. I'll get the drinks and you can fill him in on the next exciting instalment in my crappy life story.'

With colour pulsing at her cheeks, Olivia grabbed her handbag and ploughed her way towards the highly polished oak and brass bar, her stiletto heels click-clacking on the marble-veined floor. As she waited, purse in hand, for the impeccably groomed bartender to perform the famous scene from *Cocktail*, she glanced at her chipped nail varnish. Her manicure had lasted only two days this time. She must try that new Korean place in the basement of the fast food shop next to the bank – the one Hollie had recommended despite her anxieties that it was a front for human trafficking.

Harvey's attracted a myriad of local professionals. It was the watering hole of choice for the burnt-out office worker to douse their anxiety with as much liquor as it took to eradicate the pent-up pressure. At six o'clock the noise level was set at 'low hum' but as the scotch and prosecco hit the spot Olivia knew the volume would quickly ratchet up to 'screech' – competitive bragging became increasingly outrageous as alcohol oiled both vocal cords and egos. By chewing over that day's events at the coalface of British business, boasting about their expanding list of wealthy Russian clients, the value of their holiday homes in Cornwall, or their last all-expenses-paid foreign business trip, the bar's patrons were able to delay their return to empty homes where not even a cat waited to welcome them – their lifestyle was too cruel for a pet.

Well, that was true of herself and Hollie; Matteo didn't know what stress was. And if he did, he would probably regale them with the unwelcome advice that it caused wrinkles and a bad complexion and that it should be avoided at all costs. He would laugh and inform them that wine merchants had an inbuilt defence mechanism to stress hormones – or was it just easy access to the antidote?

As she watched the barman pour their cocktails into gold-rimmed glasses with a theatrical flourish, she felt disconnected from the ambient throng, as though she was on board a drone hovering against the ceiling observing the theatre unfolding below. But the dislocation was fleeting. She plastered a smile onto her lips in thanks to the barman before shuffling back to their table with three glasses balanced between her fingers.

What would Matteo's take be on her unplanned sabbatical? she wondered, glancing across to the alcove where two of her best friends waited for their drinks to arrive. Her heavy heart lightened at the sight of their heads bent together in conversation, ebony mingled with shards of ginger.

'Hi, Liv!' Matteo relieved her of two of the glasses before air-kissing her cheeks. The aroma of Chanel's 'Pour Monsieur' floated like a soothing balm in the air between them as he took an experimental sip and smacked his lips. 'Ahhhh, Chianti is heaven in a glass! You do know those Piña Coladas don't count as one of your "five-a-day", don't you?'

He smoothed a palm over his hair, perched his gym-toned buttocks back onto the sofa and crossed his ankle over his knee. 'So, how many hours has "London's Top Divorce Lawyer" put in *this* week, then? Seventy? Eighty?'

'Very funny, Matt. You know I've been frantically trying to tidy up my clients' files.'

'So, you favour the grey look for that kind of strenuous work, do you?'

'Hey, this is Karen Millen I'll have you know!'

'No, Liv, I meant your skin tone. You look like you haven't ventured out into the natural light for weeks. When are you going to slow down and ditch the workaholic tedium? Why not delegate some of your workload to Miles? You pay too high a price for your career success. You too, Hols.'

Olivia knew Hollie was just as time-squeezed as every one of the patrons in Harvey's, if not more so, with multiple demands on her time, but whenever Matteo asked her why she crammed her life with such a plethora of pursuits her retort was a well-rehearsed – 'Sanity in diversity, Matt darling!'

'Well, we can't *all* work in the crushed grape business, can we?' Hollie snapped, defensive of her troubled friend.

'Rather an alcoholic than a workaholic! Anyway, Liv, Hollie has filled me in on your mission. And whilst I think it's an excellent idea to go travelling, I'm not convinced by the whole "love makes the world go round" premise.'

Olivia watched him twist his lips into a grimace and she wondered whether he had used cosmetics to enhance their perfect shape? There was not a shadow of a doubt in her addled mind that his Mediterranean-toned skin had been assisted to produce such a healthy glow, but looking good had always been a priority for Matteo, like many of those of Italian descent.

'Why not ditch the project, and the trip to Malta, and come to Tuscany with me next month? I'm staying with Dad and Uncle Gino in Florence, then touring the local vineyards to sample some of the best wines Italy has to offer. I could introduce you to one of my cousins?' His mahogany eyes twinkled as he sipped his glass of Chianti and waited for Olivia's reaction with interest.

'Matt ...' began Hollie, shooting a warning glare in his direction, but Matteo was clearly on a roll and had no intention of listening.

'Why do this "work" project when you're supposed to be on holiday? Isn't the whole point of a "holiday" to kick back and chill? God knows the two of you could do with a slice of relaxation. You girls are so tightly screwed that you'd need a power tool to unwind. And why is it so important to find out "what love's got to do with it"? Isn't that a tad insensitive of our Rachel when ... well ... in your current position?' Matteo squeezed Olivia's hand, his expression reflecting his absolute sincerity. She rolled her eyes at him – Matteo knew that practised gaze could smoulder granite. 'Never mind, Liv, now you can be more like me. Look at all the gorgeous girls I've dated. If I'd been married just think what I would have missed out on!'

A splutter of derision erupted from Hollie's mouth.

'Isn't it more a case of you can't keep a girlfriend for any longer than four dates!' She smirked, wiping away a dribble of prosecco from her frosted lips with the back of her hand.

'Hey, Holls, that is so not true! And highly defamatory, I might add. Liv darling, can I sue her for slander? Do you still do "no win, no fee"? Anyway, too much of a good thing can be overwhelming. For the sake of humankind, I have to spread this glorious body and dashing charisma around. *Share the lerve.*' Matteo grinned as Hollie tutted, recrossing her slender legs, a gesture that caused her skirt to rise further up her thighs. 'Anyway, I had *six* dates with Bianca. A nun's existence like you've got going on, darling, is not part of my life's golden-paved pathway. It gets *so* exhausting to feign interest in someone when the initial attraction has worn off, delicious as Bianca was. Variety is the spice of life.'

'Yes, you'd know! Anyway, chance would be a fine thing. There're no decent guys around to date.'

Pointedly, Hollie swept her eyes over her shoulder and around the wine bar. Olivia followed her concentrated beam as it encompassed the whole battalion of professionals at varying degrees of inebriation; all, without exception, pale-skinned, red-eyed, and scrawny from the long hours spent behind their desks and in front of their flashing computer screens.

'Well, it's not as though I haven't told you, and told you again, the reasons for that, Holls.'

Olivia sat back in her chair, smiling at her friends' familiar bickering. She was acutely aware of Hollie's fruitless search for 'the one'.

'You do know there's no such thing as "Happily Ever After", don't you?' Matteo continued. 'Your dreams of fragranced bouquets and hand-made confectionery and never-ending romance, as depicted in those Mills & Boon-style romances you devour, are completely unattainable in twenty-first-century London. How can such an intelligent, accomplished woman as you read such drivel anyway, let alone believe in it? The rippling

37

six-packs of the guys on the front covers are enough to make anyone vomit!'

Matteo gave a theatrical shudder before becoming more serious.

'Why not pursue your musical career? You were amazing when I saw you play lead clarinet for your orchestra last month. And didn't Nathan's brother, Dan, say that if you just practised a tad more often, you'd definitely qualify for the Ladies' County Golf Team when they play in Dubai next year? If you stopped spending all your time frequenting those dreary corridors of the local Magistrates' Court with those grumbling criminals panting in your fragrant slipstream, then you'd have a better chance of seeing what you're missing out on.'

Matteo's upper lip curled in distaste at the people Hollie dealt with as a criminal defence advocate.

'If you spent as much time chatting with any one of these guys—' he flung his perfectly manicured hand over to a group of suits laughing uproariously at the bar '—as you do with those scumbags you represent, then maybe you could be as lucky as me, darling!'

'Well, the words "pot", "kettle" and "black" spring to mind, Matteo. A serial dater who shies away from the merest sniff of commitment is not in any position to …' Hollie stopped short in her circuitous retort, obviously realising she was at the top of a slippery slope towards childish squabbling.

For the first time, Olivia felt a smidgeon of envy for Hollie and Matteo's easy relationship. Matteo was Elliot's childhood best friend and therefore Hollie had known him most of her life. Ever since their carefree teens on the beaches of Cornwall, they had argued like brother and sister over steaming bowls of hand-made pasta at his parents' pizzeria or freshly caught fish and chips at her family's fish restaurant in Newquay. Hollie had even put her chosen career as a criminal defence lawyer down to her enduring love of a good argument with Matteo. Although he often infuriated her, sometimes purposely, Olivia knew Hollie loved sparring with him. It meant she could continue to hone her advocacy skills for her daily attendance at the City of London Magistrates' Court.

Olivia tuned out and sunk beneath a drape of sadness, content to listen to her friends squabble because it diverted their attention away from her own issues. Unfortunately, her sojourn of solitude didn't last long because it seemed Hollie and Matteo were determined to include her in their conversation and bolster her spirits.

'Well, I think a trip is an excellent idea, Liv,' said Hollie, a smirk playing around her lips as she examined her apricot manicure to avoid Matteo's indignant stare. 'In fact, not only will your research provide valuable insight for Rachel's research paper, but for me, too. And *you*, Matt. I, for one, would love to know what makes love last forever! Hey, Liv, you could use Matt's love life as your control sample of what *not* to do.'

Hollie's eyes widened with excitement as she tossed her marmalade waves over her shoulder and scooted to the edge of the sofa, her freckled cheeks reddening at the idea that had just dinged into her brain.

'In fact, I want you to send me regular bulletins from your travels. A list of "Olivia's Lessons in Love"! The hard evidence, as you gather it on your journey around the world in the crazy pursuit of the mechanics of "True Love". Yes! Yes! Yes! I'll follow every missive avidly, and maybe I could even try putting some of them into practice!'

Olivia had to laugh as Hollie bounced in her seat like Tigger's more energetic sister, as her animation increased. She saw Matteo rolling his eyes in disgust, especially when Hollie had used the words true love, but his lukewarm reaction only served to encourage Hollie to continue outlining her master plan.

'So, every time you stumble across a little gem of romantic wisdom, you have to email me, and Matteo, a sort of "*lesson in* love", a "*directive of desire*", a "*bulletin of adoration*" – whatever you want to call it.'

'Bulletin of Baloney, if you ask me,' muttered Matteo, an expression of complete incredulity written boldly across his handsome face.

However, Hollie simply ignored him as she warmed to her theme.

'Then, I'm going to diligently collate everything and come up with a personality portrait of what to look for in an ideal partner! So, Malta is your first stopover on the whistle-stop tour of everlasting love, is it? One of the lowest divorce rates in Europe, Rachel reckons? Now, whilst I don't profess to know much about the country, I think it still boasts a culture of close-knit families, so I bet that will be the first of "*Livvie Hamilton's lessons in love*".'

Clearly deciding that if you can't beat them, join them, Matteo leaned forward to press the case for Olivia accompanying him on his work trip to Tuscany's picturesque vineyards and wineries.

'Italy has a similar culture of "family first"! Liv can just as easily come with me to see how we Italians maintain long-lasting and love-filled relationships. Dad was married to Mum for forty years before that cruel bastard that is breast cancer stole her from us.'

It had been two years since Matteo had lost his mother, and he and his father, Antonio, had continued to feel the gaping chasm left by her loss every day. Antonio had been unable to continue to run their restaurant without his soulmate by his side, and he had sold up so he could return to his native Florence and be consoled in the bosom of his extended family. Matteo's Uncle Gino, Antonio's elder brother, had drawn him into his wine business, keeping his hands busy and his mind occupied, but Olivia knew that Matteo fretted for his father as the raw agony in his chocolate brown eyes had not diminished.

Hollie reached over and covered Matteo's smooth, moisturised hand with her own, keen to offer him a silent dose of sympathy.

'I'm sure Olivia would love to visit your family, Matt, but she already has the airline ticket for Malta, and you're not going to Italy until next month.'

Then, still clutching his palm in hers, she swung her gaze back to Olivia to resume what had now become her pet theme.

'I think two or three bulletins per trip should suffice. That should make around twelve by the end of your sabbatical – enough to build up a corpulent body of evidence, I'd say – then I intend to apply the criteria to every single guy I know and see what it throws up. I have high hopes for a long and happy marriage thanks to your timely research.'

Olivia smiled at her best friend's effervescent demeanour. The grey smudges in the hollows beneath her eyes had disappeared, or maybe that had something to do with the three champagne cocktails she'd devoured before her Piña Colada arrived.

'You too, Matt. I'm sure Livvie's research will apply just as well to guys. We'll take the findings and match them to all the girls you've dated – although a computer programme may be needed to cope with all that data!'

'Don't be ridiculous. I've never heard you spout such a load of garbage, Hollie. Lots of things cause marriages to end!'

Matt's eyes darkened as a spasm of pain shot across his face, causing his forehead to crease and a contrite Hollie to rein in her enthusiasm.

'Yes, and that might be what Rachel's research is about, but Livvie's task, on the other hand, is to explore what makes marriages *last*, enduring relationships, ever-lasting love – and I *need* to hear that advice.'

'So, what's on the itinerary after Malta?' asked Matteo, keen to move the conversation on.

'Well, would you believe it's a strike from my bucket list? Although, actually, I had expected to go there with Nathan at some point ...'

A sharp spasm of pain shot through her chest as she thought

back to the plans she and Nathan had made when they were first married to visit the tropical island, surf the waves on the famous Waikiki Beach, sample the exotic cocktails and generally chill out to recharge their depleted batteries. Now she was facing making the dream trip on her own and a deep chasm of loneliness opened up before her, whipping the breath from her lungs.

She realised that Hollie and Matteo were watching her closely and the sympathy on their faces almost caused her to crumble, but with effort, she managed to squash her emotions back into their dark, pain-filled box and snapped the lid tightly shut. There was a time and place for self-recrimination, and Harvey's wine bar wasn't it.

'Where did you expect to go?' pressed Hollie.

'Hawaii!'

'What? Wow! That's fantastic! But why Hawaii? How is that part of the mix?'

'I asked the same question. Rachel did have New York on her list as one of the US states with the lowest divorce rates. I know, I didn't believe it either, but it's true. I've been to Manhattan and the place is frenetic; a workaholic's paradise! But Rach has a friend, a former postgrad student at UCL, who lives in Hawaii and who's been issuing invitations for her to visit for years, and the US state of Hawaii *is* up there in the top five.'

'I bet I know which state has the highest divorce rate. And why!'

Matteo had adored a recent stag jaunt to Las Vegas and still raved about the brash, over-the-top, in-your-face metropolis where couples could exchange their wedding vows in a drive-through chapel in front of Elvis, Tom Jones or the Blues Brothers. It wasn't a city that ranked high on Olivia's wish list, though, especially after Matteo had regaled them with the details of his friends' alcohol-fuelled exploits.

'So, a couple of trips and a written report back to Rachel. By when?'

'Rachel has asked for it by the end of November as her paper has to be submitted before Christmas, but I'll need to give her progress reports along the way. And anyway, I'm due back at Edwards & Co on the first of December – if I have any clients left, that is. Miles Morrison is somewhat of a loose cannon.'

'Miles might be a misogynistic worm, Liv, but I'm sure he'll cope,' said Hollie, mildly.

'So you'll have plenty of time to come to Italy with me, then!' added Matteo.

'Well, it's not definite yet, but there could be other trips.'

'Like where?'

'There's a Danish Professor of Law in Copenhagen that Rachel has scored an interview with. Apparently, he's really difficult to pin down but she's managed to finally get an appointment. She might want to go herself, though. Understandably. But that's not until the end of October. And the last trip will be to Paris.'

Olivia had mumbled the last sentence, her throat constricting as she prayed that her friends would not pick up on the significance of the final destination on her itinerary. She had no chance, though, and prepared herself for the renewed onslaught of pain.

'Ooh, "The City of *Lerve*"? Hey, isn't that where you and Nathan honeymooned?'

Matteo caught the scorching glance Hollie sent in his direction and slapped his hand over his mouth in contrition for inadvertently straying into delicate territory.

'Oops, sorry, Liv.'

'Are you sure about going there?' asked Hollie gently.

'We are getting divorced, Hol. In fact, the proceedings might even be finalised by then.'

Matteo, clearly keen to make amends for his faux pas, switched back to his previous topic.

'You know, a round-the-world trip is definitely not complete without a stop-off in Italy: the land of sunshine, good food, celebrated wines, and handsome men with oodles of charisma, a stylish sense of fashion and a devout addiction to their skin-care regime.'

'Oh, God, Liv, you have no idea how jealous I am!' announced Hollie, leaning back against the sofa and folding her arms across her chest. 'I absolutely *insist* on regular updates via email, Facebook and Twitter. You've got to set up an Instagram account as well. But, if it's going to be a *truly* global jaunt, you'll need a stop-off in Asia. Just to complete the set, as it were.'

'Why don't you drop in on my mate Connor in Hong Kong?' suggested Matteo, referring to his banker friend who had joined them on the stag weekend in Vegas and had ended up getting his nose pierced, much to his wife's horror.

'No! No! I've got it!' cried Hollie, scooting forward again to re-enter the conversation. 'My brother starts his new job at the Pan Pacific in Singapore on the first of May. You can visit *him*, save on accommodation costs, and Elliot can show you around. I'm sure he'd love to see a friendly face on those days when he's not ordering his staff around the kitchen like a demented Sergeant Major. Mmm, I'm not sure what the divorce rate is like in Singapore, though.'

'Hollie, I don't think …'

'Look, it's perfect. If you fly over there straight after Hawaii, it'll be mid-July and he'll be grateful for a visit from his fabulous sister's best friend. You two always did get on.'

'Yes, we do, but …'

'You know it's a great idea, and you've got the cash. When was the last time you took a holiday, anyway?'

Finally, Hollie noticed Matteo flicking her the daggers.

'What?'

'Singapore is where Nathan is based now,' he said through gritted teeth.

'Ah … yes … sorry, I forgot. Have you two spoken since he got there?'

'No, not spoken exactly, but I've had a couple of emails: one with the address of his company's flat and the other to confirm his agreement of the valuation on our apartment. All very polite and business-like. No animosity here!'

Olivia had tried to keep her reply to Hollie's question light and upbeat, but the truth was that she was desperate to hear Nathan's voice, to ask him a kaleidoscope of questions that she had added to every day since the divorce petition had been thrust into her hands until she would need a whole day to listen to the answers. Despite the fact that they'd spent very little quality time together in the months leading up to that dreadful day, she had still felt his presence next to her every minute and every hour of each day, and he was in her thoughts constantly, even now. No, more so now, and whilst she wasn't going to admit it to Hollie and Matteo, she missed him tremendously.

'Singapore is a huge city. You don't even have to tell him you're going, if you don't want to. It's not like you'll bump into each other,' urged Hollie, still pursuing her mission to include an Asian stop on her worldwide expedition chasing down love.

'Maybe …'

'And haven't you always wanted to travel to South East Asia? I have. I love all that feng shui stuff, the oriental cuisine, the *shopping*! And you can send me your bulletins from there, too. You know, being serious for a moment, I'm actually quite excited about this project.' Hollie drained the last of her cocktail and narrowed her dark emerald eyes. 'Promise me you'll do this, Liv? Promise you'll send me your "lessons in love"? My future romantic endeavours depend on you. No, *all* of our romantic endeavours – Matteo's, Rachel's, Elliot's, that estate agent guy over there's!'

Hollie pointed to where a George Clooney look-alike was slumped on a bar stool, desperately in need of a shave and a good night's sleep, not the double whisky he'd just ordered.

'Look, you're always complaining about the five hundred divorces you've racked up. This is your chance to redress the balance, to concentrate on the positive elements of the institution of marriage. Am I right, Matt?'

'Despite my view that Hollie's idea is ludicrous, I propose you take the path of least resistance and humour her, Liv. And you never know, it could be just the exercise in positivity you need to get your life back on track.'

'Okay, okay.' Olivia laughed, shaking her head at the hopeful expectation in their eyes, like a pair of puppies keen to earn their daily treats. 'Thank you both for your invaluable advice. I'll think about it.'

'What, the trip to Singapore or the "lessons in love"?'

'Both!'

In fact, she'd already drafted the first lesson.

Olivia Hamilton's Lessons in Love: No 1. *"Never start an argument you have no chance of winning!"*

Chapter 5

Olivia glanced out of the window of the Boeing 737, listening to the low drone of the aircraft's engine as they cruised their way towards the southern Mediterranean Sea. As she loosened her seatbelt and settled back into her seat, she realised that it was the first flight she had boarded since her honeymoon in Paris seven years earlier, and the only time she had ever travelled abroad alone.

She experienced a sharp stab of regret when she thought of the surprise trip Nathan had booked for their first wedding anniversary. However, she had been cocooned in a complicated contested hearing in the High Court and unable to extricate herself from its claws in time to catch the train, and their long weekend in Bruges had been cancelled. Nevertheless, it hadn't prevented him from continuing to schedule time away in the UK – a spa break in the Cotswolds, a jaunt up to Edinburgh, afternoon tea at The Ritz – none of which had actually gone ahead.

And yet still Nathan had continued in his battle to tempt her to spend time with him. Tickets to the theatre, to the cinema, to listen to Hollie play her clarinet in a concert for 'Help the Heroes' in the Royal Albert Hall – which she had never forgiven herself for missing even though Hollie had – and those VIP Ed

Sheeran tickets. In the end, Nathan had resorted to inviting Matteo and Hollie along in the hope that Olivia wouldn't feel able to let their friends down as well as him. Sadly, he'd been proved wrong. Even Hollie, who was regularly 'on duty' for police station callouts, managed to make it in time to take up her seat at *Les Misérables*!

Then she cringed, and the needle-sharp incisors of guilt skewered her chest when she remembered the expression of hurt on Nathan's face as he watched her sprint towards him as the Venice-Simplon Orient Express's last Pullman carriage disappeared from the end of the beautifully restored station platform. The trip had been arranged at the beginning of December as part of his fortieth birthday celebrations; it was one of the items that featured high on his bucket list and they'd missed it and it was her fault. Looking back, she should have realised that that was the final candle of hope to be extinguished on the cake of their marriage.

She thanked the smiling air steward for her milky coffee, and continued with her internal monologue of self-reproach, aware that she was prodding a fresh bruise, but she couldn't help herself. She had been a dreadful spouse – not only that, but a neglectful partner and friend to Nathan. What surprised her was that he had tried for so long. How had it ended like this when their relationship, and their marriage, had started out so well? She had to concede Rachel was right when she'd thought they would be one of the lucky ones whose marriage endured. They *were* ideally suited. She had adored Nathan, still did. He had been her soulmate, and, in the years they had spent together before their careers had intervened, they'd been happy.

Nathan worked hard. He travelled extensively for his job as in-house counsel for a large pharmaceuticals company, yet he always found space in his busy schedule for her. 'A golden couple', her father had called them on their wedding day. They may have been well-paid, able to live in an apartment overlooking the river and take exotic holidays, but they hadn't been rich in that priceless commodity that everyone wished they had more of – time. Nathan's recent posting to Singapore was the ultimate recognition of his career success: promotion to General Counsel for the whole company. By rights, he should be enjoying his moment in the limelight with his wife by his side, but he'd had the misfortune to choose a partner who couldn't even spare the time to celebrate his achievement.

No wonder he had taken such a drastic step.

And would it have been easier to accept the ending of their marriage if there had been someone else? Someone delighted to share in his success, someone who would holler his accolades from the rooftops with pride in her voice and devotion in her heart? Or maybe he *had* found someone and was just too considerate to tell her. Ironically, she had spent more time thinking about Nathan, what he was doing, what he was thinking, where he was at any given moment, and who with, since receiving the divorce petition than she had in the month leading up to that fateful moment.

A wave of anguish and desolation engulfed her body as she realised that she had inadvertently stumbled upon the second item for Hollie's list before even setting foot on Maltese soil.

Olivia Hamilton's Lessons in Love: No 2. "*To stay together, you have to be together.*"

However, dwelling for too long on the reasons for her breakup with Nathan threatened to stretch the guy ropes that were holding her emotions in check to breaking point and she had no wish to succumb to a torrent of tears in the public arena of the inside of an aircraft with rows of bored passengers watching on. So she resolved, for the time being at least, to push her heartache into the deep, dark crevices of her mind and instead to savour her first aerial glimpse of the island of Malta, the great outdoor museum of the Mediterranean.

It wasn't long before they had landed at Luqa airport, and as soon as the 'Fasten Seatbelt' sign was switched off, she slung her holdall over her shoulder and joined the scrum in the aisle of pasty-faced holidaymakers, all eager to escape from their three-hour confinement, taste their first blast of warm sunshine and indulge in a few glasses of the local red wine.

It was the last week of February so thankfully there had been very few squabbling children on board the early morning flight from Gatwick. However, many of the travellers exhibited exuberant spirits for the start of their annual break from the minutiae of normal life or a visit to much-loved family. Couples held hands in the queue at Passport Control, overjoyed at being able to spend time together away from their day-to-day struggles and Olivia found herself adding a third discovery to the email she intended to send to Hollie.

Olivia Hamilton's Lessons in Love: No 3. *"Time away from the usual routine is essential to reconnect and replenish together-ness."*

As she held her passport open at the photograph page in front of the handsome immigration officer, a shard of pain sliced across her right temple. She put it down to the early morning start, mingled with the effects of her persistent battle with insomnia, which meant she was granted only snatches of respite from the contemplation of the ruins of her marriage. The last thing she wanted to do was socialise with a Maltese stranger sent to collect her from Arrivals. If it had been up to her, she would have preferred to grab a taxi to Valletta, check in to her hotel over-looking the harbour, dump her bag in her room and then plunge straight into the hotel's huge infinity pool.

She loved Rachel, but she couldn't stem the feelings of regret that she had succumbed so easily to her persuasion to get involved in her project. And yet she knew her friend hadn't done it for selfish reasons but so that she wouldn't have time to wallow in self-pity over her lost relationship or worry about what Miles was doing to her clients' files. She hadn't told Rachel, but Henry had already blasted her for calling Katrina, and he had extracted a begrudging promise from her not to contact the office unless the matter was of the utmost urgency. He had then used the rest of the telephone call to regale her with a long and detailed itinerary of his world cruise's ports of call – one of which just happened to be the ancient city of Valletta – and he'd insisted she report back with a list of the best fish restaurants and 'must-see' attractions that he could share with Jean.

How on earth had she ended up wearing three badges? Which was she? Research assistant, love guru, or tour guide? And a trip every two months was too much – Valletta, Honolulu, Singapore, Copenhagen, Paris – especially as she also had a home to sell and a whole life to dismantle and store in her parents' garage in Yorkshire.

But it was the trip to Paris at the end of November that concerned Olivia the most because in a cruel twist of fate, it was around that time their decree nisi would be pronounced. Would she hear about the formal dissolution of her marriage when she was visiting the same city she had honeymooned in?

However, there was one thing she was certain of – despite the heartache she was going through now, she didn't want to live the rest of her life alone. The night before, she had woken up in a cold sweat when a dream had conjured up an image of her as a lonely old spinster in a care home with no family to visit her. In fact, as she'd had more time than usual to think about her future, she came to realise that a life without children in it was unthinkable.

Had Nathan been right when he had asked his solicitor to put those allegations in the divorce petition?

The realisation that he was rushed at her and almost knocked her backwards. Perhaps these bulletins she had been tasked with sending home to Hollie and Matteo would not only benefit her close friends but would serve to teach *her* some valuable lessons in love as well.

With that decision made, she grabbed her suitcase from the

carousel and made her way into the arrivals hall to be met by a barrage of uniformed, tanned holiday reps and locals meeting their families. She spotted a card scrawled with "Ms O Hamilton" and she surprised herself when, despite her emotional turmoil, an involuntary gasp of delight escaped her lips as she met the eyes of the Adonis holding it between his olive-skinned fingers.

Was this her taxi driver? Or perhaps it was Nikolai Garzia, Rachel's contact in Malta? She chastised herself for sending up a prayer for the latter.

'Olivia Hamilton?'

To Olivia's uninitiated ears, the way the man wrapped his voice around the syllables of her name sounded like he was rehearsing an Italian aria. His dark brown eyes crinkled at the corners, and the tang of his cologne injected a shock to her pulse. Despite the ambient warmth, he wore buttock-enhancing black jeans and a pink and white linen shirt, fastened at the cuffs with golden links depicting the Maltese cross. His boldly drawn eyebrows were raised in question behind his long mahogany fringe, enhancing his matinee idol looks as he swept the hair from his face over his forehead. Ignoring the pounding across her brow, when he held out his palm to introduce himself, Olivia delved deep to replicate his welcoming smile.

'Yes, that's me.'

'Hello, Olivia, welcome to Malta. I'm Nikolai Garzia, but my friends call me Niko and I hope you will, too.'

'Hi, Niko, it's good to meet you,' said Olivia, relishing the pleasurable tingle of electricity that shot out from her fingertips as she shook his hand.

'Likewise, Olivia.'

Niko smiled straight into her eyes before grabbing the bag from her shoulder and tucking her arm through his to guide her out into the Maltese sunshine. The heat hit her like a blast from her hairdryer, the welcome warmth caressing her skin and seeping down into her stiffened bones. She scrabbled around in her handbag for her sunglasses whilst Niko directed their route to the car park.

'Rachel has briefed me on your requirements.'

Niko's thick, Mediterranean accent made it sound as though her requirements were not even remotely connected to the academic and she was grateful she had managed to obscure her eyes behind dark lenses. The guy possessed a smile that would be more at home in an American toothpaste commercial, and the air of a young, hip Spanish teacher – one all the teenage schoolgirls swooned over and the boys grabbed to coach the football team.

'Our time together is limited, so we must get straight down to business. I will deliver you to your hotel in Valletta, allow you to freshen up, and then return to collect you at 7 p.m. to take you to meet my family.'

Olivia smirked at the way his arrangements sounded as a waft of fresh lemony green fern scent met her nostrils, causing a surprise curl of attraction to invade her abdomen. *Good grief, Olivia, get a grip – this is not a date!*

'You have been invited to help celebrate my grandparents' sixtieth wedding anniversary,' added Niko as he slung Olivia's holdall into the back seat of his tiny red Fiat 500 and slammed the door.

'Oh gosh, no, I don't want to intrude on your family's celebrations.'

Olivia balked at the thought of spending her first evening in the intimate company of Niko's extended family. She would prefer to stick to the itinerary Rachel had devised and to interview Mr and Mrs Garzia senior in the lobby of her hotel the following morning, then spend the rest of the day indulging in the facilities of the hotel, specifically the expansive infinity pool. She could already feel the cool ripples lapping around the crevices of her body, massaging away the knots of stress that had built up over the last few months.

'My grandmother does not travel to the city now, I'm afraid, Olivia. This is the better solution. Anyway, isn't this what Rachel's research is all about?' Niko asked, flicking a shrewd glance in her direction as he navigated the narrow roads out of the airport. 'Visiting a couple who have been together for over half a century in their home environment to ascertain the factors that contribute to such an enduring partnership? My parents also will be present, of course. They have been married for forty years.'

'Well, in that case, it's very kind of your family to invite me. Thank you.'

'You are welcome. Perhaps this would be a good time to warn you in advance that my mother takes a huge amount of pleasure in complaining about the fact I have yet to settle down and enter the honourable institution of matrimony. Until now, I have preferred to focus firstly on my education and establishing my career as a lawyer. I've fought for years against their expectations that I would follow their example, marry early and produce grandchildren for them. But I will be thirty-four in December and I concede it's time. Our life goals morph with the passage of time, do they not, Olivia?'

Olivia saw Niko grin in her direction with a blast of such intense suggestion in his 'come-to-bed' eyes that she felt her cheeks redden – and he was clearly delighted with the reaction. She ignored his question and settled into her seat to enjoy the ride into Valletta, the crumbling capital city of the Maltese islands.

Every village they drove through emerged as though seen through a sepia lens. The honey-coloured façades of the architecture, bathed in the early afternoon's golden hue, appeared like dwellings from a bygone era. Dogs roamed the cobbled alleyways, sampling offerings in steel bowls placed on the worn stone steps by thoughtful store owners. Cats squinted on windowsills they shared with scarlet geraniums tumbling from terracotta pots.

She saw no evidence of spotty youths hanging around street corners displaying blank expressions of intense boredom. On the contrary, the adolescents she saw were helping their grandmothers with their shopping carts or zipping by on Vespas dressed in their all-black waiter's uniform. There was also a distinct absence of the mass migration of exhausted office workers, their faces set in a grimace of determination, up against the clock, every minute to be accounted for.

Niko swung the ancient Fiat deftly through the city walls so fast that Olivia had to cling onto the side of her seat. There seemed to be no speed restrictions in place, nor any obligation to give way or use indicators, and road courtesy was regarded as a sign of weakness to be exploited, especially by the drivers of the ubiquitous snub-nosed buses who treated all other road users as either invisible or irritating flies.

As they screeched to a halt at the front steps of the magnificent Phoenicia Hotel overlooking the cinematic Grand Harbour, a whiff of salty sea breeze tickled at Olivia's nostrils. She allowed her eyes to rest for a moment on the colourful local fishing boats, jostling for attention alongside their sleek luxury yacht cousins and cruise liner rivals, all set against a backdrop of golden spires and fortified bastions.

'Until later, Olivia.'

Niko deposited her holdall at her feet, then seized her shoulders in a strong, vice-like grip to plant a fragrant kiss on each of her cheeks. Stunned, she watched in silence as he folded his long legs back into the tiny car and sped away, dust billowing up in his slipstream. To her surprise, a sharp blast of homesickness attacked her chest until she realised why – Niko reminded her of Matteo.

Was that why she had felt so comfortable in his company?

Collecting her bag, she strode through the hotel's columned portico into the impressive lobby, taking in its mosaic floor, the stupendously elaborate chandelier overhead, and the sweeping split staircase that had been carpeted in crimson. The room even housed a grand piano, its keys currently silent.

Check-in was swift and efficient. When she got to her room, she swallowed two painkillers, dragged out the Caribbean-inspired bikini she had purchased especially for the trip, tied up her hair and made her way to the Bastion Pool deck. As she pushed through the wrought-iron gates fashioned in the shape of a peacock and caught her first glimpse of the twinkling aquamarine-blue of the pool set against the cobalt of the Mediterranean Sea, and the island of Manoel beyond, her headache drained from her temples.

She had taken only three steps into the pool area when the pool guy rushed over to place a mattress and drape the thickest, fluffiest, whitest towel she'd ever seen over a sun-lounger, before offering her a cocktail from the well-stocked bar. On impulse, she ordered a tall glass of rosé and soda with plenty of ice in honour of Hollie and Matteo, tossed her paperback onto the plastic table, dropped her kaftan to the floor and dived into the crystal-clear water.

Ah, pure unadulterated heaven!

After twenty lengths in the deserted pool she felt the compacted muscles at the back of her neck and shoulders loosen and her body relax. Thirty minutes later she'd completed her session of water therapy and flopped onto the sun-lounger, totally rejuvenated. She took a couple of sips of the waiting spritzer, lay back, closed her eyes and promptly fell asleep. When she woke, she had a throbbing head and her tongue was stuck to the roof of her mouth.

Glancing at the watch she had forgotten to remove, she shot up from her recliner. Six o'clock! No way! She only had an hour before Niko would be back to collect her.

Chapter 6

Olivia stood under the invigorating jets of the power shower, mortified that her skin had taken on an unflattering hue of post-box red. She had committed the heinous crime of forgetting to cover her lily-white skin with copious lashings of the Factor 50 suntan lotion that she had picked up from the Duty Free. Matteo would be horrified at the lapse in her skin care regime – all those wrinkles! But it was the peeling pink Rudolph nose that caused her the most immediate concern. She patted on a smudge of foundation and dusted her cheekbones with a sweep of blusher before stepping into a short, apricot-and-ivory sundress, fastening the silver-hooped belt around her waist, and then sliding her toes into her favourite sequin-bedecked sandals.

Her wardrobe decisions were not taxing – she had only had enough room to cram one outfit suitable for a family celebration into her holdall. She ran her fingers through her caramel hair, now highlighted with flaxen streaks from the sun, and tucked one side behind her ear before attaching a pair of large pearl earrings – a *bon voyage* gift from Rachel.

A glint of gold in the bathroom mirror caused Olivia to pause in her preparations. Was it okay to still be wearing her wedding ring? Should she remove it?

She wiggled off the band that had meant so much to her when Nathan had first slotted it onto her finger seven years earlier. A white line remained, so incongruous against her sunburnt fingers, and tears suddenly prickled at the corners of her eyes as she placed the precious symbol of her marriage into her cosmetics purse. However, there was no time to dissect the final conversation she'd had with Nathan before he had left for Singapore, or to worry about why he hadn't returned her calls since he'd arrived because if she didn't hurry up she would be late.

For some reason, Olivia was inordinately pleased at Niko's reaction when he appeared in the temple-like foyer of the hotel at precisely 7 p.m. and insisted she performed a twirl in the centre of the mosaic on the lobby floor. She knew her self-esteem had taken a battering over the last few weeks and she was grateful to him for his polite attentiveness.

'You look spectacular, Ms Hamilton.'

To her surprise, when Niko dropped a kiss on the back of her hand, an unfamiliar ripple of desire curled through her lower abdomen – the guy really was handsome, with smouldering chocolate-brown eyes, his hair neatly barbered into a quiff for the party, and a tight black T-shirt that showcased his gym-honed biceps to perfection. Olivia self-consciously re-tucked her hair behind her ear and forced herself not to blush when she saw Niko had noticed how the kiss had affected her.

Again, Niko drove his rust-blistered Fiat out of the city at speed, its ancient suspension objecting loudly to the wanton thrashing, a light breeze playing with Olivia's hair. The roads into the interior of the island where the Garzia family's farm and vineyard were located became increasingly narrow and winding the further they travelled and the view beyond the tiny vehicle's path was jaw-droppingly scenic. There wasn't a single high-rise sugar-cube of a hotel in sight, simply an undulating patchwork of scorched earth with swirls of golden wheat and barley interspersed with neat rows of green vines and potato crops.

They shot through ancient hamlets, their buildings blending in perfect harmony with the landscape, their stonework rinsed in a weak solution of ochre-coloured paint. Everywhere she looked there was an image that merited a gilt frame. There was no jarring intrusion of modern architecture, only pretty alleyways dotted with ceramic pots stuffed with white geraniums and tiny chapels in tranquil town squares trimmed with fairy lights. In no time at all, they were whizzing past a medieval walled town, rising from the meadows like a desert mirage, its skyline tinged with a golden halo of light.

'What an amazing view!'

'That is Mdina – you must find the time to take a trip there whilst you are here. The city was the capital of Malta until the Knights of St John arrived in the sixteenth century and chose to make Valletta their home instead. If you are interested in art, St John's Cathedral houses a magnificent painting by Caravaggio, but for me Mdina is a truly magical place.'

Olivia pondered the town set into a low hill, wondering what secrets its walls concealed as Niko continued with his tour guide soliloquy.

'It is necessary to explore its streets on foot as only wedding cars, hearses, and emergency vehicles, are permitted through the fortified gates, and it is for this reason it has been named "the silent city". A visit to St Paul's Cathedral is an absolute must; its ceiling frescoes are spectacular! I'd be happy to show you round if you like?'

'That sounds great, thank you.'

Olivia tore her eyes away from the impressive sight and smiled across at her new friend and willing chauffeur. He clearly adored his country with a passion and she immediately regretted her faded connection with her own hometown of Leeds. Of course, she still visited her parents who lived in a small village on the outskirts as often as she could, but she hadn't graced the city with her presence for over twenty years. Yet here she was, agreeing to visit the medieval capital of an island in the middle of the Mediterranean Sea with a guy she had just met.

When the sign for Zebbug appeared, Niko slowed the Fiat to a more respectable speed and Olivia heaved a sigh of relief, loosening her grip on the side of the passenger seat.

'This is a very picturesque village.' Olivia smiled, surveying the miniature church that could only have room to fit a congregation of twelve. 'Why is the bunting out?'

'In Malta, every community celebrates the day of its own patron saint with a feast, or *festa*. There's always a competition to see who can put on the biggest, the best, the wildest, the most exuberant of shows. We decorate the streets and buildings with lights and flags. We have parades and lots of fireworks. Children toss confetti from the balconies. Everyone joins in. We even have brass band concerts, which I think is a hangover from the British rule.' Niko smirked.

'Our food is shared and the wine flows freely. It's a shame you won't still be with us when my favourite festival takes place – *l'imnarja*. There's traditional music, lots of dancing and a plentiful supply of *fenkata* – a wonderful rabbit stew. There are horse and donkey races – I can just see you perched on the back of a donkey.' Niko nodded down at Olivia's silver sandals with four-inch heels and she laughed – practical they were not! 'Okay, at last, we arrive!'

Niko swung the steering wheel to the left and the little car bumped down a cypress-lined avenue, the land to either side carpeted with fennel and dotted with purple and white clover, wild irises and rows upon rows of lush green vines and vegetables. Then, just a few seconds later, the Garzia family's three-hundred-year-old farmhouse came into view, the burnished stone of the house's crumbling façade reflecting the final golden rays of the evening sun.

Olivia jumped from the passenger seat, a smile tugging her lips. To her untrained eye, the building's architecture held a

Moroccan feel, built around a central courtyard that would no doubt provide an oasis of shade and calm on any other day but this. Carved niches in the surrounding walls were adorned with blue-and-white ceramic pots filled to bursting with bright, fragrant geraniums. Chiselled plaques and terracotta urns completed the illusion that she had inadvertently stumbled into a film set.

The evening's celebration was well underway. Maltese music tinkled in the background from speakers dangling from an upstairs window, and necklaces of fairy lights hung from the eaves like floral garlands. Two long wooden tables, bedecked with red and white gingham tablecloths, were laden with bowls of salad, couscous and chunks of rough brown bread, interspersed with well-used earthenware jugs filled with the Garzia estate's red wine. At least thirty people were either devouring the delicious food at the tables or chattering at the kitchen door before delivering even more dishes to the tables. Children in their smartest shirts and party dresses, their hair combed so neatly they looked comical, chased pet cats away after tempting them forward with morsels of ciabatta dipped in home-pressed olive oil.

The rich fragrance of home-cooked cuisine drifted to Olivia's nostrils and caused her stomach to growl, but the cacophony of laughter and high-pitched gossip, coupled with crying babies, shrieking children and barking dogs made her feel like an intruder. As she was absorbed into the throng of Niko's family, she was surprised at the frisson of nerves that tingled through her veins, so she took a quick step backwards, her heel crushing down on Niko's toe and causing him to expel a yelp of pain.

'Oh, Niko, I'm so sorry!'

Olivia reached up to tuck her hair behind her ear again, her go-to reaction whenever she felt anxious. She suddenly felt as though she had no right to be there, as though she were gate-crashing a private family celebration, and envisioned the gathering falling into a horrified silence that she'd had the audacity to intrude on the joyous occasion – but of course they didn't. Niko immediately grasped the situation, linked his arm through hers and led her to where the party's guests of honour presided at the head of the largest food-laden table.

'Hi, Nanna, Pops, this is Olivia Hamilton.'

'Ah, Olivia, it's good to meet you. Welcome to our home!' declared Niko's grandmother, a petite, well-rounded woman, her ash-coloured hair set into neat rows of curls in honour of the auspicious occasion. She reached up with her thumb and forefinger outstretched to pinch Olivia's cheek. 'My husband and I are thrilled you could join us to celebrate our anniversary this evening, aren't we, Filip?'

Olivia couldn't prevent a giggle from erupting when she saw Niko's grandfather, who had an enormous linen serviette tucked into the neck of his shirt, pause theatrically, a huge barbecued chicken leg at his lips. He smiled a welcome at Olivia, rolled his eyes at his wife, then resumed his enjoyment of the family feast, every dish prepared with a well-practised hand and a soupçon of affection.

'Thank you so much for inviting me, it looks like a great party!'

'Ach.' Mrs Garzia waved her arthritic hand as though it was nothing before switching to speak to Niko in speedy Maltese. From her tone, Olivia imagined her saying something along the lines of 'Fetch the girl a glass of wine, Niko, and make sure she eats some of your mother's *fenek*. She looks like one of those anorexics. A plate of your mother's home-cooking is what she needs.'

Despite her lack of understanding of the local language, Olivia was left in no doubt as to the old lady's dim view of her slender frame and washed-out complexion. Whilst Niko went off to do his grandmother's bidding, she perched on the edge of a wooden bench at the adjacent table, next to a small boy who immediately fixed his dark brown eyes on her, clearly wondering who this strange woman was that his Uncle Niko had brought to dinner until he was distracted by the arrival of the anniversary cake, topped with a fanfare of candles.

She couldn't eat the mountain of *kapunata*, a sort of Maltese ratatouille, that Niko placed in front of her, but relished the *pastizzi* – tiny diamond-shaped parcels of flaky pastry wrapped around spinach and ricotta. She savoured the flavours with a gusto she had forgotten she possessed, before moving on to slurp on an over-ripe nectarine, its juice trickling down to her arm and dripping from her elbow. She caught Niko's mother watching her, smiling with vicarious pleasure as her creations disappeared into a grateful stomach, and Olivia slowly reacquainted herself with the power of good food and welcoming company.

As Niko had been commandeered by his father and uncle to discuss the state of their vines, she decided to return her plate to the kitchen where the women of the Garzia family had congregated. She grabbed a tea towel, anxious to repay their generosity. She smiled as Mrs Garzia senior plunged her hands into the porcelain sink, repelling all objections from her daughter and gesturing to Olivia to take her place next to her.

'So, Olivia, you want to know why our marriage has lasted for so long?' she asked, her dark eyes filled with sharp intelligence. 'Why there has *never* been a divorce in the Garzia family? Well, I'll tell you why, and it's not just one reason, it's lots of things. My family and Filip's family grew up together, with many other Maltese families in the area. We shared family events such as this, celebrated each village's *festas*, the collecting in of the harvest, the saints' days. We all know each other, we share traditions, we live in the same culture, we have the same expectations and belief in God.'

Ella Garzia handed an engraved glass jug to Olivia to dry.

'Our match was approved and supported not only by our parents, but also by our extended families, and therefore we were accepted as a couple straight away. Because we know each other's histories, we can communicate and understand each other with

63

the minimum of effort. Oh, not in an American-style talking-about-your-feelings kind of a way, but by being sensitive to each other's moods and non-verbal signals. It's these things, I believe, that have seen us through a terrible war and all the hardships the post-war years brought, the loss of a treasured son, and the numerous plagues that have befallen our crops. Life on a country farm is not an easy one.'

Mrs Garzia removed the plug from the sink, wiped her hands on her flower-bedecked apron before untying it and folding it into squares.

'The river of marital happiness does not always flow smoothly; sometimes there are pebbles, sometimes rocks and occasionally great boulders to navigate, but we each know our roles in our marriage and accept them without question or resentment. After the heart soars, contentment follows.' Ella tapped the side of her nose with her index finger, then walked to the kitchen door, turning her lined face over her shoulder, a glint of mischief appearing in her watery eyes. 'All the reasons for a contented marriage I've outlined are true, but of course you mustn't forget to include the obvious one in your research project.'

'What's that?' Olivia smiled, warming to the old lady's frank disclosures.

'Sexual attraction!' announced Ella, giggling like a schoolgirl when she saw the expression of astonishment on Olivia's face before sweeping out into the courtyard to join her family.

As her glass was constantly replenished, Olivia began to relax. She marvelled at the cohesive unity of the multiple generations of the Garzia family and how their easy interactions percolated into the evening's humidity. From her vantage point on the periphery, she was well placed to observe the variety of relationships: mother and daughter, father and son, uncle and nephew, sister and brother, grandmother and grandchild – everyone was comfortable in the company of their family *and* in their own skins.

There was not one guest lurking in the shadows, feeling awkward and out of place as she had when she'd arrived. Their various communications were conducted as though part of a communal dance, a family waltz – brother sauntering over to cousin to discuss a new Vespa, uncle gossiping with a great-nephew about his choice of hairstyle, sisters cackling with laughter at a shared secret before then executing a seamless transition to chastise the cluster of children teasing the cats and the teenagers bent on substituting their own music in the audio equipment.

Olivia realised that every family member present that evening knew the others intimately. They all possessed a shared history, a knowledge of each other's personalities gleaned from years of attending similar get-togethers, which served to keep them connected and the family intact. Filip Garzia was clearly the uncontested head of the family, even though he had retired from running the farm in order to hone his palate on the local wine and renew his acquaintance with the boules court and, similarly, retired friends from as far back as his school days.

Olivia had to delve way back into her memory to recall the last time she had experienced a similar feeling of well-being; it was one delicious summer in her late teens filled with a combination of music, hope and a great deal of giggling. She and her friends had been savouring the feeling of freedom after spending the previous three months revising for their A levels, safe in the knowledge they were on the precipice of adulthood, which they would spend marvelling at the elegant spires of Oxford, or the bridges of Newcastle, or the cathedral city of Durham. She had relished her holiday job as a waitress in a local café – crammed daily with tourists sheltering from the incessant Yorkshire rain – and the opportunity it offered for her to study its customers.

A pang of regret wormed its way into her heart as she sipped on her glass of wine. That was over twenty years ago! What had happened to the girl with the rosy cheeks and the toffee-coloured hair made frizzy by the rising condensation in the café from the warm bodies and damp cagoules? Her teenage self would hardly recognise the woman she had become, loitering in this pretty courtyard in the middle of the Mediterranean, wondering how soon she could escape back to the anonymous five-star hotel where she was staying – alone.

Thankfully, she was jolted out of her spiralling monologue of despair by the timely arrival of Niko.

'Enjoying the evening, Olivia?'

She experienced a repeat of the lower abdomen lurch at the way he pronounced her name. Or could that just be the fact that she had lost count of how many jugs of the family's red wine she'd consumed at dinner?

'I am, thank you. Your grandparents are very generous to have included me this evening.'

She glanced across to where Ella had pecked her husband on the cheek before shooing him off to join in with an impromptu game of boules. Unexpectedly, the tenderness between the couple sparked tears in her eyes.

Nothing escaped Niko. Without saying a word, he reached out, slid his palm gently into hers and led her out of the courtyard, dodging the chaos as the wooden tables were dragged away to allow the dancing part of the evening to begin, laughing at his cousins who were lugging two huge loudspeakers, attached to a tiny iPod, onto the cobbles.

'Everyone looks so happy, so relaxed in each other's company.'

'I'm sure my grandmother has explained to you why our extended family remains intact, unaffected by the spectre of separation or divorce. As you already know, they consider me a little peculiar because I've chosen to remain single for so long. But, unlike my sisters, I've relished the opportunity this choice has afforded me to study abroad, to experience a little of the wider world before returning home to settle down.'

For a few precious moments, as they sauntered along the neat rows of vines, Olivia allowed her gaze to rest on the horizon, enjoying the way the last ripples of violet light vanished into inky darkness leaving only the moon and the eternal canopy of stars to illuminate the vineyard.

'It's the same in many other Maltese families, particularly those living in rural communities. Look around you tonight and you will see many enduring relationships – not only marriages but relationships between the generations, between friends, between neighbours – we love each other. Our shared personal history, a deep knowledge of our family's traditions, is the reason why marriages in Malta survive. Of course, our religion plays an important role in that endurance, too – pre-marriage pregnancy is rare here, but the stability of our childhoods, and witnessing our parents and grandparents strive to ensure a secure home, provides us with a formidable example to emulate.'

'Mmm, I think you're right.'

Niko's words catapulted Olivia's thoughts back to her own parents' celebration of their forty years of marriage a year ago. As their only child, she had garnered every spare moment of her sparse reserves of time to hire a room at Newby Hall – her mother, Julie's, favourite stately home in North Yorkshire – to make sure they celebrated in style. She adored her parents, both of whom had supported her every dream without question or complaint, no matter how wacky. Looking back on that joyous occasion, she realised with a stab of guilt that it had been the last time she had spent a whole weekend in Nathan's company.

As the silvery moon played hide-and-seek with the clouds, an errant gust of air funnelled by the vines sent a shiver through Olivia's silent contemplation.

'You're cold. Here, take this.'

Niko draped his jacket over her shoulders and the faint aroma of tannin, mingled with his unique cologne, infiltrated her senses. Goose bumps skittered across her forearms and she marvelled at the kaleidoscope of sensations one person could feel at the same time. As she took in the sensuous curve of Niko's lips paused inches from hers, the soft sigh of his breath tickling her cheek, her thoughts became an unintelligible melee of chaos; her heart bounced at the way he was looking at her, yet her body and her brain were telling her that the feelings swirling through her veins were of affection, friendship, and nothing more. She took a step backwards, lowering her gaze, and Niko took the hint.

'Come on, let's rejoin the party. I hear music!'

Niko slotted his arm through hers again, and they emerged from the shadows into the courtyard where the muffled burble of conversation and laughter was rudely interrupted by the first notes of 'Gangnam Style' blasting from the speakers. Every member of the Garzia family under the age of fifty flooded the makeshift dance floor and performed their own individual version of the Korean dance routine.

'Come on!' yelled Niko, grabbing her hand and dragging her into the melee.

'Oh, God, no!'

But she found herself joining in, copying the actions until the music moved on to an Ibiza Mix. Perspiration gathered on her temples and beneath her breasts and she begged to be released from the throng to go in search of a glass of water.

She perched on an upturned bucket, kicked off her sandals and continued to watch the Garzia family party, revelling in the surge of happiness that broke through the armour of anxiety she had worn since Nathan had dropped the bombshell of their divorce. She had been welcomed into Niko's family celebrations with open arms and there was a warm fuzzy feeling floating inside her chest and, when she glanced at her watch, she was astounded to find it was well past midnight. Only the younger generation had continued to dance – until the introduction of slower, smoother rhythms had served to clear the courtyard of the teenagers.

'Want to dance with me?' asked Niko, clearly unsure of her reaction after what had happened amongst the ripening grapes.

The evening air had retained the day's warmth and the younger children had long since been chased off to bed so that their parents could enjoy a smooch to replenish the coffers of togetherness. Olivia smiled and stepped into Niko's arms, their bodies moulding together perfectly as they swayed to the music beneath the candlelit lanterns that cast a romantic amber glow over the dancers. However, after only one dance, exhaustion began to grab at her bones. She was so worn out by the trauma that had been dumped in her path over recent weeks that she wished she could simply fall asleep, secure and protected by these strong arms, even though they weren't the arms she wished were holding her.

The music had to end some time, and when it did the couples reluctantly broke apart.

'Night, Niko!' called Anna, Niko's twin sister, raising her eyebrows in a clear question. Her mane of glossy hair, an identical shade to her brother's, had broken free of its sophisticated up-do, but she looked happy at the success of the evening's celebrations.

'Goodnight, Anna. See you at the *Kalafrana Festa* next Saturday, and you two little monkeys had better behave this time or you'll have your Uncle Niko to answer to.'

Niko kissed his sister on the cheek, hugged his brother-in-law, Joseph, and watched the couple disappear into the darkness with two bleary-eyed little boys in tow, the tallest wiggling his fingers in Olivia's direction.

'Okay, it looks like the party's over. Come on, I'll drive you back to Valletta, or you could stay here at the farmhouse if you wanted?'

The intensity of Niko's eyes as he searched her face for a clue as to how she felt about his invitation caused her to waver whilst she flicked through her options. She struggled to fathom the reason she felt so drawn to Niko – after all, they had only met that day and yet she felt like she had known him for years. But hadn't she felt exactly the same way when she'd first met Matteo? That unconditional, *uncritical* acceptance of a good friend? Niko was handsome, intelligent, and he was clearly attracted to her, but her heart refused to budge from its place on the perch marked Nathan Fitzgerald.

'Thanks, but I think I'll go back to the hotel, if that's okay.'

'Sure.'

She hooked up her sandals with her index finger and trotted with Niko to where he'd abandoned the Fiat, ignoring the swoop of regret in her stomach. However, she knew it was because she was leaving the warm embrace of Niko's large, extended, *happy* family rather than anything at the romantic end of the spectrum. Fortunately, Niko knew the roads back to Valletta like his family tree and they were soon drawing up in front of the magnificent portico of her hotel where the over-attentive doorman leapt forward to open Olivia's door, leaving no time to linger beyond a friendly goodnight peck on the cheek.

'May I offer my services as your tour guide on Monday? A trip to Mdina, perhaps?'

'Sounds great, thank you.'

Olivia waved until Niko's little car disappeared from sight then mounted the steps to the lobby, the siren call of her bed drowning out any other cogent thought. As she slipped between the cool cotton sheets, the final image to flicker across her mind was one of her dancing with Niko in the courtyard and she knew that he would be a friend and nothing more, because whilst he was attentive, not to mention incredibility sexy, he was not Nathan.

Chapter 7

That night Olivia slept better than she had for years, and she refused to put it down to the copious amount of alcohol she had been plied with at the party as she often drank more than that when she met Hollie and Matteo at Harvey's. For the first time in as long as she could remember, there had been no waking in the early hours, anxiety gnawing at her stomach and points of advocacy being rehearsed on a ticker tape loop around her brain.

Sunday morning had dawned without her, and she regretted missing the Mediterranean sunrise, watching the salmon-pink fingers of light banishing the darkness to welcome in another sun-filled day. And yet she had woken refreshed, luxuriating in breakfast in bed before taking a long, hot shower to wash away the remaining cobwebs of sleep. She intended to spend the whole day stretched out by the pool, this time under a parasol and a floppy straw hat, with her laptop, a paperback, and a regular supply of cocktails.

Ignoring the impish voice whispering in her ear that she was, once again, resorting to the analgesic that alcohol provided to ensure that her habitual tendency to fret about life and all its challenges was kept at bay, she selected a sun-lounger in a quiet spot and settled down, her laptop resting on her naked thighs. Before she indulged in her first swim of the day, she needed to write up the notes of her interview with Mr and Mrs Garzia, send them to Rachel, and then compose the next of her promised *Lessons in Love* for Hollie and Matteo.

After a slow start, her fingers whizzed over the keyboard as she detailed the evidence that she had collated from talking to not just Ella and Filip Garzia, but also the other members of Niko's extended family: his twin sister and her husband, his uncle and aunts, and his married cousins, as well as his parents. Happy with the conclusions she had drawn in the first of her reports to Rachel, she paused for a long time, her eyes lingering on the hypnotic undulations of the bobbing yachts and fishing boats in Valletta's northern harbour as she tried to disentangle the essential ingredients of her findings for her email to her friends. Eventually she managed to compose her next pearls of wisdom and began to type:

Olivia Hamilton's Lessons in Love: No 4. *"A shared cultural background ensures mutual interests and social networks which, in turn, supports harmonious partnerships."*

Olivia Hamilton's Lessons in Love: No 5. *"Growing up in a stable extended family, with an enduring parental marriage to emulate, provides an increased likelihood of your own relationship lasting."*

A possible sixth 'lesson' sprang into her mind when she recalled the comfortable interaction and joyful togetherness exhibited by the whole Garzia family, from great-grandparent to mischievous toddler, but she realised that she had already covered this revelation in Lesson No 2, so she must be on the right track.

She clicked the 'Send' button and closed her laptop, finishing off her second mojito and signalling to the waiter for a third, relishing the sensation of the ice-cold cocktail slipping down her throat. The view from the swimming pool terrace was sublime, from the hotel's meticulously pruned gardens to the angular, honey-hued architecture crammed onto the peninsula upon which Valletta had been built and the rippling sapphire of the Mediterranean Sea beyond, the whole panoramic vista set to the symphonic chirp of the local crickets.

Olivia knew she was experiencing a little slice of paradise and it struck home with lightning force everything she had missed out on in favour of the treadmill of corporate life. She sighed, a sound tinged with regret, and as the heady mixture of the midday sun and alcohol took their toll, her demons escaped their guy ropes and refused to be corralled, issuing a sharp sting of misery as she recalled the details of her one and only conversation with Nathan before he had left for Singapore.

'Liv, I'm so sorry the papers were served in that way! I specifically instructed Eleanor Garfield, Ralph Carlton's colleague, to write to you in the first instance to advise you that the proceedings were about to be issued. I know it's no consolation, but I've demanded an immediate written apology to be sent to you. I hadn't realised Ralph Carlton could be so vindictive!'

'Really, Nathan? The leather-scaled ogre I've been moaning about for the last ten years? The rabid rottweiler of the divorce courts?'

'But I didn't engage *him* to act on my behalf. I insisted on dealing with Eleanor. I felt sick when Katrina filled me in on what had happened in the Edwards & Co foyer. I can't apologise enough, Liv. Look, I intend to lodge a formal complaint about his blatant breach of the code of conduct with the OSS.'

'No, Nathan, please don't do that, it'll only make things worse. It's okay. What's done is done.'

There had been a pause in their discussion of more formal matters during which question after question chased around Olivia's exhausted brain, causing her to feel slightly disorientated. There were just so many things she needed to say, a whole list of things she was desperate for the answers to: was he missing her just as much as she was missing him? Did he feel as though he'd lost a limb? Was he regretting his decision to end their marriage? Or was his life in Singapore so hectic that she barely breached his thoughts? But before she had slotted her brain into gear, Nathan had grasped the conversation baton, his tone softer, more hesitant.

'I really didn't want things to come to this – you know that, Liv – but we've spent less than six weeks in the whole of the last six months doing things as a couple. I know, I know, we've both been busy with work, me with my travel commitments after my promotion and you with your clients and then volunteering at Women's Aid and the soup kitchen. We seem to have prioritised everything else but our relationship.'

She heard the ragged intake of breath down the phone line and she knew Nathan was dragging his palm across his jawline, scratching at the blond stubble on his chin in that familiar gesture she loved as he contemplated his next sentence before he spoke. She knew him so well and it was clear he was finding the situation just as difficult as she was, a fact that only served to enhance her sadness and regret. However, she definitely wasn't prepared for the next grenade he tossed into the melee of emotions that were circulating through her veins.

'What it boils down to, Liv, is that I want a family. I thought that if you agreed to come out to Singapore with me, we could escape the London rat race for a while and work on taking the next step in our lives. Having children is the one thing I can't compromise on. So, when you said you couldn't join me over here, even for a couple of weeks, it seemed like as good a time as any to start the ball rolling. It'll allow both of us to move on before it's too late. But if it could have been *any* other way …'

She had been shocked by the depth of feeling in his voice, and her heart performed a somersault of sorrow. She knew Nathan wanted a child, that it wasn't only women who experienced the insistent tick of the biological clock. She wasn't sure whether it had been something he had been contemplating for a while or whether the catalyst had been his approaching fortieth birthday or his best friend, Stefan, adding a third son to his growing brood and appointing him as godfather, but whatever it was, she hadn't felt that same urgent tick-tock.

Whenever the question of when they were going to start a family had come up, she had either changed the subject, or when that hadn't worked, told Nathan she wasn't ready or that she couldn't afford to take the time away from her career right then. Over the years, she had grown to understand that she had to start working on the flaw in her make-up that demanded everything she did had to be perfect, and that the only way to do that was by giving it 100 per cent of her time and effort. How could she be an amazing mother *and* an accomplished lawyer?

'There's no panic to respond to the papers,' Nathan had continued, clearly keen to bring their conversation back to more practical topics. 'It's not as though either of us are desperate for the decree nisi to be pronounced. I hope you don't mind sorting out the sale of the apartment? Getting it valued and on the market? If it sells quickly, I'll ask my dad or Dan to come over to collect my stuff, if you don't mind boxing it up?'

There would be no undignified squabbling over Royal Doulton ornaments or the Gordon Ramsay kitchen knives for them, thought Olivia ruefully, because there had been no Saturday afternoon saunters around the labyrinth of consumerism that was John Lewis.

'Singapore is going to be my last overseas posting, Liv. I've negotiated with Andrew to co-work the head of legal post with Cordelia. Now that her children are both at uni she's keen to start travelling again. There may be the occasional trip to Paris or Berlin, but essentially, I'll be London-based, and I'll start viewing properties in Guildford as soon as there's an offer on the apartment.'

When she heard the wobble in Nathan's voice, Olivia's throat had tightened as she battled to keep her own emotions in check. At the time, she had resolved not to mention her own, albeit enforced, sabbatical from Edwards & Co because she hadn't wanted her surprise change in circumstances to influence their discussions in any way. They had said a swift goodbye, promising to keep each other informed of any important developments. When she'd ended the call, Olivia had never felt so bereft, so lonely, in her whole life and even sitting amongst the palm trees and the tropical gardens of Valletta, the pain was still there like a glowing ember refusing to be doused.

She tipped her sunhat over her eyes and leaned back against the lounger, conjuring up an image of Nathan in her mind's eye: an irresistible combination of sexy, charismatic and intelligent, coupled with a calm, attentive and generous character. She imagined him now, standing at his office window high above the Singapore skyline, running his fingers through his honey-blond hair, and a surge of sadness washed through her chest that he had been right – as a couple they'd become like a pair of rotating coracles, spun together for brief encounters before diverting onto their own preferred waterways.

Unlike her, Nathan had never been in control of his emotions; he was always much more vocal in expressing his hopes and dreams, and in declaring his love for her. No matter how busy he was, he always made a point of putting others first in his thoughts and was much better at sticking to his work-life balance mantra. In fact, despite preparing for his trip to the Far East, he'd still managed to find the time to single-handedly organise his mother's sixtieth birthday bash, whilst Olivia had barely been able to grace them with her presence, a situation that even now caused an uncomfortable feeling of shame. She knew Nathan was filled with regret that their lives together had unravelled and that the cavernous void between them had become unbreachable – not only had he lost his soulmate, he'd also lost the place he had called home.

But would either of them really miss their pristine apartment on the top floor of the glass-and-steel building they had called home for the last five years? When had the beige walls of the high-rise dwelling ever reverberated with laughter? She prodded her memory but couldn't recall a single instance. The Fitzgeralds were too busy to entertain, and their verbal exchanges had morphed into scattergun instructions before one of them rushed off to do something else with someone else.

What had they been thinking? What dull lives they lived. No friends round for dinner, no nights out at the renowned London theatres, no sampling the sensational menus handwritten on blackboards by the latest celebrity chefs in the restaurants across the West End. When had *she* last laughed with abandon that hadn't been instigated by overindulgence in prosecco?

When their friends had found out about their impending divorce, there had been none of the usual trite soundbites that Olivia had so often heard uttered by her clients' sympathetic companions who came to support them at their first consultation with a solicitor – a terrifying event in anyone's life. 'You're much better off without him/her' or 'it's probably for the best', and 'now you can move on, start afresh, be happy, take that longed-for holiday, pursue that interesting hobby, become vegan, take up fell-walking or sprint cycling or travel the Silk Road on horseback'.

Olivia wondered idly whether Fiona Farnham had actually completed her challenge, made a new life for herself by stepping outside her comfort zone and learning how to rely on her own wits instead of her ex-husband's credit card. She hoped so. She admired every single one of her clients who faced their imminent separation with stoic, or enthusiastic, determination to pursue their dreams, or simply just begin a new chapter of their lives; there were others who chose the route of bitter recriminations, making it their mission to challenge, argue, contest and rage over the most innate, inconsequential little thing imaginable purely on a point of principle.

'Can I get you another drink, madam?'

'Oh, yes, please, but could I have a sparkling water this time?' She smiled at the friendly barman with the neon smile, but her thoughts remained at the far end of the memory super-highway.

It had never ceased to amaze her what some people would do in the name of revenge. She thought of the case of the distressed spouse who cut off the sleeves of her adulterous husband's Savile Row jackets, and another who paid for a steel band to play outside his ex's window at 4 a.m. every morning, and then there was Rosemary Farrington, another of her 'scorned' clients who'd had to endure the indignity of watching her husband of thirty-five years frolicking with his new girlfriend, his former secretary, on the beaches of Barbados when their family had only ever enjoyed an annual break in a caravan in Cleethorpes.

The story made Olivia smile now, twelve hundred miles away reclining on a sunbed in the gorgeous Maltese sunshine, but at the time she had been relieved that Rosemary had only told her about what she'd done to assuage the pain of separation during an interview *afterwards*, adamant that she had no regrets because the incident had forced her to seek much-needed coun-selling.

Having found out that her husband's affair with his secretary had been going on for over three years, Rosemary had decided to hit her philandering husband where it hurt the most: via his beloved scarlet Porsche 911 Cabriolet – a symbol of his supposed virility if ever there was one. Apparently, Geoff Farrington loved the car more than he had ever loved his family, so one Saturday night when he was out, allegedly celebrating a win at his golf club, Rosemary had carefully unpicked the leather upholstery of the passenger seat and placed a freshly smoked kipper inside before sewing it back up again. It was a few weeks before the stories started to filter through to her and when they did, the injection of satisfaction at his reaction went a long way towards helping her to move on.

Yes, Olivia had seen it all.

Clients instructing her in all seriousness to correspond with their former spouses over issues as diverse as who should get custody of their iguana, to who should be responsible for running the home-made gin stall at the local village fete, an annual institution that both parties had been an integral part of. One client, Francesca Barton, had even informed her that she had sat up at three in the morning – that ungodly hour when, Olivia now knew from her own experience, the pain of separation was almost too much to bear – plotting, in step-by-step detail, precisely how she would get away with her husband's murder. Francesca had truly believed that she had thought about it for so long that she had come up with the perfect solution and had actually wanted Olivia to scrutinise her copious handwritten notes so that she could advise her – from a legal perspective – whether she had overlooked anything!

Olivia remembered being completely horrified – not least because what her client had come up with had sounded plausible and achievable, although she had to admit that despite being a lawyer for over fifteen years, she was no expert in the field of criminal litigation. After Francesca had left with, she hoped, a very brusque professional warning ringing in her ears, Olivia had rushed downstairs to talk to her fellow partner, James Carter – rugby-toned and an astute advocate in the field of criminal defence. His sharp grey eyes had gleamed with interest as he contemplated a new dimension to his typical day in the local Magistrates' Court where he usually dealt with a long line of punters who couldn't come up with any more detailed a defence other than 'it wasn't me, mate'.

Olivia reached out to take a sip of her San Pellegrino with a twist of lemon, rolling an ice cube around her mouth as she continued her introspection on her professional career. Over the years, she had heard some heartbreaking stories, some truly inspiring stories, and stories of women, and men, who, after a long and unhappy marriage, had gone on to find love. Like Tina, who had never been allowed to own a pet due to her husband's aversion to animals of any kind, who after her divorce met a fellow dog-walker in a local park and was now living her dream parading her prize-winning Lhasa Apso at shows across the country.

Whilst at Edwards & Co she had listened to bereft clients for hours, offering sympathy, tissues and endless cups of sugared tea. Some clients thanked her profusely, treated her as a friend and asked for advice beyond the realms of what a competent solicitor could offer, later sending flowers and cards in grateful thanks. Others, of course, couldn't wait to end of their consultations, seeing her as the 'bad guy' who was responsible for helping to end a marriage they had hoped would last forever. She hoped that her involvement had offered a modicum of solace to someone buried under the avalanche of emotion, and that she had in some small way eased their passage into a new phase of their lives.

However, in order to do these things properly, she had to work long hours and put a great deal of herself into her work, which inevitably meant that the other areas of her life suffered. She had neglected her friends and her family, she knew that, and the great irony was that she had been living in a world filled with stories that weren't her own. Now look at her, on an enforced sabbatical, in Malta of all places, doing everything she could not to think about the scattered remnants of her marriage, wondering what to do with herself when all she'd ever known was the hurly-burly of a high-octane environment where people depended on her for their very sanity.

What was she going to do to keep hers?

Katrina had suggested she started a blog, wrote about her

experiences. But she couldn't do that; there was the confidentiality thing to start with, and how would writing help her to keep a grip on her sanity? However, there was another reason she had balked at Katrina's suggestion to write about her life at the coalface of matrimonial disharmony, whether with wicked humour or searing realism, and that was because she still felt raw and vulnerable about what had happened, and her natural instinct was not to brazen it out but to run away and hide – which was probably why she was sitting on a sunbed in a hotel in Valletta on the pretext of collecting evidence for a project for her oldest friend.

What would people's reactions be when they read about a self-confessed workaholic and the winner of the Top Divorce Lawyer accolade being served with her own divorce petition? That it served her right? That an intelligent woman like her should have at least had an inkling that something like that was about to happen? That to be successful a marriage needs work from both its participants and they had no sympathy for what happened to her?

Or would they empathise? All she was doing was trying her best to help her clients during what were often very difficult and painful circumstances – like a surgeon who wants to do as many life-saving operations as possible but in the process forgets that he has a family at home waiting to have supper with him or a bedtime story read to them. What a choice to have to make!

No, she wouldn't write a blog. She had no desire to poke her head above the parapet and have rotten fruit thrown in her face. She might be a coward for thinking that, but she had no wish to embarrass her family – none of what had happened was their fault. In fact, the last time she had seen her mum, she had actually warned her, gently but firmly, that it might be time to think about cutting down on the hours she spent at work and to take some 'me-time' for the sake of her mental health.

However, what would she do if she did? She had no hobbies

because she had no time to pursue them – unless she was allowed to count drinking wine at Harvey's with other exhausted and disconsolate professionals, all pasty-faced from lack of sunlight and their bad diet choices of grabbing a takeaway on the way home because there was never anything in the fridge.

To this day, Katrina still teased her about the time she had invited her to her flat one Saturday night so Olivia could surprise her with a home-cooked meal. Of course, she'd worked all day at the office, but had promised faithfully she would be back home by eight o'clock and they had celebrated the fact that she was only fifteen minutes late – carrying takeout. Katrina had suggested they keep the food warm in the oven whilst they set the table and had howled with laughter when she'd discovered that, even after living in her top-floor flat for over two years, there were still polystyrene blocks in the oven.

After that indignity, Olivia had had no intention of going on to confess that neither she nor Nathan had the first idea how the dishwasher worked because it was such a hi-tech, multi-functional model that only a person with a degree in physics would be able to master the controls without ploughing through the instruction booklet – a weighty tome that could have been a sequel to *War and Peace*. Who had the time? Anyway, as neither she nor Nathan cooked at home – either dining out or eating takeaway – they didn't have many dishes to wash and it was never an issue.

She thought about the dinner parties she and Nathan had attended at their friends' homes, those Saturday nights sometimes the only time they would actually sit down for a meal together, and she mourned the fact that she wouldn't be doing that for a while now. When they had found out about their impending divorce, every one of their friends without exception had expressed their heartfelt sympathy, their sadness at the surprising news, and most agonising of all, that of all the couples they knew they had thought that Olivia and Nathan would be the one to stay the course.

Sadly, it wasn't to be, and all she could do now was move forward, pursue her own challenges and weave new stories into the tapestry of her life. And yet sorrow threaded its gloomy tendrils through her heart and tightened the cord, because, despite everything that had happened over the last six weeks, she still loved Nathan.

Chapter 8

Later that evening, after Olivia had rinsed away the day's sunscreen from her still-reddened skin, she selected her favourite scarlet shift dress and golden gladiator sandals and decided to treat herself to an artistically presented meal in the hotel's Phoenix restaurant.

At the suggestion of the head waiter, who could have been Hercule Poirot's younger brother, she chose to dine *al fresco* on the terrace overlooking the gardens where she could listen to the crickets tuning up for their evening sonata. The sky had left twilight behind and in the distance, she could see tiny squares of amber lights flash on and off as the city's residents went about their night-time exploits.

She relished every mouthful of the sea bass dressed in a jus of sweet chilli, ginger, and spring onions on a bed of fragrant jasmine rice, and savoured the sharp, crisp flavour of the Pinot Grigio. However, the meal was not a patch on the home-made feast she had tasted the previous evening, and the thing she missed most was the welcoming company. Even the view, with the backlit pool resembling a crumpled sheet of turquoise foil, did not compensate for the swirl of relaxed family banter of the Garzias' celebration. And she might have been sitting amidst the elegance of starched linen tablecloths, silver cutlery and crystal glasses, and serenaded by soft classical music, but she couldn't fail to notice that she was the only one in the restaurant dining alone and her heart contracted painfully that this was how it was going to be for the foreseeable future.

Feeling awkward and conspicuous, she refused dessert in favour of a speedy getaway, almost sprinting back to the sanctuary of her room and heaving a sigh of relief when she closed the door on the outside world that suddenly seemed to be completely made up of loved-up couples. Had it always been thus, or was she just noticing it now because of her current situation? As she lay against the tumble of pillows she had selected from an extensive menu, waiting for sleep to whisk her into oblivion, she mulled over what she had learned over the last two days.

She loved Malta.

The tiny island had welcomed her, a fraught, stressed-out executive on the brink of divorce, draped her shoulders with a soft mantle of sunshine and friendship and enveloped her nerve-jangled body with its rustic charm and easy-going acceptance. She'd had the honour of meeting some extraordinary people whose paths she was never likely to have crossed if she hadn't accepted Rachel's challenge, and her contact with the Garzia family had punctured the bubble of sadness she had been inhab-iting for the last two months.

Before she knew it, she was once again drifting off into a dreamless sleep, and she couldn't believe it when she was woken up by a call from Niko at eight thirty the next morning, demanding that she met him in the hotel lobby immediately. Once again, when she leaned forward to greet him with the traditional kisses and caught a whiff of his cologne, she had to work hard not to close her eyes and revel in the fresh, crisp, orange-blossom-esque scent that sent a fizz of interest through her body.

'Sorry, Olivia, there's no time for breakfast. We'll grab some *mqaret* on the way to the bus station.'

'What are *mqaret*?' asked Olivia as Niko slid his hand into hers as though it was the most natural thing in the world and guided her down the marble steps at the front of the hotel at speed. 'And why are we going to the bus station?'

'*Mqaret* are a bit like those *pastizzis* you were cramming into your mouth at my grandparents' party on Saturday night, except these are sweet, stuffed with dates and deep-fried.'

'Deep-fried?'

She wrinkled her nose in distaste and Niko laughed.

'Trust me, there's no other way to start the day. Every bar in Valletta serves their own home-made version, but the best ones are to be found at the bus station.'

'So we're breakfasting at a bus station?'

'Yup. And then, Miss Snooty, we are catching a bus.' Niko grinned, clearly enjoying her reactions to his plans for the day. 'When was the last time you rode on a bus?'

'When I was a teenager! What's happened to your Fiat?'

However, when she thought about Niko's little rusty roller skate, she realised that she probably didn't need to ask that question.

'Nothing's happened to my car. I just thought you might like to take a trip on one of the old snub-nosed buses we have here in Malta – they're part of our culture, as much a tourist attraction as the medieval architecture. Come on, keep up!'

Olivia trotted in Niko's wake, enjoying the view of his buttocks flatteringly encased in a pair of tailored navy-blue shorts, and congratulating herself on her foresight of pairing her white Capri pants and Breton T-shirt with a pair of red flatties – if she had worn her stilettos on the cobbles she would have been walking like a demented duck! With the skill of a seasoned local, Niko led her swiftly through Valletta's higgledy-piggledy streets, every spare inch lined with parked cars and discarded scooters, until they reached the edge of the city.

'Here, taste this!'

As Olivia had come to accept, Niko was right again – the tiny, flaky parcels were delicious and the injection of sugar to her system fuelled her energy levels and lifted her spirits. She even grabbed a packet of *Qubbajt* – nougat made with honey and almonds whose history dated back to when the Arabs occupied the islands – to share with Niko on the journey to Mdina.

Sod the sugary calories, I'm on holiday, she argued, relegating the image of a tutting Matteo to the back of her mind.

They climbed onto the bus, selected a seat at the front, and just as she was beginning to think her bones were about to rattle into dust and she could no longer feel her backside, the suspension-less bus rolled into Malta's most beautiful city. That morning, however, it was teeming with tourists who had arrived on more sophisticated, air-conditioned transport.

'Mdina is one of Europe's finest examples of an ancient walled city,' explained Niko with pride as they sauntered towards the entrance into the town – a soaring columned gate topped with a baroque-style crown of russet and ivory. 'Its origins can be traced back to the Phoenicians – they chose this particular site for its strategic importance because it's on an elevated rocky plateau and as far inland on the island as you can get. Come on, this way.'

They climbed to the top of the fortifications and the view that greeted Olivia was breath-taking. She could see the whole of Malta, and even the tiny island of Gozo beyond, spread out before her in a haphazard patchwork of emerald and mustard, and she stood for a while, shoulder-to-shoulder with Niko, in silent contemplation of the medieval town shrouded in mystery and oozing a history that stretched back over thousands of years. Unfortunately, the spell was broken by Olivia's growling stomach and heat rushed into her cheeks.

'Gosh, I'm so sorry. You know, at home I don't normally eat breakfast and lunch is usually a latte or an espresso depending on exhaustion levels and whether I have an afternoon court hearing to prepare for.'

Olivia tucked her hair behind both ears and was relieved to see that Niko was smirking at her embarrassment.

'Then, Ms Hamilton, would you do me the honour of allowing me to buy you lunch? I know the perfect place.'

'Thank you, I'd love that.'

They meandered together through the winding cobbled alleyways with Niko still wearing his tour guide hat and regaling Olivia with random facts about the many inhabited palaces and monasteries they walked past. Every one of them was steeped in history and conflict, their secrets buried deep in the crumbling fissures in the stone, their height ensuring the air remained cool and still.

'Here we are. *Ciappetti* happens to be my favourite restaurant in Mdina.'

Olivia took in the hand-painted sign announcing the well-hidden restaurant; its name was scrawled on a white ceramic tile surrounded by hand-painted images of pears and lemons and grapes. She liked the place already. And, as if to agree with her conclusions, her stomach produced another noisy confirmation.

What was going on? She was never hungry.

The waiter seated them at a corner table in the restaurant's courtyard, its high walls ringed with an impressive balustrade. Large terracotta urns sporting miniature palm trees laced with pretty fairy lights had been strategically placed to add a touch of colour and privacy to the oasis of calm, and a low burble of chatter added to the relaxed ambience. Within moments a carafe of house wine arrived, accompanied by a tiny dish of black olives.

'So, what do you think of my country, Olivia?'

A shiver of delight shot down her spine at the sound of her name on Niko's tongue and she smiled at him as she took a sip of the rough Merlot.

'I love it, Niko, and I love your amazing family, too. I enjoyed seeing the way each generation interacted so easily with the next, how relaxed everyone was in each other's company. The warmth and genuine respect were humbling to witness – it's something I haven't experienced since moving to London and I didn't realise how much I miss it.'

Why had she discarded her Yorkshire roots so carelessly? Even her northern accent had been buried under years of rounded southern vowels, only popping up when she was angry or had enjoyed a few drinks – the former rare, the latter not so.

'The spirit of love dances in all our souls, Olivia.'

A waft of warm, roasted garlic floated on the air as a generous platter of antipasti was delivered to their table, preventing Olivia from adding anything further that her karma-infused state would cause her to regret later. Instead, she dug into the food, every mouthful a serenade on the lips. The young Merlot improved with every sip, and the tranquillity of the little enclosed patio cast a mellow mood over the meal.

Later, when they were toying with tiny cups of bitter black coffee laced with brandy and a plate of home-made *mqarets*, Niko confided in Olivia about his parents' growing frustration at his refusal to settle down and add more grandchildren to the expanding Garzia family.

'They were okay with me pursuing my education, even with me choosing a career outside the family's farm or vineyard, and when I qualified as a lawyer they were the proudest parents in the whole of Malta. However, when I dropped the bombshell that I wanted to study for my Masters in London I think they were worried I would meet someone at UCL and never come home. I did meet many beautiful girls, and made some great friends, Rachel amongst them, but I am happy to be back home, surrounded by the people I love and who love me.'

A flash of guilt tore into Olivia's heart. Were her own parents so different from Niko's in their hopes for their daughter's future to include children? Or were they just too reticent to mention it? And if so, why? Had she drifted so far beyond the outer realms of her family that her closest relations, the two people she loved without reservation, couldn't speak their minds?

The thought made her uncomfortable, but fortunately Niko hadn't noticed because he was distracted by the arrival of their check. After refusing her offer to contribute, he gave Olivia one of his devastatingly attractive smiles, shoved his chair back from the table and stood up.

'Come on, we can't leave Mdina without a visit to St Paul's Cathedral. I promise to ditch the "tour guide" commentary. We can simply soak up the atmosphere.'

Olivia returned Niko's smile, and followed him out of the restaurant, down a shady alleyway, and into a large rectangular piazza in front of the most beautiful Baroque-style cathedral she had ever seen. Its twin bell towers – each adorned with a white clock face – presented a pleasing symmetry to the columned façade, and beneath the rays of the afternoon sun, the ochre-hued stone seemed to emit a golden glow.

When she stepped through the magnificent entrance door of the cathedral and raised her eyes skywards, a gasp of incredulity escaped her lips; the ceiling frescoes defied description. Craning her neck, she feasted her eyes on the vast central lantern, filled with intricate portraits enriched with ornate gold cornices surrounded by eight soaring-arched alcoves, each depicting a scene from Maltese history.

'Wow! Just … wow!'

'That's the famous Shipwreck of St Paul painted by Mattia Preti,' said Niko, pointing to the largest mural on the ceiling, deep pride suffusing his words.

'It's … it's absolutely amazing!'

The paintings were more than just works of art – they were creations born of devotion and love and, as any conversation seemed to melt away into the cavernous dome, Olivia chose awed silence in the presence of such exquisite craftsmanship until it was time for them to leave.

As they made their way back through the stone gate to catch the last bus to Valletta, Olivia slotted her arm through Niko's, revelling in the warmth of the early evening sunshine after the coolness of the cathedral, giggling at the increasingly hilarious family anecdotes he was sharing with her. Any passing tourist, or member of the nobility who still resided in the many palaces of Mdina, would have been forgiven for thinking they were a couple.

In love.

And Niko must have been thinking the same.

'You know, I promised Rachel I'd take care of you whilst you were here, and I'm honoured she felt able to trust me with such an important role. Perhaps, if you'll allow me, I could help you begin to smooth over at least some of the cracks in your heart?'

Olivia loved the way Niko's eyes lingered on hers for those few extra seconds, loved being in his easy company, enjoyed being the focus of his attention. She couldn't deny the connection they had formed from the moment he'd taken her by the hand and dragged her into the buzzing courtyard to share in his family's celebration. Just being there at the farmhouse, in the bosom of his family, had gone some way towards soothing the burning mortification she felt at the termination of her marriage, at least for the time being, and the concrete-heavy block that pressed the breath from her lungs had definitely lessened.

Under the benevolent glare of the Maltese sun, her spirits were lifting, and she was able to see her future in glorious Technicolour instead of the former monochrome. She felt as though every single one of her frozen senses had been woken by the dazzling light of the Mediterranean.

So what was stopping her from moving her friendship with Niko on to the next level? To all intents and purposes, she was a free agent, and for all she knew, Nathan could, at that very moment, be acquainting himself with the delights Singapore had to offer and there was no reason why she shouldn't do the same here.

And yet she couldn't.

As much as she appreciated Niko's charismatic magnetism, the cute way his fringe constantly flopped into his eyes, and his intelligent, attentive conversation, there was still something missing, and whilst she was loath to admit it, she knew what it was.

He wasn't Nathan.

Nathan, who hide silly notes around the apartment for her to find when he was away on business. Nathan, who had saved a leaf that had blown into her face on their first date and preserved it in clear plastic resin. Nathan, who knew what she was going to order at a restaurant even before she had glanced at the menu. Nathan, who sent lunch to her office because he knew she wouldn't bother otherwise. Nathan, who left her favourite songs on her voicemail instead of messages. Nathan …

Chapter 9

'Sooooo? Spill the gossip!' coaxed Hollie, her green eyes sparkling as she scrutinised Olivia's reddening cheeks under her practised cross-examination techniques. 'And don't try to deny that anything happened. You have a sickeningly healthy glow that cannot be explained away by the effects of a short sojourn in the Mediterranean sunshine.'

'I think you've scored a direct hit, Hols!' Matteo laughed, scooting forward onto the edge of his seat, jiggling like a puppy who had just been promised a long walk in the park. 'Come on, Liv darling, you don't have to spare our blushes, just give us the full, unabridged version!'

'You two are so immature!'

Olivia sighed and rolled her eyes at their juvenile shenanigans. Her Maltese trip had been the sole topic of conversation since she had plonked her behind onto the familiar leather sofa at Harvey's. She had tried to stay away from the wine bar and its addictive atmosphere where stress hormones danced in the air like fairy dust until sluiced away by a deluge of alcohol and offloaded gossip – the antidote that powered their lives. However, she could resist anything except the promise of a glass of ice-cold prosecco, and Matteo had made it his mission to ply her with her favourite fizz in the hope of loosening her tongue.

Okay, so her friends were right to want all the details and she had failed miserably in her attempt at nonchalance as she sat there in the hot seat, struggling to mask her irritability. She was still struggling to come to terms with the grenades that life had thrown in her path recently, as well as the insights her liaisons with Niko and his family has produced. Self-knowledge was an uncomfortable gift and she hated to admit that she was a neglectful daughter, as well as an inattentive spouse and below-par friend. She had to accept that the lingering sense of guilt would probably never fade – the past could not be changed – but she *could* make a fervent promise that if she did nothing else she would spend more time with Malcolm and Julie Hamilton – her wonderful parents who had sacrificed so much to see their only daughter fulfil her dreams.

And then there had been the bullet to her heart when the taxi from the airport had drawn up outside her apartment and she had seen the 'For Sale' board in all its red-and-white glory. She felt confused, cast adrift from the anchor her routine of 'all-work-and-no-play' had offered her. Despite her fatigue, her battle with insomnia had returned with a vengeance. She woke every night at 4 a.m. just as the spring dawn began to slice its way through the crippling darkness, her mind a whirl of turmoil about her approaching divorce, the loss of her home, what damage Miles was doing to her reputation, her inability to accept Katrina's assurances that all was well, Henry's refusal to allow her access to her office, the state of the universe …

Katrina, bless her, had invited her to a barbecue in her back garden the next day to celebrate her mother's birthday. She was pathetically grateful to have something to look forward to. Without the distraction of work, her days stretched endlessly into the distance, empty and lonely, with only the cooking programmes to prevent her from succumbing to the grasping claws of misery. She had no intention, or inclination, to attempt any of the delicious-looking recipes – she still had no food in her fridge – but their culinary guidance provided a homely feel she had never been able to replicate herself.

'Cooking porn', Matteo called it.

Her mind wandered to the flirty emails she had received from Niko in the weeks since she'd got back from Malta, asking whether she planned to return, suggesting a possible visit to London in August. Yes, they had a great deal in common, had connected in a way she hadn't expected, and his vibrant company had pierced her desolation – his liberal scattering of tiny nuggets of affection had definitely caused a beginning thaw in her frozen emotions, delivering the hope that, one day, her battle scars would heal.

She pulled her mobile from her bag now, and offered Hollie a chance to drool.

'Wow, Liv, I'm surprised you came home! He's George Clooney twenty years ago. Do you think you could introduce me to his brother, or his cousin, or maybe even his uncle? *And* he fulfils the criteria of No 3 and No 4 on your list for a long and happy marriage! Drive us over to Gatwick now, Matt!'

'Don't talk to me about that stupid list!' grumbled Matteo, leaning back into his seat and crossing his ankle over his thigh. 'Liv, you have no idea what you and Rachel have created here! From the way Hollie's been going on – and Pippa, and Harriet, and Jodie, and everyone else who's been reading your bulletins of balderdash – it's as if you're writing the definitive tome on relationship nirvana!'

Olivia laughed at the belligerent expression on Matteo's face and decided that attack was the best form of defence.

'No date tonight, Matteo? What's happened? Run out of willing participants?'

'Funny lady. As it happens, I'm meeting someone in here

later on. It'll be our third date, so you might say we're going steady!'

Olivia heard the hint of sarcasm in Matteo's voice as he ostentatiously picked a speck of cotton from his shirt cuff. She took in his polished good looks, the black Armani jeans, the hand-sewn Italian-leather loafers, the pink gingham shirt, immaculately laundered and open at the neck to reveal a tuft of mahogany hair. His skin glowed from the Clarins facial he'd indulged in that Saturday afternoon, and a whiff of his favourite spice-infused aftershave drifted in the air between them. Clearly his Italian heritage had blessed him with a genetic predisposition for effortless elegance and sartorial style, and next to him she felt a little dishevelled.

'Well, Niko certainly *is* movie-star handsome, Liv, but you're right, it's not the ideal time to start a new relationship – and he does live a three-hour flight away. Sadly.'

Hollie reluctantly handed Olivia's mobile back to her, curling her lower lip in regret before resettling herself on the sofa and raising her eyebrows in Matteo's direction, sending him a silent signal that caused Olivia's caution radar to start squealing.

'What's going on?' she asked, swinging her head from one friend to the other.

'Well …'

'Come on. You two have been exchanging meaningful glances all night.'

'It's probably just vindictive gossip, bearing in mind the source is Ralph Carlton.'

'Oh God, something tells me I'm not going to like this. Come on, just get it over with.'

Just as she did every time the anxiety demons circled, Olivia reached up to select a coil of hair to twist between her fingers, her eyes fixed on Hollie, trying to read her expression for a clue as to what she was about to reveal.

'I bumped into Ralph at court yesterday, schmoozing with one of his wealthy clients. He joyfully regaled me with fairy stories about Miles undergoing a complete personality transplant over the last six weeks. He couldn't wait to declare his delight that, at last, Edwards & Co has "seen the light" in the way they conduct their matrimonial cases.'

'What does *that* mean?'

'It means that Miles has morphed from pampered poodle into rampant rottweiler and has ditched the softly-softly approach to divorce. Apparently, his correspondence is abrasive and threatening and he's taken to issuing proceedings without any prior negotiation or mediation.'

'Oh, the devious little—'

'Hang on,' interrupted Matteo, placing his hand on her arm.

'What? There's more?'

'I'm so sorry, Liv, he's been bad-mouthing you, too. He's been preaching to anyone who'll listen that the way you practise is a sign of a weak negotiator, and that, in your enforced absence, Edwards & Co is now a firm to be reckoned with.'

'Oh my God, this is exactly what I thought would happen.' Olivia reached down to grab her mobile from her bag, her heart pounding as her trembling fingers mishit the screen. 'I'm calling Henry. He *has* to let me come back now! I've spent ten years building our reputation and it's taken Moronic Miles just a few weeks to destroy it!'

Matteo gently removed the phone from Olivia's hand, his forehead creased with concern.

'Unlike Hollie, I only know Miles from the golf club where Dan gave us some coaching over the winter. What I do know is that those with a mediocrity of talent – and I've no doubt you could squeeze Miles's natural attributes into a thimble – often possess a well-honed skill and a vindictive penchant for belittling the achievements of others. However, we can't overlook the fact that it was Ralph Carlton who said these things.'

'So?'

'Firstly, we have no evidence that Ralph was telling the truth – he's an arrogant piss-taker at the best of times, and he loves conflict and stirring up bad karma. It's just malicious prodding, Liv, and Hollie promises to check out the truth with James first thing on Monday morning, don't you?'

'Yes, absolutely!'

'And secondly, if you're still not convinced, it's Saturday night. You know Henry and Jean have dined with their friends at the tennis club every Saturday night for the last twenty years and he wouldn't thank you for interrupting that tradition with a call about work. Anyway, Miles can't have done that much damage over six weeks, can he?'

Matteo's attempt to reassure Olivia provided scant comfort, but she shook her head.

'I suppose not.'

'Great, because your break from the grindstone seems to have done you the world of good. There's a glow in your cheeks and a little more flesh on those bones, but even so, you're still working that "haunted ghost" look, which will only give credence to the rumours Miles is spreading about you personally.'

'About me *personally*? What about me *personally*?'

'Ahhhh. Ooops.'

Now it was Hollie's turn to roll her eyes at Matteo before leaning forward to lace her fingers through Olivia's and meet her gaze.

'Now don't go ballistic, but Ralph also hinted that Miles is telling Edwards & Co clients that you had a sort of breakdown after being served with your divorce papers, and that you've gone off "*to search for the meaning of life*".'

'Oh God, oh God, oh God!' she gasped, struggling to speak because her breath had suddenly been whipped from her lungs as she tried and failed to douse her rising anger. 'Wait until I get my hands on that scrawny little—'

'Hi! I hope I'm not late. Matteo?'

A young woman, with hair the colour of dark espresso, had materialised at their table, flicking her enhanced sapphire eyes from Hollie to Olivia before resting her gaze on Matteo with a question that clearly asked why there were two other girls on their date.

'Hi, Jess. Meet Olivia and Hollie, my two BFFs. Girls, this is the super-gorgeous Jessica Simmons. Isn't she delicious?' Matteo leapt from the couch to sling his arm around Jessica's slender frame.

Good grief, I'd hate to be labelled 'delicious', thought Olivia shooting Jessica a sympathetic grimace.

However, Jessica ignored Olivia's attempt at friendship and simply tossed her locks over her shoulder in a practised gesture, then hooked her carefully bronzed arm through Matteo's, and gifted the two seated women with a possessive glare, her heavily kohled eyes narrowing in a blatant warning to back off from her guy.

Olivia suddenly understood why Matteo never got beyond the first few dates if this was the type of jealousy he attracted. Nevertheless, she rose from the sofa to air-kiss Matteo's new girlfriend, whilst Hollie remained seated and just nodded a welcome. Olivia was also anxious to continue with their conversation about the ratbag that was Miles Morrison, but Jessica's presence had usurped her command of her audience.

'Didn't you say we had a table booked for eight o'clock at Pierre's, Matteo sweetheart?'

'Yes, but I was just …'

'Well, it's seven forty-five and it'll take us a good twenty minutes to get there. We don't want to lose our booking, do we?'

Jessica placed her bejewelled hand on her hip, her lips forming a perfect pout and her demeanour signalling to anyone watching that she couldn't wait to get out of there and have Matteo all to herself. When Olivia had arrived at the wine bar, Matteo had told her that he had pulled in a couple of favours with a friend who was the sommelier at Pierre's to get a reservation at the hottest restaurant in town in return for a discount on their wine order, so it wouldn't be polite to be fashionably late.

With an apologetic smile on his face, Matteo shrugged his shoulders and grabbed his silk-lined jacket, bending forward to deposit noisy farewell kisses on their cheeks.

'Bye, girls. Be good. Don't do anything I wouldn't do.'

'Gives us lots of scope,' muttered Hollie.

Olivia stared after them as they drifted towards the door, stopping occasionally for Matteo to exchange a few words with other regulars in the wine bar, much to Jessica's annoyance as she waited, clutching on to his arm as if she expected him to do a runner. However, Olivia had more pressing things on her mind than Matteo's love life.

'Hollie, I can't just sit back and let Miles trash my reputation. It's taken me years to build up my practice and get the message out about our approach to litigation.'

'Look, Liv, you should try to put it out of your mind. Why don't you come down to Surrey and watch me play in the Ladies' County Golf Competition tomorrow? My trip down to Royal Birkdale last month has reinvigorated my ambition to win another trophy for the cabinet. Dan says that if I put my mind to it, I might be in with a chance of qualifying for the Ladies' Amateur Open next year!'

'That sounds great, Hollie, but no thanks.'

'What about next weekend? Can I tempt you with a train journey down to see my parents in Cornwall for Elliot's farewell dinner at the restaurant before he jets off to Singapore?'

'Can I take a rain check?'

'If it's really bothering you that much, why don't you wait until tomorrow and talk to Kat about Miles at the barbecue?'

'Yes, I think I will. But if that toad—'

'Hi! Great to see you, Olivia.'

Good grief, not another interruption, thought Olivia, but she knew that's what happened when you were practically a fixture at the local wine bar. However, when she turned her head, she was relieved to see that the dulcet tones belonged to Grace, Hollie's ever-cheerful flatmate, who was leaning forward to envelop her in a warm hug.

'Sorry to hear about you and Nathan. I thought if any couple could make it to their golden wedding anniversary, it would be you two.'

'Thanks, Grace,' muttered Olivia, swallowing down on a sudden surge of emotion as she saw the genuine sadness in her friend's piercing blue eyes.

Olivia knew that raven-haired Grace, a set designer at the Theatre Royal, adored Nathan. She was thrilled by his keen interest in her work, evidenced by his life-long love of all things theatre, and was a willing plus-one whenever Olivia had cried off due to work commitments and Hollie, Nathan's usual 'first-reserve', was away playing her clarinet in a concert. She had to smile when she recalled Nathan's delight the previous November when, after being stood up once again, Grace had wangled it for him to have a guided tour backstage, and he had even met a few of the cast members.

'Look, it's my night off – and heaven knows I owe you for all those tickets Nathan has shared with me over the last few years. Why don't I treat us all to dinner? Oh, that's if you're not waiting for dates?'

'Well, my dinner date tonight is with the "delicious" Prince Pepperoni from the Principality of Pizza Hut,' announced Hollie, wiggling her eyebrows in a suggestive manner. 'If either of you fancy double-dating with the Duke of Dominos or the Count of Carluccio, I'd be happy for you to tag along?'

Olivia caught Hollie's eye and her brief dalliance with melancholy was replaced by an unexpected fit of giggles. Through the ensuing laughter another item for her lengthening list of lessons in love appeared fully formed.

Olivia Hamilton's Lessons in Love: No 6. *"In order to have a long-lasting relationship, you have to first of all find a date!"*

Chapter 10

The following day, clutching a bottle of champagne, Olivia gingerly navigated the paraphernalia of modern toddlerhood that was scattered along the path leading to the sunflower-yellow front door of Katrina and Will's renovated Victorian terrace house. As she waited for the door to open, she took in the discarded prams, naked Barbies, bikes, wheelbarrows and variously shaped balls – the place looked like a battleground of heroically fallen toys. She drew in a deep breath and savoured her last moments of calm in the tiny oasis of the front garden before the onslaught of noise and boisterous banter that invariably engulfed any visitor to the Windwood household.

A faint tinkle of music, punctuated by high-pitched screams, informed her that the Saturday afternoon barbecue was already in full swing, and when a waft of smoke, mingled with the aroma of charcoaled meat, floated on the early May breeze to her waiting nostrils, her stomach growled in complaint at the lack of breakfast.

Looking down at her attire she felt slightly ridiculous jiggling on the doormat in her stilettos and neat scarlet shift dress. Why hadn't she chosen something more practical for a garden party colonised by excited toddlers? She hugged the bottle of chilled

Moët to her chest as she continued to wait on the Welcome doormat, wondering if she should spin round and head for the hills. After few seconds of serious deliberation, she decided that Katrina would be disappointed if she didn't show her face and jabbed again on the doorbell, letting it buzz until she heard a loud shriek from behind the door, accompanied by a low reassuring tone belonging to Will.

'Yay! Auntie Livvie! Auntie Livvie! Auntie Livvie!'

Katrina's eldest daughter flung her whole body at Olivia. The little girl, in full-on 'Disney-Princess-and-tiara' mode, wrapped her slender arms around Olivia's waist and rested her cheek on her abdomen whilst Olivia stroked her hair, an identical shade to Katrina's. In fact, Olivia was prepared to bet her pension on this mini-person developing into a carbon copy of Katrina.

'Hi, Ruby, it's great to see you. I love your dress! Which Princess are you today?'

Ruby stared at Olivia as if she had just landed from Planet Mars. 'I'm Elsa, of course!'

Will laughed at his daughter's indignation, his moss-green eyes crinkling at the corners.

'You can let go of Aunt Olivia now, Rubes. Great to see you, Liv. Come through, I'll get you a drink.'

Will leaned forward to deposit a kiss on Olivia's cheek before she was unceremoniously dragged by the hand down the hallway, through the light and airy kitchen that was currently strewn with culinary chaos, and out to the rear garden where a brand-new trampoline presided over the proceedings.

'Yay, Auntie Livvie, Auntie Livvie! Come on the trampoline with us,' cried Imogen, Katrina and Will's four-year-old, the blonde curls inherited from her father bouncing into the air like a mad mini-Medusa.

'I'll join you later, Immie. Just need to say hello to your mum.'

Beyond the rectangle of lawn, this little oasis in the suburbs that Katrina called home was ablaze with spring colour, the teal-and-cream summerhouse had been festooned with home-made bunting and balloons, and the place was packed with the Windwood family's guests. As Katrina and Will had been together since university, and had then produced three children in quick succession, their circle of friends had blossomed to include not only their respective families but colleagues, neighbours and the parents of their children's friends from the local primary school.

Unaccustomed to the cacophonous turmoil of family life, the high-pitched chatter scratched at Olivia's delicate senses. Of course, the fuzzy feeling in her brain could also have something to do with the amount of prosecco she had consumed with Hollie and Matteo the previous evening. She reached out to steady herself on a garden bench, painted blue-grey to match the shed, to gather her strength and survey the gathering. Every guest seemed to be part of a pair or the dual nucleus of a family unit around which their offspring circulated like satellites. Olivia suddenly felt exposed, vulnerable, abandoned to the periphery of the happy throng and an unexpected stab of loneliness invaded her chest.

'Liv! I didn't know you'd arrived. Here, take this.'

The Welsh lilt of Katrina's familiar voice broke through Olivia's tumbling contemplations, but despite engaging tremendous effort, she was unable to hide her discomfort from her friend. She accepted the proffered crystal flute with a grateful smile and took a sip.

'Thanks, Kat, I needed that. Great turnout!'

'I think it's because the sun's decided to grace us with its presence at last! I have no idea what we would have done if it had rained. The house is a mess, and now we've got to find room for another new arrival!'

Katrina's eyes sparkled with happiness and Olivia's heart skipped a beat before ballooning with delight as she drew her friend and colleague into a warm embrace, tears smarting at the corners of her eyes.

'Oh, my God, congratulations, Kat! I'm so happy for you! When's the baby due?'

'Just before Christmas. Will and I are so excited – and the children are insisting that we christen this one Santa. So, by the time you return to Edwards & Co from your sabbatical on the first of December, I will be on maternity leave. Again!'

Katrina rubbed her stomach, an expression of pure joy spreading across her features at the prospect of spending a whole year at home in a house full of boisterous children and a new-born baby. Olivia was genuinely thrilled for her friend, but she had to confess she was bewildered that after having graduated with a first-class honours degree and then being courted by all the big City firms, Katrina wasn't more intent on pursuing her career to the next level. Despite her continuing avid consumption of legal textbooks on a plethora of subjects, as well as being a keen supporter of legal charities alongside Olivia, Katrina was content with her part-time paralegal position and relished her time at home buried under a mountain of domestic bliss instead of paperwork.

But who was she kidding? She *did* know the reason for Katrina's choices. There they were, leaping like ferocious frogs on the trampoline under the watchful eye of Katrina's mother in whose honour the party was being held. And Will, a broad smile on his face as he chatted to a colleague from his stockbrokers' business with their youngest child, Archie, balanced on one arm and holding a bottle of alcohol-free beer in the other hand.

Clearly, it was Olivia who was missing something, not Katrina.

'Come on, Liv, let me introduce you to Sarah and Graeme. Will and I were at uni with them. They both volunteer for Women's Aid in Birmingham – helping anyone who needs legal advice after an incident of domestic abuse, including forced marriage. No kids. Can you tell?'

With the sleeves of her mauve and fuchsia kaftan flapping behind her like angel's wings, Katrina made a beeline for a thirty-something couple who were loitering next to the drinks table. Olivia recognised the look of abject horror scrawled across their faces as they observed the antics of two small boys, armed with plastic buckets and spades, in the process of removing chunks of turf from the middle of Katrina's lawn.

Olivia smirked at the horticultural duo before a tsunami of sadness threatened to overwhelm her. Was she really intending to miss out on all of this? She became aware of a pause in conversation and saw that everyone looking expectantly at her. With a Herculean effort, she dragged her thoughts back to the present.

'Sorry, I ...'

'Sarah was asking about your forthcoming trip to Hawaii?' said Graeme, a six-foot-four beanpole of a man with a shock of red hair who was in the process of pulling the ring on a can of Guinness.

'Oh, sorry, yes. The trip's actually part of a research project I'm involved in with a friend of mine, Professor Rachel Denton, from the Family Law Department at UCL.' Olivia paused to drain her glass and help herself to a refill. Sarah and Graeme certainly knew how to choose the best spot at a party. 'Apparently, Hawaii has one of the lowest divorce rates in the US. Would you believe that the top five States are—'

'Yes, Katrina mentioned you were going over there because Sarah and I were married on the island, weren't we, darling?' Graeme interrupted, leaning forward to rub his overlong beard on his wife's cheek, oblivious to Olivia's badly concealed grimace. 'In this amazingly romantic non-denominational church right next to Waikiki Beach surrounded by tropical plants, palm trees, and the most fabulous backdrop of Diamond Head.'

'Oh, it was adorable,' sighed Sarah, dragging the sides of her hand-knitted cardigan over her pinafore dress, completely unconcerned by her husband's rudeness. 'Would you believe that the walls of the chapel were made from canvas so they could be rolled up for an open-air ceremony.'

'It sounds wonderful. I'm staying at the—'

'We had our wedding breakfast at the Royal Hawaiian Hotel – "the pink palace" they call it. It was the best week of my life.'

Olivia decided not to try again and instead she watched as Sarah laced her fingers through her husband's and the couple exchanged a private message of adoration. Her stomach performed an uneasy lurch – she was clearly the third wheel here.

'Excuse me. Bathroom.'

She wasn't sure whether they had even heard her as she made her escape through the French doors and into the peaceful coolness of the lounge. Once again, she wished she had made an excuse so she could have remained ensconced in her apartment, with the blinds drawn against the offensive sunshine, to wallow in self-pity and grieve over the loss of her marriage. *Everyone*, everywhere she looked, was part of a couple. She hadn't appreciated what it felt like to be a singleton when Nathan had been at her side – yet another unforeseen adjustment to come to terms with.

A surprise image of Niko floated into her mind. What would it be like to arrive at a party with a new partner in tow and have to begin the ritual of introducing him to her friends, of gauging their reaction to him, and his to them?

However, she knew precisely why she had forced herself to don her red dress and towering heels. She needed to speak to Katrina about Miles and the sickening rumours he was allegedly spinning about her mental frailty. The thought of his treachery must have temporarily clouded her judgement because before she knew what was happening, she had tripped over the lip of the French doors and launched herself into the lounge, sinking to her knees before grasping at the back of the rose-and-fern chintz sofa to break her fall.

'Someone indulged in too much fruit punch, methinks?'

'Of course not!' Olivia shot back in annoyance until she saw the deliverer of the comment was none other than James Carter – one of her partners at Edwards & Co.

'Ooo, a little cantankerous today, aren't we, Olivia? I would have thought a break from the relentless pursuit of matrimonial misery would have soothed over your prickles by now?'

James took a sip from his glass of warm Guinness, leaving a thin moustache of brown froth along his upper lip, which he removed with a languid flick of his tongue. A cream-and-brown Siamese cat lounged on his lap; its blue eyes narrowed with pleasure as he scratched between its ears.

Olivia liked James. Unlike the personality-challenged Miles Morrison, James Carter was excellent company, and an accomplished criminal advocate to boot. He was well respected in the legal community and his soliloquies in court were frequently discussed and analysed by those seeking to emulate his persuasive arguments – even Hollie was known to seek his advice when she was flummoxed by a difficult case. In his late forties, his salt-and-pepper hair and come-to-bed eyes bestowed him with a certain Ryan Reynoldsesque appearance in a dim light. Resolutely single in order to take advantage of these attributes, he preferred to skip from one adoring girlfriend to the next, studiously avoiding commitment. A bit like an older version of Matteo, Olivia realised for the first time.

'Sorry, James. Just feeling a bit ragged today, that's all.'

'Yes, all this "touchy-feely" togetherness is a tad vomit-provoking, isn't it? Good God, the thought of all these children running amok in my beautiful mews home, sliding their sticky palms down my pristine windows or fingering my CD collection is enough to give one an attack of the vapours!' James shuddered, pushing his tortoiseshell glasses up to the bridge of his nose to better study Olivia as she flopped down on the sofa next to him.

Olivia selected a strand of caramel hair to twist between her thumb and index finger, quickly reforming the questions she had intended to fire at Katrina for the consumption of James. In fact, it was actually fortuitous that James was there because she suspected Katrina and Will would have chosen to protect her with soothing words of reassurance instead of delivering a blow-by-blow account of how Miles was single-handedly destroying her caseload and reputation. James, in contrast, would have no such qualms.

'Is it true that Miles has been bad-mouthing me to all and sundry?'

Olivia saw James glance at her out of corner of his eye under the cover of taking a reluctant swallow of his drink. As a wine snob, she knew he would have inspected the labels on the bottles of red wine before choosing the Guinness instead.

'Well, believe it or not, I'm not in the habit of listening to salacious gossip. As you know, I much prefer the false protestations of innocence spurted by the criminal fraternity to the emotional outpourings of marital doom that accompany those in the throes of divorce. However, I have to confess to overhearing our esteemed colleague in the advocates' waiting room burbling on about something, but I'd advise you take whatever you've heard through the grapevine with a large gulp of saline.'

'What exactly has the arrogant little worm been saying?' demanded Olivia, ignoring James's advice and drawing her lips inwards – thinking of Miles left a rancid taste in her mouth.

'Nothing to get yourself in a twist about. On a professional level, it seems Miles has morphed into a clone of his idol, Ralph Carlton, that bolshie bulldog we all know and love, and is offering a certain cohort of our clients the "tenacious terrier" approach rather than the "cashmere-soft" service you prefer.'

'Oh God …'

'Look, Miles's eye for detail may be in dire need of the services of an optician, Olivia, but he's a competent enough lawyer. Okay, so a few of your clients have left the firm; it's no big deal. In fact, conversely, others have welcomed the shift in approach – an accurately directed threat of exorbitantly expensive court proceedings can concentrate recalcitrant minds. I know you probably don't want to hear this, but new instructions are up, despite the deserters.'

'But, James, we've signed up to a Code of Conduct that promises a conciliatory approach! If Miles has changed the whole ethos of our matrimonial practice, we'll lose our membership and ...' Olivia paused, surprised at James's relaxed attitude. She had always believed him to be a supporter of her more conciliatory approach. 'James?'

'It's client numbers that count, as I think Henry discussed with you when you agreed to take your sabbatical. This recession has struck harder and deeper than any of us expected. The coffers are depleted. Now there's been an upturn, slight yes, but a step in the right direction; more clients mean a higher fee income. Look, let Miles have his fifteen minutes of fame playing the starring role in his career after years of being a supporting actor. Yes, his ego has swelled to the size of a pumpkin, but there's only another few months until you return. We'll reassess the figures in October or November and decide which way to go then.'

James smiled at Olivia, his eyes softening at her dismay.

'You've got to learn to curb your obsession with all things legal, Olivia. Ditch the domination of divorce in your life! Now, if you'll excuse me, this pint has the taste and consistency of burnt tractor tyres, and there's a young lady waiting inside that summerhouse desperate for my company. Toodle-oo.'

James was clearly anxious to avoid further cross-examination and Olivia had not even had the chance to ask him about her suspicions that Miles was behind the instigation of the rumour that she was in the throes of a nervous breakdown. As she watched James disappear into the garden shed, she knew all thought of his erstwhile friend's trauma had evaporated. Ten years to build up a reputation as a sympathetic divorce lawyer; six weeks to toss it in the garbage! And what was more, even James, a confirmed bachelor, had managed to snag a date to his colleague's afternoon barbecue.

A swoop of despondency squeezed her heart and tears threatened – everyone had someone with them! She couldn't stay and watch the happy throng any longer, so she tiptoed through the scattered plastic toys to the front door and let herself out into the welcome tranquillity of the street beyond. At least her visit to Katrina and Will's had one positive outcome – she had stumbled upon another lesson to add to Hollie and Matteo's list.

Olivia Hamilton's Lessons in Love: No 7. *"A blinkered addiction to career progression shatters the dream of a stable family life."*

Chapter 11

Olivia couldn't sleep. The guy in the seat behind her must have been a basketball player because his knees were wedged so snugly into the small of her back that no amount of eye-rolling or tutting was going to make him move. She had been on the plane to LA for over nine hours and she was still annoyed with Rachel for ambushing her with her own special brand of persuasive argument.

Okay, yes, she *had* agreed to embark on this crazy pursuit of what people called love, and it *was* important to complete the project when there was grant money involved, but travelling halfway round the world just to interview a former student about marriages in Hawaii? That wasn't crazy, it was lunacy as well as being very un-environmentally friendly! Hadn't Rachel heard of videoconferencing?

However, she had to admit that her anxiety over climate change wasn't really what was scratching at her craw. Rachel had held off emailing her flight tickets and intended itinerary for as long as possible and now she knew why. Careful scrutiny in the check-in queue at Heathrow airport had instigated a frantic call to her so-called oldest and most treasured friend, and she was seriously considering renaming her Ruthless Rachel.

'What's the problem, Liv?'

'The *problem* is that I did not sign up to travel thousands of miles *around the world* on my own!'

'You don't want to go on a round-the-world trip?' asked Rachel, all innocence. 'Lots of people would kill for an opportunity like that! Anyway, as I explained to you in the email, the ticket was cheaper than a return ticket to Hawaii via LAX.'

'You don't fool me, Rach. Just because I've been temporarily shoved out of the legal profession does not mean I have lost my edge, thank you very much! I'm fine with the stop-off in LA, and I'd already agreed to meet up with your friend Alani in Oahu. What I'm objecting to is the stopover on the way back!'

'What's wrong with Singapore? I've heard it's a fabulous city, great shopping, too.'

'Ah, my friend the comedienne! You know exactly what I mean. Have you spoken to Nathan?'

'No, but I *have* spoken to Hollie who tells me that her brother is ecstatic about getting a visitor from home. Elliot's been over in Singapore for weeks, and apparently he's hardly set foot out of the kitchen. He's desperate to do a spot of sightseeing and who better to join him than one of his sister's best friends? Tell me that's not a win-win.'

Olivia could hear the familiar tapping of Rachel's silver earrings against the screen of her mobile and despite her irritation at being well and truly stitched up, she had to smile. She could imagine her oldest friend sitting in her paper-strewn office at the university, sipping a stone-cold Caffè Misto whilst she searched for the half-eaten sandwich left over from yesterday so she didn't have to leave her desk to forage for lunch.

'Swear to me you have not set anything up with Nathan.'

'What harm would it do for the two of you to meet and talk? On neutral ground, so to speak?'

'I'm *not* meeting him, Rach!'

'Okay, okay, I get it.'

There had been a pause in their conversation whilst Olivia handed over an exorbitant amount of cash for a bottle of water and a tiny croissant, more than enough time for Rachel to rethink her tactics and launch an attack from a different angle.

'Look, Singapore is one of the countries on my list for the project. Yes, yes, so it was a little way down the list, but when this absolute bargain of a ticket became available, I jumped at the chance to include South East Asia in the report – a truly global perspective!'

Olivia sighed; she knew what Rachel was saying was just a thinly veiled ruse because she could have easily broken her trip back home in Tokyo where she had to change planes. What she couldn't fathom out, though, was whether Rachel had spoken to Nathan, and if she hadn't, whether she'd be able to resist the temptation to call him once Olivia was in Singapore.

Rachel and Nathan had always got on well together, with Nathan taking an avid interest in Rachel and Denise's desire to one day deliver a faultless Argentinian Tango, or a smooth and elegant Viennese waltz, or a charismatic Rumba. In turn, Rachel had willingly tagged along when Nathan had wanted to spend a night in the freezing Brecon Beacons stargazing, and she had been instrumental in persuading Olivia to accompany them one summer weekend two years ago so that Nathan could unveil a star he had named for her – an overwhelmingly romantic gesture that even now caused Olivia to gasp with emotion.

'Okay, getting back to the point of your visit, Alani is really excited about meeting you and she's even promised to organise a traditional Hawaiian welcome at Honolulu airport. So why don't you try to get some sleep on the way over from LA to Oahu so you can enjoy it and take a few photos for your Instagram page. It'll be lots of fun, something your recent months in London have been chronically short of.'

'That's not true …' Olivia began, but stopped abruptly, because it so was.

'Promise to keep me posted, Liv?'

'Will do.'

Some chance of grabbing a couple of hours sleep! thought Olivia, adjusting her seat and pushing it as far back as it would go, turning to glare at the leggy passenger who simply gifted her with a white toothy smile and a shrug. Perhaps he *was* a basketball player, she thought, noticing for the first time his strong athletic build, elegant fingers and neat manicure.

As there was nothing on the in-flight entertainment system she wanted to watch, she toyed with the idea of ordering a bottle of Laurent-Perrier, Matteo's favourite tipple, but reluctantly decided against it. It hadn't been until she had retreated to her self-imposed hibernation that she had taken the time to calculate the number of units of alcohol the three of them had been consuming each week, and she was horrified to discover that they all exceeded the recommended weekly intake three times over. She'd vowed to make a concerted effort to cut down, but she still experienced the pull of the fizz whenever she was stressed or irritated – clear evidence of how much she depended on a 'quick fix' in which to deposit her emotional baggage.

And whilst she was under the spotlight of self-analysis, she also had to accept that if Rachel hadn't presented her with a neatly structured plan spanning the whole ten months of her career-break, with the next leg of her journey chasing love always in the not-too-distant future, then she might just have sunk into self-absorbed depression. Or maybe she was doing herself a disservice and would have used the time off to travel up to the Yorkshire Dales to scramble through the undergrowth of her life in search of her roots, ever hopeful of spotting fresh branches upon which to hang her shattered dreams.

Eventually, almost twenty hours after leaving Heathrow, she set her foot on the solid ground of the marbled Arrivals Hall of Honolulu International Airport. Due to the long, tiring flight, as well as her involuntary disconnection from her old life, her body felt like it didn't belong to her; her arms were weak, her ankles were swollen and her head was pounding – the latter probably caused by quaffing an entire bottle of champagne that the mischievous imp on her shoulder had not allowed her to refuse.

Nevertheless, giving herself a pat on the back for travelling with only carry-on luggage, Olivia inhaled a deep breath, plastered a smile on her lips, and stepped through the glass doors to receive her traditional Hawaiian lei greeting from a slender, mahogany-haired young woman, with an orange hibiscus tucked behind her ear.

'Aloha! Welcome to Hawaii, Olivia.' The woman beamed, placing a garland of fragrant, lilac-flecked orchids interspersed with tiny pink shells around Olivia's neck with a sigh of contentment. 'I'm Alani Newalu, it's great to meet you.'

'Thank you, Alani, it's great to meet you, too.'

'I hope you like your lei – it's a symbol of love and friendship; two things we have an abundance of here in Hawaii, and something I believe you have come to experience? How was your journey?'

'Well—'

'Yeah, I know it's a trek from London. Believe me, I've done it so many times I never want to see the inside of a plane again. Oh, I really enjoyed studying in England, though. Of course, Professor Denton was my favourite lecturer, but that was three years ago and she's still not come out for a visit!'

'Oh, I—'

'But now we have you! And I guarantee that you'll love Hawaii so much that Professor Denton will not be able to resist my next invitation.'

'I'm sure she'll—'

'Right, just to let you know that I've taken a few days' leave from my uncle's legal practice so I can be at your disposal whilst you're here. Come on, I'll drive you to your hotel in Waikiki so you can get some rest, then tomorrow we'll hit the beach!'

Does this girl understand the rules of conversation? wondered Olivia, feeling as though her participation was superfluous. Still, she thought she would try again.

'Oh, no, really, I'm here to research—'

'You need to acclimatise to our islands. A long journey, jet lag, the time difference, your brain will be like wet sponge cake! You can't possibly be expected to apply your full attention to intellectual pursuits under those conditions. I've tried everything and believe me only a day at the beach helps.'

As they shot through the suburbs of the high-rise state capital in Alani's luminous green Jeep, a kaleidoscope of emotions tumbled through Olivia's body. The onslaught of the intense heat, coupled with the maniacal driving, produced a light-headedness that made her nauseous and she was grateful her contribution to the constant chatter was not required.

When at last the beach paradise of Waikiki loomed, the melee of exhaustion, the cloying perfume of the lei scratching at her neck and chest, together with the hum of the Jeep's engine and the rhythmic music on the stereo caused her head to loll to her shoulder despite the verdant tropical scenery beyond the dusty windscreen.

'Tell me, Olivia, have you been to Hawaii before?'

Sensing the pause in Alani's monologue rather than hearing the question, Olivia dragged her drooping senses back to the surface of the treacle-filled pond she had been swimming in.

'Sorry?'

'Have you visited the Hawaiian Islands before?'

'No, no, I haven't but it's been at the top of my bucket list for years – which is probably one of the reasons I think Rachel selected this US state.'

Olivia gasped, pushing herself into the back of her seat as a decrepit truck whizzed past as close to their little Jeep as primer and paint. She elected to keep talking rather than watch the road.

'I recently met a couple who were married here in Waikiki – in a tiny chapel by the beach. Sarah and Graeme were so envious when I told them of my trip, but I have to admit that I seriously underestimated how far the islands are from the US mainland – the flight over from Los Angeles just about finished me off.'

'Well, the Hawaiian Islands are the most isolated archipelago in the world. We also have the world's most active volcano, Kilauea. It's been erupting continuously since 1983.' And then Alani was off again, delving back into her monologue of extolling her homeland's many virtues. 'And I have great news, Olivia!'

'You do?'

'I absolutely adore the whole tourist trail gig so I intend to be your personal guide for as long as you are here on our beautiful island of Oahu. I love your choice of hotel, by the way – the Pink Palace is amazing! The hotel was one of the first hotels to be built on Waikiki, so it's nearly one hundred years old! It has *the* best spot on the whole beach and a fabulous view of Diamond Head. I promise to let you settle in today, but in honour of your hotel's most famous visitor, Duke Kahanamoku, tomorrow we'll hit the water. Is that okay with you?'

'Great,' murmured Olivia vaguely as she battled the waves of exhaustion threatening to drown her.

'Prof Denton has filled me in on her research project. I know you're meeting up with Jacques Ferrer at some point to talk to him about it, but if you want *my* take on true eternal love,' offered Alani, pausing to scrunch up her ski-slope nose, 'it's that there's no such thing. What's the point shackling yourself to one person? My cousin Mahina just got engaged and she's organised a huge family celebration at my grandparents' ranch to announce it to the world. And she's the same age as me! Life is for surfing, dancing, drinking and, most of all, having fun with *lots* of guys. "Live wild and live free" is my motto. Then, only when you're old and decrepit, should you grab the least offensive guy who's still available and settle down to a life of mortgages and slippers. What's the point of this project, anyway? Most marriages end in divorce, so why bother in the first place? Am I right?'

Alani's perpetual burble continued along the same vein and Olivia zoned out until the screech of tyres signalled their arrival at the hotel and she was catapulted back to the present. What she saw out of the window made her jaw drop.

'Welcome to The Royal Hawaiian Hotel!'

To Olivia, the iconic candy-pink hotel, crouched low in gardens filled with banyan trees and bougainvillea, was more akin to Barbie's wedding cake than a luxury resort, but she loved its quirky architecture instantly. The building had been designed in the Moorish style, but over the years, it had become completely dwarfed by a crowd of modern, high-rise cousins. Rachel, who had suggested the hotel, had informed her that she would be following in the footsteps of the Rockefellers and royalty and now she was standing, staring up at its impressive façade, she could understand why. With a rush of renewed energy, she reached into the back seat, grabbed her holdall, then slammed the door, causing crumbles of rust to dribble to the ground.

'Thanks for meeting me at the airport, Alani.'

Alani leaned over to the passenger side to shout through the open window.

'Pick you up at ten tomorrow. Hang loose!' She wiggled her thumb and pinkie finger before shooting off.

The tranquillity of the hotel's lobby soothed Olivia's prickling skin and raging turmoil. Overwhelmed by fatigue, she was grateful she had taken the decision to plunder her savings instead of accepting the very generous offer of a bed at Alani's parents' ranch. She could still hear Alani's dulcet tones swirling through her addled brain as she checked in and refused assistance with her sparse luggage.

Dumping her bag on the super-king-sized sleigh bed, she drew back the doors to the balcony and descended into awe-filled silence. The tropical tableau spread before her was a beach lover's paradise. All thought of grabbing a quick nap vanished at the sight of the glistening sapphire of the Pacific Ocean and the bleached whiteness of the sandy beach dotted with flamingo-pink umbrellas. Wooden loungers, shielded by rows of swaying palm fronds, surrounded the circular pool as the sun cast its golden rays over the whole idyllic scene.

Of course, these essential elements of any vacation had been available at most of the hotels she had stayed at over the years, but the panorama before her sagging eyes was made unique by the spectacular beauty of the jutting Diamond Head mountain over to her left, coupled with the ducking and diving of the multicoloured gems that were surfers riding the world-famous Waikiki waves.

However, despite the magnificence showcased by Mother Nature, hot tears smarted at Olivia's eyes and her heart contracted painfully. This wasn't how she had envisioned fulfilling the item at the top of her bucket list and the experience of a lifetime felt tainted by the absence of anyone to share it with – specifically Nathan.

But then, wouldn't everything she did from now on qualify for the same observation?

That brutal realisation twisted a knife in her stomach and a surge of emotion breached her defences. She stepped away from the glorious view just in time as her knees crumbled beneath her, sending her crashing onto the huge super-king-sized bed for one, where she sobbed until she had no more tears left to shed.

Everything that had happened to her was of her own making, everything. Even though it hurt, she forced herself to remember the evening when Nathan had arrived home carrying a pineapple in one hand and a coconut in the other, a grin stretching his cheeks, his eyes sparkling with excitement.

She'd laughed. 'What's going on?'

'Guess!'

'We're having Piña Coladas?'

'Where we're going you can have as many Piña Coladas as you like, made from freshly harvested pineapple!'

'What do you mean?'

Nathan had then reached into the inside of his suit jacket and produced a glossy travel brochure, flicking it open at a page extolling the exotic beauty of the Hawaiian Islands. Just thinking of the look on his face when she hadn't squealed with delight sent a firework of agony through Olivia's veins.

Why, oh why had she shaken her head, dousing his happiness with the ice-cold water of the work-commitments excuse? Surely she could have taken two weeks away from her desk to replenish the coffers of marital harmony? Visiting Hawaii had been *her* dream, not Nathan's – his bucket list was topped by a return trip to Paris, his favourite city in the world. Her wonderful husband had done this for her and what had she done? She had thrown it back in his face – or that was how it looked with the benefit of hindsight.

She had learned a salutary lesson: caring about her clients was important, but she had to care about those closest to her too, and included in that list, she was surprised to realise, was caring for herself. Nathan had known this; he had been trying to tell her in as many ways as he could think of until he had run out of ideas and all that was left was for him to move on.

A sharp pang of regret threatened to overwhelm her in her exhausted state. She needed to talk to him; she needed to tell him that she got it now, that she understood what he had been trying to do, and why he had been trying to do it. She knew it was too late for them, and the lesson she had learned had been an extraordinarily high price to pay, but she needed to thank Nathan for sticking with her for so long, and to tell him she wished him well for the next chapter of his life, and that ... and that she hoped he would find love again.

Because if anyone understood the *lessons in love* she was collating, Nathan did.

Chapter 12

'Aloha, Olivia. Are you ready for a visit to Hawaiian Fire?'

Standing next to Alani – petite, lithe, tanned, her dark hair twisted into a ponytail secured with a fresh crimson hibiscus blossom and dressed in trendy cut-off denim shorts and a scarlet string bikini top – Olivia felt like a geriatric giraffe. She wasn't quite old enough, but she felt as though she could easily be mistaken for Alani's mother in her faithful white Capri pants and Breton-striped T-shirt.

Shoving her sartorial inadequacies to one side, she was excited about the promised tour of the island. Alani had been right: her brain did feel like a soggy sponge cake and she was grateful for her suggestion that they should do the tourist trail before she met with Jacques Ferrer, the eminent retired divorce attorney recommended by Alani for his in-depth knowledge in the field. Getting a feel for the islands would enhance her understanding of its inhabitants and the reasons behind the longevity of their unions – just drinking in the paradisiacal scenery spoke volumes.

How could couples *not* be happy living here?

Olivia hopped into Alani's Jeep and quickly fastened her seat-belt, another action that made her feel like a feeble old grandmother, but she shoved her insecurities brusquely away – today was all about having fun!

She assumed that the first place on their itinerary – Hawaiian Fire – was related to the fact that Oahu was one of a chain of 'fiery' islands that made up Hawaii. She hoped part of the tour would include a stop-off at Diamond Head, the volcanic crater she had gazed appreciatively at whilst devouring a plate of croissants and sliced mango on her balcony that morning – there was not a whiff of the swamplands and rice fields from whence the luxury resort had sprung over a hundred years ago.

However, as they swerved through the busy Waikiki streets, teeming with tourists, honeymooners, street vendors and beach lovers clutching colourful surfboards, Olivia realised Alani was not pointing her Jeep in the direction of the mountain. Before she could enquire about their destination, they drew up at the eastern part of the beachfront where they were met by two of the hunkiest guys Olivia had ever had the pleasure of setting eyes on. Both stood over six feet tall in their flip-flops and knee-length Hawaiian surf shorts, their rippling six-packs displayed without inhibition or arrogance – and they smelled of coconut and sunshine!

'Aloha, Alani! And you must be Olivia? Great to meet you,' said the tousled-haired Adonis, offering Olivia his fist to bump.

'Hi!' she squeaked, sending a blast of warmth to her face.

The surfer guy smirked, clearly used to the reactions of females, before running his baby-blue eyes over Olivia's conservative attire.

'Okay, Olivia, you can change over there.'

'Change?' Her voice sounded like she'd swallowed helium.

'Sure. You weren't thinking of surfing in pants, were you?'

'Surfing? Oh, I don't think we are here to …' Olivia shot a nervous glance at Alani.

Alani smiled. 'It'll be fun, Olivia. Have you never surfed before?'

She had no need to verbalise her answer; she knew it was

written in great big letters in the expression of horror scrawled across the width of her face.

'No worries. Brett and Steve are not only surfing instructors, they are firefighters and qualified lifeguards, too, so you'll be ultra-safe.'

'Oh, I'm not sure I ...'

'Safety is our number one priority, Olivia,' confirmed Brett, a dark-haired New Zealander with the physique of a rugby player. 'There'll be five instructors out there on the waves this morning and we have a class of eight students. Our instruction is clear and, for beginners like you, it will be one-to-one until you get the feel of the waves.'

'Come on, Olivia,' urged Steve, casting his eyes towards the swell of the ocean. 'It's going to be an exhilarating experience in the most beautiful location in the world. Who wouldn't want to try out surfing on Waikiki Beach?'

Olivia couldn't argue with his taste in scenery – it was truly spectacular and the water was already sprinkled with a confetti of swimmers. But surfing?

A twist of nerves coiled through her stomach and her heartbeat quickened, although that could be to do with the fact that Steve had slid his palm into hers and was leading her towards the stand where a plethora of coloured boards awaited selection. She was shocked to find a flare of physical desire shoot through her body and head southwards as she met his eyes, the thick curl of honey-coloured eyelashes adding a sweep of jealousy to the mix. Why did guys get such great lashes?

Steve selected a long, wide surfboard made of lightweight fibreglass perfect for the gentler waves of Waikiki, pointing out the three fins on the underside, which enhanced stability.

'This is the best type of board for beginners.'

Olivia knew when she was beaten. She swapped her clothes for a navy and white one-piece she bought from the surf store, its varnished wooden shelves also crammed with the ubiquitous

Hawaiian shirts emblazoned with tropical palms and red and yellow parrots and the wildest, most exuberant swimming shorts she had ever seen. The spirit of 'Aloha' was obviously commercial nirvana. She trotted back to the beach where the other surf novices were lined up in front of the instructors.

'Start with your board on the sand like this.'

Steve demonstrated the skill by lying flat on his stomach, imitating the action of paddling in the water with his arms and hands, then he strolled along the line correcting technique. Olivia never expected to be so grateful to her father for those weekly jaunts to the local swimming baths in Leeds as she was growing up. She had always moaned on the journey there but glowed on their way back home with a hot chocolate inside her and her hand clutching the next certificate of achievement.

When Olivia had mastered the theory, she followed the other surfing students across the talcum-soft sand to the shallows of the turquoise ocean to practise her newly acquired paddling technique, and it wasn't long before she moved on to whipping her legs up onto the board in a crouching position, whooping with delight at being able to ride the surf, if only for a few seconds. She knew the sea there was shallow, and that the waves were the equivalent of nursery ski slopes, but Olivia didn't care. The thrill of being carried forward by the power of an immense curl of crystal-clear water fired her energy levels, and she remounted her orange-and-yellow board repeatedly to squeeze every ounce of enjoyment from the two-hour lesson, which came to an end before she knew it.

'Thank you, Steve.' Olivia smiled. 'I had fun!'

'You're welcome!'

'*Mahalo nui loa*, Steve!' called Alani. 'Will I see you at my cousin's luau Saturday night?'

'Sure will, Alani.'

Steve's impressive shoulders glistened in the sunshine as he said goodbye and trotted off to deliver his next tutorial to another eagerly waiting group of beginners. Surf dude wasn't Olivia's usual type, but she could easily make an exception, especially as she took a moment to appreciate his muscular physique from the rear. Had she just stumbled upon another lesson to add to Hollie's list – perhaps accompanied by a photograph, merely to illustrate her point, of course?

Mmm, how to phrase it?

Olivia Hamilton's Lessons in Love: No 8. *"Sexual attraction and the frisson of physical desire in a partnership must surely contribute to enduring love."*

'Wow, what an exhilarating experience.' Olivia laughed as she rubbed her body dry in the tiny wooden hut round the back of Hawaiian Fire's cabin and dragged her clothes back on.

'Can't come to Hawaii and not surf the waves!' declared Alani, twisting her luscious hair into a top-not. 'And you've never partied until you've partied Polynesian-style, either. Why don't you join me and my family on Saturday night to celebrate my cousin's engagement at our ranch?'

Olivia dumped her soggy costume in her bag and jumped into Alani's Jeep. Already her under-used muscles were seizing up from the unexpected exertion.

'That's very generous of you, Alani, but I'm still shattered from the trip. And I'm interviewing Jacques Ferrer on Saturday afternoon, then I'll need to write up my notes.'

Even to her ears it sounded like a lame excuse delivered by one of the 'old and decrepit' women Alani had referred to the previous day, who had exited life's superhighway of adventures and settled down to marriage and mortgages. Nevertheless, what Olivia had said was true: a morning's surfing had drained her limited physical resources because she'd paid no attention to her fitness levels for years and her muscles were screaming their objection to the onslaught.

But then, to someone like Alani, she *was* old, she reminded herself. She would be celebrating her fortieth birthday on the twelfth of December. She wondered how old Steve and Brett were? Twenty-five? Twenty-six?

Olivia chanced a glimpse at Alani, her suntanned arms outstretched on the steering wheel, her wavy hair drying naturally around her shoulders, Ray-Bans guarding her eyes against the glare of the sun. This sprite of a girl had collected her from the airport, given up her time off to take her surfing, and was now extending the hand of friendship further by adding her name to the guest list of her family's celebration.

She thought back to her visit to Malta, to Niko and the way he had included her in his own family's party. She hadn't been to a similar family gathering at home since Nathan's fortieth birthday and a swirl of regret caused her to reconsider Alani's generous invitation.

'Sorry, Alani. What I meant to say was, I'd be honoured to attend your cousin's engagement party. Thank you for inviting me and thank you for giving up your time to make me feel welcome. It's working.'

'No problem!'

They arrived at the hotel in one piece, and Olivia thanked Alani again, then spent the next hour meandering through the ten acres of garden that encircled the Pink Palace. She adored the lush tropical diversity of the bougainvillea, gardenias and hibiscus fighting for supremacy next to banana and koa trees whose trunks, a tiny brass plaque informed her, were used to make canoes. There were even pineapple plants that for some reason she thought grew on trees like coconuts but in fact grew close to the ground, as well as examples of the coffee plant that produced the world-famous Kona coffee: the main crop – the only coffee grown in the United States – being cultivated commercially in the Mauna Loa's rich volcanic soil on the Island of Hawaii.

Olivia spent the rest of the day swimming in the pool and relaxing on the sun-loungers trying not to gaze at the honey-mooning couples smooching beneath the palm trees. After a taste-bud-tingling meal of parmesan mahi-mahi with baked artichoke and red peppers, and a rich passion fruit soufflé scattered with caramelised macadamia nuts, she returned to her room, tired but replete and happier than she had been for a while – which she put down to the fact that she was no longer skipping meals and had spent the whole day outside in the fresh air and taking part in physical exercise.

With the uplift in her spirits came a surge of confidence. She reached for her phone and scrolled through her contacts until she found the one she was looking for, pressing the call button before she lost her nerve. A few moments passed before she heard the familiar buzzing sound, her heart pounding out a concerto of trepidation as she waited for Nathan to answer. However, her call went to voicemail and when she was asked to leave a message she panicked and hung up, refusing to listen to the demon on her shoulder calling her a coward.

But what she had to say to Nathan couldn't be summed up in a voicemail.

As shards of indigo twilight darted through her balcony windows, Olivia grabbed her laptop and slipped between the delicious coolness of the sheets, intent on diverting her thoughts to composing an email to Rachel, but all she managed to type was 'arrived safely' before she tumbled into a dreamless sleep, awaking the following morning to yet another glorious cascade of dawn's pale sunlight streaming through the gap in the tropical-themed curtains.

She swung her legs to the floor and groaned; every muscle in her body felt like it was encased in concrete. She hobbled into the bathroom but couldn't straighten up to tug on the shower, so she grabbed the bath taps and managed to release a gush of hot water, tipping in a whole bottle of the aromatic bath cream.

As she soaked away her aches and pains, she had an unexpected revelation. Just as it had in Valletta, her constant battle with the insomnia monsters had been overcome. Yes, she was physically drained, but that alleged antidote to anxiety had been tried before in her five-year 'war' on sleep and had never produced results – just deeper exhaustion.

The simple realisation that she had enjoyed another unbroken night's sleep, mingled with the floral scent of the chin-high bubbles, delivered a shot of adrenalin to her veins. With a smile on her face and a spring in her step, she jumped out of the bath, towelled herself dry and slipped into a peach chiffon summer dress for that day's meeting with Jacques Ferrer, the lawyer who shared Rachel's interest in the ramifications of divorce from this side of the world.

She wondered what he was like.

Chapter 13

Hi Rachel,

What a fascinating man Jacques Ferrer is. As soon as the taxi pulled up outside his beachfront home, I realised what a privilege it was for me to be interviewing him. Did you know Jacques was a divorce attorney in Honolulu for over forty years? Forty years! He was practising law before I was even born! I didn't tell him that, of course, not sure whether it was so as not to appear impolite or because I didn't want him to know how old I was. He must be approaching seventy, but he still swims in the ocean every day and plays beach volleyball with his partner! And he's sooo handsome – thick silver hair and steel-grey eyes that swirl with unspoken wisdom; he had me at 'Fancy a Mai Tai, Olivia?'

Ooops, sorry, Rach. Back to the task in hand!

I mentioned to Jacques my theory that in such a paradise where the sun always shines and natural beauty is abundant, romance is bound to flourish. Long-term relationships obviously have a better chance of surviving under a Hawaiian sky than, say, under the leaden rainclouds of London or Manchester. But Jacques referred me to the other states competing for the accolade of the US's lowest divorce rate and my arguments in support of the sun-sea-and-sand combination did not stack up. New York and Massachusetts are no tropical Edens yet they've edged Hawaii from the top slot.

According to Jacques' research, a common trait in enduring marriages is that both spouses have a college education. Over 80 per cent of Hawaiian residents finish high school and a significant percentage go on to college where they achieve a higher level of education. Look at Alani whose family supported her for five years whilst she studied abroad. (By the way, she won't stop nagging you for a visit, so you and Denise might want to start saving up! I can just imagine you both dancing the hula in grass skirts and leis.)

Anyway, Jacques argues that most students wait to marry until their studies are completed. This has the knock-on effect of college graduates marrying later. Statistics apparently record teenage marriages are two to three times more likely to end in divorce. Jacques points out the earliest, most favourable age to marry is around twenty-five, after the parties have finished college and had the chance to gain experience in their chosen profession and accumulate maturity, wisdom and finances. The effect of age difference between the spouses is negligible; all college graduates are more likely to marry, their marriages last longer, and they are less likely to divorce.

Also, choosing a partner of similar educational ability results in a higher earning capacity for the partnership and, therefore, enhanced economic stability. Again, Jacques' research has shown that couples with an income of over fifty thousand dollars are at lower risk of divorce than those earning under twenty-five thousand. A steady job and a steady income means a stable life and partnership. The family enjoys better, healthier lives, smarter kids, less financial anxiety, which in turn produces more understanding, tolerance and increased enlightenment. This translates into sound marriage values where partners stick together naturally or persevere more effectively.

And, would you believe, Jacques also found that married couples inherit a higher than average percentage of their family's wealth than their single or cohabitee counterparts? Apparently, relatives believe a marriage contract contributes to a greater sense of trust, stability and permanence, hence an increased willingness to pass on family wealth.

Olivia paused in her typing. Jacques had also shared with her the fact that the growing gender gap in the education system meant exceptionally intelligent women were experiencing increased difficulty in meeting similarly educated men. Her thoughts meandered back to her own college days. She had known Rachel for over twenty years and in that time her friend had never introduced her to a partner. Had she been guilty of moaning about her own relationship when Rachel had struggled for years to find a suitable mate to share her life with?

Guilt tore into the crevices of her heart. Again, she chastised herself for being a neglectful friend, unworthy of the support and affection Rachel lavished on her to prevent her from succumbing to the tentacles of self-pity.

She decided to press 'Save' and finish the report to her oldest, wisest friend the next day, then opened an email from Niko, received only yesterday, inviting her return to Malta in August for their village's *festa*. Simply reading his words conjured up a desire to be standing in that sun-soaked vineyard again, staring up at the stars with Niko's arm wrapped around her shoulders. And yet it wasn't *his* handsome features that floated across her vision and caused her emotions to churn, despite the undeniable chemistry that had drawn her to him and the splash of carefree fun he had brought into her life. The person in that romance-infused image was blond, with soft grey, intelligent eyes and a way of looking at her that made her feel like she was the only woman in the world.

Oh, God, what had she done?

Before she could descend into another helix of remorse her phone chimed with a text from Hollie demanding her next fix of the lessons in love soap opera. She sighed, but the missive had caused her lips to twitch upwards. She had no intention of applying the montage of marital harmony she was amassing for Hollie and Matteo to her own life – she didn't have the courage to deal with what it would reveal – but it was obvious that Hollie had clambered on board the love boat big-style and seemed to be taking what Olivia had discovered so far seriously.

Olivia remembered that Matteo had left for Italy at the same time she had flown to LA, so she knew Hollie would be cast adrift from the moorings of his unswerving friendship despite her euphoria at having just been informed of her selection for the Ladies' County Golf Team. Keen to step into the role of supportive friend at last, she quickly reread her email to Rachel and decided to ping back the next two bulletins for Hollie's delectation.

Olivia Hamilton's Lessons in Love: No 9. *"Marrying after your mid-twenties reduces the risk of divorce."*

Olivia Hamilton's Lessons in Love: No 10. *"Once married, couples with a university education are more likely to remain married because they achieve a higher income and their enhanced economic stability translates to a more stable partnership."*

Olivia pressed 'Send' and snapped her laptop shut.

To her surprise, she was assaulted by a sudden surge of self-reproach. Writing those last two observations brought home to her with a vengeance the fact that she and Nathan had indeed had a better chance than many to make a success of their marriage. They had both been thirty-two when they married, well outside the risk-laden teenage years, and they'd both been fortunate enough to have a university education.

But what was the point of regret?

The past was a place that refused re-entry and she realised for the first time that no good could come of wallowing in the mire of misery that was of her own making.

So, she made a decision.

She was going to spend the evening at Alani's luau in the company of friends who had no knowledge of the way her selfish obsession with her career had destroyed her marriage.

Chapter 14

The engagement celebrations were in full throttle when her limo-taxi swooped up to the front porch of the Newalu family ranch. A white picket fence laced the sprawling property, and a procession of tiki torches lit the driveway to the house beyond from which the booming base of a live rock band throbbed.

Olivia took a moment to chastise herself for her clichéd expectation of hearing the elegant and graceful swirl of Polynesian hula music! A waft of white ginger floated in the humid night air as she strolled towards the hub of the party, past a gathering of palm trees, and a huge mango tree, its branches weighed down with ripe fruit and various other flora and fauna she didn't recognise.

Stick a broom in the fertile soil here and it would produce flowers, she thought.

'Good evening, Madam,' said a teenage cocktail waiter handing her a glass filled with a neon-coloured liquid.

'Good evening. Erm, what exactly is this?'

'Maui blanc, pineapple wine.'

She took a tentative sip, enjoying the sudden burst of fruity zest and optimism it delivered.

'Mmm, it's delicious, thank you.'

The waiter directed her towards the Olympic-sized swimming pool around which glamorous couples giggled and dozens of braziers spurted amber flames, which cast a rich golden glow over the assembled partiers. Exotic colognes and perfumes swirled through the air, mingled with the enticing aroma of roast pork that made her stomach growl and again she smiled at the fact that her usual missing-in-action appetite had returned with a vengeance in Hawaii. For a woman who never ate breakfast, she had surprised herself by indulging in the cornucopia of tropical splendour at the hotel's morning buffet – kiwi, papaya, guava, passion fruit and, of course, pineapple – as well as partaking in a lunchtime feast of sushi prepared by Jacques Ferrer's housekeeper, and yet here she was drooling over what she might find on the barbecue!

'Hey, Olivia! Glad you could make it. Love the shoes! Come on, the guys are getting the batons fired up.'

Olivia followed in Alani's fragrant wake to where a raised dais had been erected as a temporary dance floor in front of a bamboo-and-thatch pagoda, its eaves dressed in a garland of fairy lights. The rock group had given way to a troupe of Hawaiian musicians; the women, in full-length dresses, wore colourful leis and circlets of orchids in their hair, and were performing the *hula kahiko* to the slack-key strains of the ukulele.

'Those instruments the men have lashed to their thighs are called *pahu* – it's a coconut tree drum covered in shark skin. And those bulbous drums over there – *ipu heke* – are made from hollowed-out gourds,' explained Alani, her eyes wide in excitement.

Olivia was transfixed by the performance. The familiar Hawaiian rhythm began slowly to the accompaniment of the *pahu* as well as the striking of bamboo poles, an overture that drew the entire party crowd to the edge of the stage in anticipation of the floorshow. Five minutes later, four muscular fire-dancers leapt, barefoot and bare-chested, onto the dais, twirling double-ended batons of flames like pyrotechnic cheerleaders, the scent of burning paraffin wafting through the humid night air. All the men wore loincloths, dog-tooth ornaments around their knees, and talisman leis of shells, teeth and feathers around their necks. A powerful bolt of lust shot through Olivia's lower abdomen when she realised one of the Hawaiian fire-dancers was Steve – wow, he really was a man of multiple talents!

'Are you drooling, Olivia?' Alani nudged her and giggled.

The tempo of the music continued to climb, and the beat of Olivia's heart matched it. Despite being aware that Steve was an experienced firefighter, she found herself holding her breath, her heartbeat pounding through her ears, grimacing every time the fiery wand was flung into the air and she saw one of the dancers poised to catch it with his toes.

With the first dance at an end, a different Polynesian performer strode onto the stage, his long baton lit on one end only. Olivia's jaw hung loose as, in mesmerised silence, the audience watched the fire-eater begin his repertoire. Over and over, he swallowed the blazing pole, and when the show concluded Olivia made as much noise in appreciation as everyone else in the crowd.

'Come on. They're opening the *imu!*'

Alani grabbed Olivia's hand, skipping off to where her grandfather was getting ready to perform the ceremony of opening the underground oven in which the *kalua* wrapped in banana leaves had been baking for hours. The mouth-watering aroma of roast pork and baked potatoes snaked through the air.

'We don't have *kalua* often enough!' lamented Alani, digging into a plateful of food, her eyes bright with appreciation. 'I adore it, but you've got to try it with a dollop of this, Olivia. It's a traditional Hawaiian dish we call *"poi"*.'

Olivia wasn't sure she wanted to taste-test the unappetising-looking, purple-grey sauce, but this trip was all about trying new things, breaking out of her comfort zone and experiencing life outside her carefully constructed bubble. In fact, she was beginning to relish the challenge her travels had brought to every one

of her senses and realised that her life over the
become dull, drab and mundane.

Once again, an image of Nathan floated across
a whoosh of contrition followed in its wake whe
kind eyes filled with pleading for her to spend
indulging in all the good things life had to offer with
of stubbornly putting her career before anything else.

Had it been worth it? She now knew the answer to
'Olivia, are you okay?'

'Oh, sorry, yes, I'm fine. So, what is this exactly?'

'It's made from the root vegetable called *taro*. We bake them,
like potatoes, then mash them into this paste. It's believed that
when a bowl of *poi* is on a Hawaiian table we are dining with
our ancestors.'

Under Alani's watchful gaze, Olivia wrapped her tongue
around the offered fork. Inbred politeness, especially after hearing
of the food's connection to Hawaiian culture, prevented her from
spitting it onto her plate, but try as she might she couldn't control
her facial expression.

Alani let out a shriek with laughter. 'Disgusting, isn't it? My
grandmother absolutely refuses to prepare it with added sugar
or milk. Prefers it the traditional way. Why don't I go and get us
some drinks?'

'That'll be great, thanks, Alani.'

Olivia watched her young friend float off towards the house,
stopping every now and again to chat to a guest, giggle with a
relative or deposit kisses on the cheeks of her grandparents. With
her eyes still filled with the flashing swirls of fire and her mouth
rancid from the *poi*, she decided to take a stroll around the
expansive gardens to continue her contemplation of how her
outlook on life had changed, but *only* because change had been
forced upon her.

If she hadn't been so wrapped up in other people's woes, she
could have been surfing the Waikiki waves, drinking Mai Tai

cocktails under the brooding shadow of Diamond Head or enjoying freshly roast pork straight from the traditional pit oven – accompanied by home-baked pineapple bread and aromatic sticky rice – with Nathan by her side. With a blast of agonising insight, she knew that she was still in love with him, that he was and always would be her soulmate, the only person she would ever want at her side as she travelled down life's highway.

She was ashamed of the drastic lengths he'd had to go to for her to see the light, and, in a way, the delivery of the divorce petition had been a gift, an unwelcome one at the time, but one that had sent her on this journey of self-discovery. Even in his darkest hour, Nathan had still put her wellbeing first. Tears sparkled along her lower lids and she suspected she might have lost her grip on her emotions had Alani not skipped into view.

'Ah, there you are!' she cried, handing her another glass of Maui blanc, completely oblivious to Olivia's flirtation with sadness. 'So, tell me, how did you get on with Jacques? What a guy, hey? What he doesn't know about the institution of marriage is not worth knowing – and he's gorgeous too!'

Alani's giggles rang out into the night and the flickering ribbons of amber from the torches reflected in her dilated pupils as they strolled back to join the party via the impressive swimming pool, its surface shimmering aquamarine from the coloured backlights. The whole estate was stunningly beautiful, and Olivia chastised herself for her dalliance with gloom when she should be taking advantage of the friendship that was on offer at the Newalu home. She pinned a smile on her face and tuned back in to Alani's chatter.

'You're right, Alani, he is incredibly handsome.'

'But what I want to know is, why are you and Rachel so intent on researching marriage? Why not research the positives of remaining single – that'd be a great project! There're loads of benefits – the freedom to travel wherever you want, to study abroad, to go wild, to simply sway in the unpredictable current of life without having to allow for someone else's dreams. I love my independence and I don't intend to give it up for anyone.'

She cast a glance over to where Mahina and her fiancé were holding hands as they toured their guests, accepting heartfelt congratulations and warm wishes for lifelong happiness.

'Not like my cousin over there. And Keon. Look at him – he's like a cow-eyed puppy! Although I suppose he *is* ancient. Did you know, he's chucked in his stockbroking career in Manhattan to come back home and get married? What an idiot! But then, I suppose when you get to thirty-five you can't hang with the in-crowd anymore.'

Olivia cringed, feeling like the resident elderly aunt. She was grateful for the low lighting as she felt her cheeks grow hot.

'I intend to squeeze every last ounce of fun out of life, to party until the "peeps squeak" as my brother says. Poor thing, he's already under pressure from my parents to settle down.'

Olivia took in the stubborn tilt of Alani's chin, which then froze as her new friend's eyes landed on Brett who was laughing with Steve and a bunch of fellow firefighters at the pool bar. *Mmm*, she thought, *doth the young lady protest too much?*

Alani realised Olivia had seen her reaction and smirked.

'Rules are made to be broken, though, aren't they? I met Brett at high school after his family emigrated here from New Zealand. But then, as you know, I travelled over to the UK to go to college and stayed on to do my post-grad doctorate at UCL. We didn't see each other for five years. Now he's a firefighter and a surfer, and well, how can you not feast your eyes on those abs! Catch you later!'

Olivia received a quick hug before Alani flounced off to join the riotous gathering of her friends and she continued her saunter towards the house. The music had switched to a serene lull and as she stepped onto the wooden veranda that during the day afforded the most panoramic view, she considered ordering a taxi back to the hotel until she was snapped out of her reverie by the return of Alani with Brett and Steve in tow.

'Let's dance!'

And before Olivia could marshal her arguments, she had been dragged onto the dance floor to be taught the hula. She was completely useless, but grateful the instruction wasn't in the art, or was that the science, of fire-eating! She possessed no discernible rhythm but was able to add yet another unique emotion to her treasure box – that of true abandonment to the poetry of music, with the assistance of copious Maui blanc and Mai Tai cocktails, of course.

Steve, on the other hand, was a fabulous dancer, his muscular physique evident as he gyrated his hips in sync with Olivia's under the guise of demonstrating a difficult move. Unlike her experience with Niko, with whom she had felt a connection, Steve made her senses zing with what could only be described as physical desire.

And yet, still there was something missing, something that took her a while to put her finger on – and when she did her cheeks glowed with embarrassment. Steve was twenty-five, she was thirty-nine, and whilst she had nothing against an age gap in a relationship, the sad fact was that they had absolutely nothing in common; he had not asked her anything about herself, nor had she been in the slightest bit interested in finding out more about him beyond showing her the next dance moves.

Back at the Pink Palace, she threw herself across her bed, exhausted yet exhilarated, all traces of her earlier melancholy eradicated by the soothing antidote of dancing, laughter and friendship. She glanced at her bedside clock and was shocked to see it was 3 a.m. Tomorrow was her last day and she had to be up early as there was no way she was going to leave Hawaii without visiting Pearl Harbor and paying her respects to the USS Arizona Memorial.

Chapter 15

Olivia walked out onto the balcony, rubbing the sleep from her eyes and hugging a cappuccino to her chest. She felt privileged to be there, to witness the apricot fissures of dawn break over the inky black of the Pacific Ocean whilst she stood in quiet contemplation of the day ahead. The USS Arizona Memorial was one of the reasons a visit to Hawaii had topped her bucket list. Her grandfather, Arthur John Hamilton, had served with the Royal Navy in the Second World War, and although deeply reluctant to talk about his experiences, he had shared one story with her father, recited on numerous occasions as dementia thrust his memories back to the past.

During the first year of the war, Arthur had served with an Australian midshipman by the name of Frederick Garrett. Freddie was a poet and a skilled strummer of the guitar. He was also an accomplished narrator, constantly regaling his fellow soldiers with stories of his trips to see his elder brother who had emigrated to join their aunt and uncle in Hawaii. Many a wretched night in the Atlantic had been survived by listening to Freddie's Aussie accent curl around tales of pretty girls and exotic food.

Her grandfather had survived the war and, in 1946, had gone

on to marry the nurse who nurtured both his physical health and psychological well-being as he recovered from the amputation of his left leg. Arthur and Dorothy Hamilton produced one precious son, Malcolm, and had been married for fifty years when breast cancer stole Arthur's beloved Dottie, an event which launched the beginning of his downward spiral of spirits even the war had not crushed. He'd died six months later with a smile on his face, secure in the knowledge that he was on his way to join his beloved wife.

During her father's visits to her grandfather's care home, the story of Freddie Garrett had often been repeated, sometimes three times in an afternoon. Her father had not objected, but the main thrust of Arthur's reminiscences was a request that his son find out for him what had become of Freddie and his brother, Charles. As Olivia's mother, Julie, had recently registered on a course to trace her own family tree, she had volunteered to undertake the task, not realising the complexity, or the heartbreak, she would encounter.

Olivia knew the story well. Freddie had survived the war, too, and had been relatively easy to trace as he'd gone on to publish some of his poetry before moving on to song-writing. Sadly, his brother Charles had not fared so well and his name was amongst the 1102 engraved on the white marble of the *USS Arizona* Memorial. Olivia had made a promise to her father, and sent up a silent assurance to her grandfather, that she would pay her respects to Charles Donald Garrett who'd died serving his adopted country on the seventh of December 1941.

The Visitor Centre at Pearl Harbor opened at 7 a.m. and she intended to be first in line to grab one of the two thousand tickets made available on the day. Although she would have preferred to spend as long as possible visiting all four of the historic sites and to catch a cab from there straight to the airport, she decided to store her meagre luggage with the concierge because the increased security measures demanded a strict 'No Bags' policy.

Olivia was repulsed by the thought that anyone could even consider attacking such a memorial.

Her first glimpse of the white, bow-tie-shaped memorial floating in the middle of the deep-blue harbour would remain forever imprinted in her mind's eye. After viewing the documentary film depicting the attack on the harbour and taking the audio tour of the exhibit recited by Jamie Lee Curtis, she boarded the first US Navy boat of the day to shuttle visitors to the offshore memorial. Their volunteer guide informed them that the permanent monument had been formally dedicated in 1962 and that over one and a half million visitors came to Pearl Harbor in a pilgrimage of commemoration, honour and respect each year.

'The memorial was designed by Oahu architect, Alfred Preis, and consists of three main parts: the entry, the assembly room where you are all now standing, and the shrine. Notice the seven, open barrel-shaped windows on each side of the walls and the ceiling. You may also like to take a look through the floor, which overlooks the sunken hull of the USS Arizona. We ask you, please, not to throw floral tributes into the water, but you may leave your offerings on the guard rails around the shrine.'

Olivia moved over to one of the windows to stare down into the depth of the waters, still bleeding black tears of oil from the sunken carcass of the battleship, and the voices around her became muffled by sadness. At the far end of the assembly hall, behind red velvet ropes, was the shrine. She struggled to gulp down her rising emotions as she contemplated the enormity of what had taken place there whilst reading the inscription:

'TO THE MEMORY OF THE GALLANT MEN
HERE ENTOMBED AND THEIR SHIPMATES
WHO GAVE THEIR LIVES IN ACTION
ON DECEMBER 7, 1941 ON THE U.S.S. ARIZONA.'

And, as she ran her eyes down the long list of names, halting at 'Garrett, Charles Donald', she could suppress her tears no longer. She hooked the lei she had brought with her around the post and moved away to allow other visitors their moment of solitude.

She stared out over the verdant landscape of Oahu, so at odds with the carnage of eighty years ago, thinking of the sacrifices Charles Donald Garrett, his brother Freddie, and her own grandfather had made to guarantee her and her generation the freedoms they took for granted. It was time to get her life in order – to put her loved ones first, just like her ancestors had done with such tragic consequences.

The experience of the tour, taking in the 'Remembrance Circle', the original *USS Arizona* anchor and ship's bell, guided by a wheelchair-assisted veteran, would remain etched in her heart until the day she died.

Chapter 16

Alani hugged Olivia, crushing the petals of the 'farewell' lei she had just strung around her neck and releasing the pungent odour of the flowers Olivia wasn't sure she liked.

'Please, please, please persuade Rachel to come over and visit us, Olivia, especially now that you can report back first-hand just how beautiful Hawaii is.'

'I will, Alani, and thanks so much for your time and your family's hospitality. I love it here. I will definitely be back, if not with Rachel, then with my parents.'

This had been a decision she had taken on the short taxi ride from Pearl Harbor to the hotel. She had made herself an unbreakable promise that as soon as she arrived back in London, she would shoot up to visit her parents in Yorkshire. She squashed the squirm of guilt that she had not yet factored a trip to Leeds into her itinerary, but she intended to rectify that straight away. Malcolm and Julie Hamilton favoured the local independent travel agents to plan and book their occasional holidays abroad, and she would arrange for the three of them to honour her grandfather's memory together by booking a holiday to the Hawaiian Islands.

'Why not ditch the research into the academics of love, Olivia?

All you have to do is let fun to preside over your life choices and happiness will surely follow. Don't fret the small stuff. Hang loose!'

The young girl planted a kiss on each of Olivia's cheeks, waved her fingers and sped away leaving Olivia feeling as though she had been discharged from the vortex of a whirlwind. With a rueful smile, she slung the handles of her bulging holdall over her shoulder and made her way towards Departures, but sadly the relief of her release from the high-octane excitement that emanated from Alani did not last long.

She had hoped to spend the next leg of her journey from Honolulu to Tokyo – where she had a seven-hour stopover – asleep or at least dozing. However, as soon as she had boarded the plane, a snake of dread usurped her new-found serenity as she wondered what would be waiting for her when she arrived at her eventual destination.

Should she contact Nathan whilst she was in Singapore? Or should she try to ignore the fact he was in the same city and just meet up with Elliot, do some more sightseeing, and then jet off back home?

Whilst she hadn't tried to call Nathan again, she *had* sent him an email – short, friendly, upbeat, with a photograph of the view from her balcony out over the Pacific Ocean. But she hadn't received a reply. Okay, so she knew that he would be busy settling into his new job, a new home, a new life, but she had expected a response, however brief, especially as he would have known she had also tried to call him even if she hadn't left a message on his voicemail.

She knew the geographical distance from their old lives in London would enable them to discuss their respective future intentions in a civilised and balanced way without the risk of adding to the carnage of their marriage. Knowing Nathan as she did, she was sure they would be able to have an adult conversation over dinner somewhere, which would go some way to ensuring that, after the divorce proceedings had been finalised, they could continue to be friends.

But as she boarded the plane that would take her to Singapore, her confidence started to unravel and she became terrified of what the meeting would reveal. Maybe it *would* end in the dreaded animosity or, even worse, in the confirmation of that niggle in the back of her mind that was morphing into a giant elephant – that he had met someone else.

She ordered a Mai Tai, and then a second. After her fourth, she promised herself she would stop the procrastination and come up with a definitive decision before the plane touched down at Changi Airport. Irrespective of anything else, the squirm of indecision was nauseating, but it grew until she liberated her luggage from the carousel and made her way out into the scorching July air of Singapore.

'Hey, Livvie! Over here!'

Hollie's twin brother waved at her from the middle of a knot of anxious travellers, then began to weave his way towards her, grinning from ear to ear before pulling her into a bear hug. She happily handed over her holdall and followed him out of the airport that had been voted the best in the world an incredible six times in a row, towards a sleek, black limousine waiting at the kerb outside.

'Welcome to the Lion City! How was Hawai'i?'

Olivia smiled at Elliot's pronunciation of 'Hawaii' – with a break between the 'a' and the 'i' – just as Alani had done.

'I absolutely loved it. It's been a dream of mine to visit Waikiki since I had a teenage crush on Tom Selleck in *Magnum PI*.' She laughed, but had no intention of revealing that her obsession with the Hawaii-based detective had never truly evaporated. 'You didn't have to order a limo, Elliot, an ordinary taxi would do, you know!'

She was overjoyed to see Hollie's brother and loved how she felt as though she was in the company of a good friend even though she hadn't seen him for well over a year. Like his sister, he had inherited their mother's Scandinavian colouring and wore his marmalade-coloured hair cropped short with a smidgeon of gel to enhance the quiff at his forehead.

'Oh, actually it's the hotel's – the title "Head Chef" at one of the most popular hotel restaurants in Singapore does have some perks, you know, and I thought it was about time I took advantage of them.'

'How's the new job going?' she asked as she settled in the back seat of the fabulously air-conditioned car and leaned her head against the headrest.

'Oh, I adore the job, Liv. The opportunity to try out new recipes is amazing – and there's not an order of boring old battered fish and chips in sight! I'm in the Match Restaurant and Lounge, which is mainly modern American cuisine. There's Open-Faced Lobster Ravioli and Brick-Flattened Chicken on the menu. But we also offer a more personalised dining experience.'

'Really?'

'The dinner guest first has a choice of New Zealand Angus steak, Australian striploin or Wagyu Ribeye and there's also Norwegian salmon, wild Atlantic cod or Maine lobster. Sadly not Cornish lobster, the best in the world in my humble opinion. Next, the ravenous diner gets to select from a list of accompanying sauces such as Morel Mushroom and Merlot or Roasted Jalapeño Chimichurri for the meat or Salsa Verde for the fish. Then, we have the side dishes like Rhubarb and Dry Cherry Chutney or Squid Ink Risotto Cakes.'

Olivia recognised the feverish glow in Elliot's deep blue eyes. It was exactly the same as his sister's when she was worked up about a criminal case she was handling or recounting the finer details of a symphony she was rehearsing. And, just like Hollie, his West Country accent thickened as his passion for his chosen profession shone out from his very soul.

Olivia thought back to the time when she had first met Elliot when she and Hollie had become friends after she'd qualified as a solicitor and landed a job in London. She had spent many summer days sunbathing on the beaches of Cornwall and the evenings waiting on tables at Hollie and Elliot's parents' upmarket fish restaurant, Marbles, in Newquay. As a child from a northern industrial city, Olivia had envied Hollie, Elliot and his best friend Matteo, growing up in such idyllic surroundings – swimming, fishing, drinking with friends on the beach.

It had been an ambition of Elliot's for as long as she'd known him to work as a chef at an internationally renowned hotel, and she was thrilled that his dream had come to fruition in an exotic South East Asian destination. Okay, it wasn't Raffles, one of Elliot's favourite hotels, but it was close. However, when she glanced across at him as they made their way towards the hotel overlooking Marina Bay, the happiness she saw fizzing in his eyes couldn't only be attributable to his culinary passion and the fact that his sister's best friend had arrived to stay for a few days.

'What are you looking at me like that for?' asked Elliot.

'There's something else, isn't there, El? Or should I say *someone* else?'

Olivia smiled in satisfaction as he sucked in his lips and ran his fingers through his hair.

'Did Hollie tell you? I warned her not to gossip.'

'She didn't have to tell me anything. I can see there's something going on just by looking at your expression. Come on, spill the details to Auntie Livvie, "love guru extraordinaire".'

'I don't know what you're talking about.'

Olivia saw Elliot flash a quick look at the chauffeur before lowering his voice to a whisper.

'Okay, okay, if you must know, I've met a girl out here. We've had a couple dates … erm, no, actually, we've seen each other every day since I've been here. She's a receptionist at the Pan Pacific, a native Singaporean, but we're being cautious. Not only because we both work at the hotel – it's not a great idea to date a colleague, is it? – but because she's been hurt before – divorced, actually. Also …' He paused, unsure whether to continue with his confession. '… Ying's only twenty-six.'

'What does age have to do with it?'

Surprisingly, her academic brain whirled into action and began dissecting what Elliot had just confided in her – Rachel would be proud, and surprised – and a twinge of anxiety crept into her thoughts. According to her research so far, Ying's age was not the problem – no, it was her divorce that scored the negative strike against the relationship, but, of course, she maintained her counsel.

'I know it makes no difference, but she's ten years younger than me. It's a huge gap when you say it out loud, but when we're together it means nothing at all.'

Elliot sighed, shook his head, and turned his attention back to Olivia, reaching over to lace his fingers through hers.

'You're going to love Singapore, Liv. As soon as Rachel told me you were coming, I asked for a couple of days off so we can do the zoo, take a Junk ride to Kusu Island, and a trip over to Sentosa Island via the cable car from Mount Faber. I definitely want to see the Gardens by the Bay – they look awesome. We can hit the shops in Orchard Road if you like, and then eat at Clarke Quay. Oh, and of course, we mustn't forget to slurp Singapore Slings in the Long Bar at Raffles or partake in afternoon tea in the Tiffin Room.'

Olivia laughed at Elliot's bubbling enthusiasm for his new home. As she glanced out of the limo's tinted windows at the ordered, sparklingly clean streets and the neighbourhood parks where elderly residents were practising their t'ai chi, she completely understood why. She vowed, there and then, to place a moratorium on the internal cross-examination of her flaws and constant reprimanding for the way her life had recently dive-bombed into the slurry of misery. Instead, she resolved to rekindle her enthusiasm for new discoveries and her natural curiosity in her fellow traveller.

'All those things sound great, El. But would you mind if we just "hang loose" for a day or two first? I've overdosed on sightseeing in Hawaii and I've got a full ten days here so there'll be lots of time to fit everything in.'

'Sure. Oh, and we need to add a visit to Little India to our list – I've got to see the Sri Srinivasa Temple. It's one of the oldest in Singapore. You must have seen photos of it? The entranceway is decorated with hundreds of Hindu deities; each one is unique and painted in such intricate detail. And whilst we're in the area we can grab a curry – I'm craving an authentic chicken Madras!'

The town car was now cruising past the futuristic skyscrapers of the Financial District, their roofs stretching like giant crystal shards into the clear sky. To Olivia, their soaring modernity appeared so incongruous next to the lush tropical palms and the vibrant architecture of the three-storey shop houses huddled in their shadow.

A mere thirty minutes later, they glided to a stop under the Pan Pacific's portico. Elliot ran around to grab her holdall from the boot whilst Olivia waited for him on the red carpet in front of the revolving doors that led into the lobby.

'Does your schedule include meeting up with Nathan?' asked Elliot, studiously avoiding her eyes.

'It does not.'

She had finally made her decision as the plane taxied to the gate at Changi.

'Okay. Cool.'

Without questioning her further, Elliot strode towards the reception desk in the hotel's central atrium, which extended thirty-five floors into the sky, his broad smile lighting up his attractive features. There was no mistaking the mutual attraction between Elliot and the pretty, ebony-haired receptionist dressed in the hotel's uniform.

'This is my sister's good friend, Olivia. Olivia, this is Ying.'

The young woman offered her slender fingers and a perfect smile to Olivia, her dark almond-coloured eyes betraying no special relationship with Elliot to her colleagues.

'Welcome to Singapore, Mrs Fitzgerald. I hope your stay with us will be enjoyable.'

Olivia was taken by surprise at the intensity of her reaction to being addressed as 'Mrs Fitzgerald'. Another note on her list – she had to change her passport back to "Hamilton".

'Please, call me Olivia.' She smiled.

Elliot carried her luggage to the external, high-speed glass elevators, which offered a stunning panorama from the façade of the hotel. Twilight was beginning to descend, and a myriad of twinkling lights flickered from the futuristic glass and steel buildings, as well as a kaleidoscope of ships and junks plying the harbour. It was all a bit too much after her long flight and as the lifts whisked them skywards, Olivia felt a little light-headed.

'I hope this is okay, Liv. I managed to upgrade your room to a Harbour Studio. The thirtieth floor has the best view of the bay and the South China Sea beyond.'

Elliot dumped Olivia's bag onto the pristine white sheets and strode across to the window to pull back the blinds and reveal the high-rise metropolis in all its glory.

'There's the Gardens by the Bay I was telling you about. And that's the Marina Bay Sands Hotel. Amazing, isn't it?'

Olivia went to stand next to Elliot in front of the full-height glass window, drinking in the stunning view of the most original hotel she'd ever seen, completely awed by the architect's vision.

'It looks like a set of cricket stumps with bales balanced on the top. What is that skateboard-like thing perched on the roof?'

'That's the Sands Skypark. It's the world's largest elevated swimming pool. I've only seen photos but there's an amazing infinity pool with the most spectacular panorama beyond. We've got to go to the Observation Deck up there, too!'

With his Cornish accent and irrepressible good humour, Elliot reminded Olivia so much of Hollie it was like having her best friend alongside her. Yet, a sudden wave of tiredness caused her to swoon slightly and she reached out to grasp hold of Elliot's arm before lowering her numb, traveller's buttocks onto the bed that had been expertly turned down, a foil-wrapped luxury chocolate placed on the crisp cuff.

'Sorry, El, I feel so disorientated. I don't know whether it's breakfast time, dinner time or bedtime. My body clock is totally wrecked.'

'Why don't you grab some rest. I'm working this evening and tomorrow anyway, but I have the following two days off, so we can explore then, and maybe have dinner one night at Clarke Quay?'

'Sure I won't be intruding on your relationship?'

'Ying is working tomorrow, too, but if it's okay with you she'll join us for dinner on Friday night?'

'I'd love that. I'm excited to get to know her so I can report back to Hollie and Matteo. You know what they've got me doing, don't you?'

'No, what?'

Olivia quickly filled Elliot in on the research project and the lessons in love they had cajoled her into sending home, before hugging him goodnight and locking the hotel room door behind him. She padded into the sleek bathroom, well stocked with a selection of Elemis products and a pyramid of the ubiquitous white towels and ran herself a bath filled to the brim with fragrant bubbles. With the grime of her journey sloughed from her pores and her body ensconced in a fluffy robe, she raided the minibar for a glass of Australian Sauvignon blanc.

'Ahh,' she sighed as she took the glass to the enormous window overlooking Marina Bay.

Evening had now fully descended over the city and the vista was truly enchanting, like a fairy-tale metropolis, and she couldn't wait to get out there and explore. The guide book she had studied on the flight had told her that Singapore was the 'Gateway to the Orient' – a melting pot of eastern cultures: Chinese, Indian, Malay, with a large dollop of western elegance – British, Dutch, Portuguese – thrown in for good measure. But the Singaporean philosophy of 'Unity in Diversity' was appropriate – it was clear the country, like its very beginnings, still boasted a robust economy, with a skilled workforce and efficient Government.

Despite this being her first visit to South East Asia, she loved the place already. Much of the city she had glimpsed from the limousine's tinted windows had seemed familiar; the Supreme Court, the Old Parliament House, the cricket pitch, the quayside and the Glaswegian-designed bridges were all relics from British colonial rule. However, you only had to scratch the surface and a fusion of Oriental and Asian traditions and cultures shone through.

Excitement tingled in her fingertips at the anticipation of gathering a few more experiences to add to her expanding treasure trove of memories, but as her swollen eyelids began to droop and she dragged the duvet up to her chin, that persistent niggle of doubt refused to be extinguished.

Was she a coward for refusing to meet with Nathan?

Chapter 17

For the last two nights, Olivia had been gifted with refreshing, uninterrupted sleep. She didn't want to jinx the welcome injection of energy that gave her, but could her insomnia finally be cured?

'So, are you ready to be amazed?'

Elliot bounced from the taxi towards the cable car that would fly them from the summit of Mount Faber across to the playground of Sentosa Island like Tigger's younger brother. Olivia was surprised to see that there were different versions of the glass bubble pods to choose from – from crystal-studded VIP cabins, to dining cabins, to superhero cabins that projected images of the various intrepid characters flying past the windows; thankfully, Elliot chose the natural wonders of the Singapore skyline as all the entertainment they needed.

As their car sped smoothly away from land, Olivia's jaw slackened. The views over the harbour, complete with luxury cruise liners docked side-by-side with traditional Chinese junks, across to Sentosa Island and beyond were eye-popping. But she wasn't the only one in their cabin to be rendered mute in amazement. She remembered this expedition was also Elliot's first day away from the kitchen since he'd arrived and she was excited to be exploring the multiple attractions on offer together.

'Sentosa is almost an entirely man-made island,' said Elliot, launching into his tour guide spiel immediately as she peered out of the window to the ground below. 'The beaches were constructed from imported sand, the boulders are fake, and some of the attractions might be a little cheesy, but I intend to do everything! I'm even going to climb to the top of the Merlion. And Ying says it's worth hanging around for the fountain-and-laser show this evening before we head back for dinner.'

'So we won't be dining at Raffles tonight, then?' Olivia teased.

'Have you robbed a bank?' Elliot smirked, as he held out his hand to steady her exit from the cabin before scampering like an excited toddler towards the flashing lights of the Imbiah Lookout.

'Aren't we starting with the culture show?' she asked, her face straight and serious. 'I was hoping to explore Fort Siloso, maybe ponder a while over the fascinating historical exhibits in the museum and explore the underground passageways. Didn't the Japanese invade the island when the British Army's cannons were pointing the wrong way, and then use the fort as a prison?'

Elliot paused, his eyes anxiously searching Olivia's.

'Ah, I get it! Funny lady! Come on!'

Olivia giggled and allowed herself to be dragged along in Elliot's wake to watch him ride the MegaZip. She refused to join him whizzing through the jungle canopy, suspended seventy-two metres from the ground on a zipwire, but he was in his element. His exuberance brought back happy, carefree memories of the trips she and Nathan had taken down to Cornwall to visit Hollie and her family before they were married, before their respective careers nudged their sharp elbows into their lives and plonked their fat butts in the space where fun and laughter should have resided.

Next on the agenda were Underwater World and Dolphin Lagoon where they fed the stingrays and marvelled at the sea dragons and fur seals.

'Fancy a dive with the sharks, Liv? Only a hundred and thirty dollars? Or what about a spot of fish reflexology?'

Olivia laughed. 'I'll give the water a miss if you don't mind. Did I tell you about the surfing lesson Alani organised for me on Waikiki Beach? Anyway, I'm starving, let's go and grab something to eat.'

'How does a carton of fire-seared noodles with chilli crab and soy sauce sound?'

'Delicious, lead me to it, Chef!'

'You've got to try the pork rib soup, too. Oh, and the chicken rice – it's the Singaporean national dish. Perfect with cucumber salad, and a little soy or chilli sauce dribbled on the rice. And the fruit here is amazing! There're mangos and passion fruit, but also lychees and dragon fruit and jackfruit. And you've got to experience the taste of the durian!'

Olivia grinned at Elliot's heightened enthusiasm whenever the conversation turned to food.

'I think I'll give the durian a miss, thank you. I read in the in-flight magazine that they smell so foul they're banned from public transport.'

'Yeh. It's sort of a cross between your dad's sweaty socks and rotting custard, but they taste phenomenal!'

They'd arrived at the end of their meander through the Dragon Trail Nature Walk to the more authentic experience of the Butterfly Park and Insect Kingdom housed in a tropical rain forest.

'Okay, we're not putting it off any longer. Come on, we're climbing to the top of the Merlion.' Elliot shot off in the direction of the incongruous, thirty-seven-metre-tall, carved stone icon of Singapore. 'It's the guardian of Singapore's prosperity and well-being. I'm not sure about you, but I intend to take my turn ringing the Prosperity Bell. Go on!'

Olivia struck the gold bell as ordered then followed Elliot up the steps to the mouth of the Merlion from where they were gifted with a full three-hundred-and-sixty-degree view of Sentosa Island and the spectacular city of Singapore beyond.

'Come on, my feet are killing me. Let's go for a paddle.'

They raced across the pristine sand of Siloso Beach, splashing their toes and each other with the cool rippling water of the Singapore Straits before plonking themselves down on the sand to dry off and wait for the nightly 'Wings of Time' water, laser, and fire extravaganza to begin.

'So, you've decided not to contact Nathan whilst you're here?' asked Elliot, his gaze fixed on the horizon where ribbons of pink and apricot floated into the early evening sky.

Olivia tipped her head back and closed her eyes, marvelling at how her previously short, glossy bob now brushed her shoulder blades. She knew Elliot meant well, but she really didn't want to venture down that avenue.

'There's no point, El. I've got to move on.'

Silence was never uncomfortable when she was in Elliot's company and she appreciated his decision not to press the issue. They sat for a while longer, contemplating their own thoughts, until the glow of the setting sun spread its warmth across the rippling harbour waters.

'Come on, the show's about to start. We need to grab a good spot!'

Elliot took her hand and they sprinted like teenagers to position themselves in the perfect place to watch the multi-sensory story of courage and friendship played against a water-screen backdrop upon which the characters were projected, and the fact that the girl character was called Rachel, a young girl who persuaded her reluctant friend, Felix, to travel the world in search of answers, held a certain ironic resonance for Olivia.

Chapter 18

Olivia's sojourn in Singapore whizzed by. Whenever Elliot was working, she stepped into the shoes of an intrepid tourist. She found the public transport system clean, safe and easy to use and some of the warning signs in the stations made her laugh. One reminded passengers not to chew gum or to carry the pungent durian fruit on board the MRT. There were even fines levied for failing to flush the loo.

Away from the fierce blast of air conditioning, the heat was stifling and the high humidity meant that she perspired incessantly. She made sure she had a plentiful supply of water and a sightseeing trip planned every day to prevent the intrusion of her internal monologue, always bubbling beneath the surface, asking her to examine the veracity of her reasons for not meeting Nathan whilst she was there. These usually happened whenever she stretched out on a sun-lounger, particularly by a hotel pool where alcohol was readily available, and she would not be fooled into falling into the trap.

On one of the days when Elliot was busy, she enjoyed the peaceful sanctuary of the Singapore Botanic Gardens with its fountains and waterfalls giving the illusion of cool. She had not expected the orchid-filled grounds to be overrun by wedding couples taking advantage of the picturesque photo opportunity and so, in the afternoon, she abandoned the flora and fauna for the Jurong Bird Park where she spent the rest of the day marvelling at the Waterfall Aviary, the World of Darkness, and giggling at the daily penguin parade. She even loved the simulated tropical thunderstorm until the real thing ambushed her on her way back to the hotel. Within minutes she was soaked through to her knickers.

The following evening Olivia took special care of her make-up for the celebration dinner Elliot had arranged with Ying at Clarke Quay. In honour of the auspicious occasion, she'd splurged in the designer shops on Orchard Road and invested in the crimson Stella McCartney dress now hanging on the front of the wardrobe door, which she would pair with a fake Gucci handbag. She'd met Ying several times when passing through reception, but this was her chance to get to know her properly.

For the first time since she could remember, Olivia found she was humming to herself. She gathered her purse and key and made for the glass elevator to enjoy another spectacular night-time view of the city as she sped down to the lobby. As she waited for Elliot to join her in the foyer, she took in the beautiful Italian glass mural of an orchid, Singapore's national flower, and her stomach growled. Along with her battle with insomnia, it seemed she had also conquered her lacklustre appetite on this leg of her crazy pursuit of love, and she was anticipating a great dinner in good company.

She felt lighter, too; her go-to expression was now a smile and not the frown or grimace of time-pressed anxiety, and her brain ticked instead of whizzed. She wished she could wrap up these achievements with a red ribbon and transport them back to London.

Her thoughts swung to Niko. She enjoyed their regular, chatty emails in which she could hear the sexy tone of his voice curling around the written words and she was transported back to their time together. She hadn't accepted or declined his invitation to return to Malta, and whilst he'd made it clear how happy he would be to see her, she knew he understood her situation.

Elliot arrived, looking dapper in his black dress pants and white linen shirt, and for the sake of discretion, Ying joined them as they hailed a taxi to take them to Clarke Quay. The whole place buzzed with diners and strollers, and the air thrummed with the sweet fragrance of Indonesian spices mingled with the tang of chargrilled steak and wok-fried noodles.

'So, what is authentic Singaporean food?' asked Olivia as they strolled along the promenade, soaking up the atmosphere.

'It's not one thing, but a blend of several cuisines – Malay, Indian, Chinese – and many recipes have been in families for generations, copied and adapted as tastes and the clientele in the restaurants change. Here, this is it.'

Elliot motioned them over to a restaurant where the perimeter lights looked like pearls on a giant's necklace, and indicated a table overlooking the canal. When they were seated, he ordered a bottle of prosecco rosé and poured three glasses.

'A toast to two of my favourite people in the world.'

Ying smiled shyly at Elliot, the dark fringe skimming her eyelashes projecting an aura of youth and beauty, which caused a frisson of envy in Olivia's chest. Did she really wish she was twenty-six again? As she had been exactly that age when she had started dating Nathan the answer was a resounding 'yes'. After all the things she'd learned over the last six months, she was certain that if she could turn the clock back to that precise moment in time, she would have done things differently and her destiny, and Nathan's, would have taken a different route.

She sipped her wine, allowing the bubbles to tickle the back of her tongue, and chastised herself. What was she doing? Wishing on a star that was stuck firmly in the past – that wasn't healthy! Hadn't she promised to begin a new chapter in Singapore? Tonight was a celebration, not a regretfest!

She plastered a smile on her face, giggling at Elliot's anecdotes about life in a high-end commercial kitchen, and by the time the fireworks burst into the sky and their post-dinner brandies had oiled the wheels of friendship, the conversation inevitably turned to Olivia's quest to uncover her lessons in love.

'That sounds so exciting!' said Ying, leaning forward, her chin in the palm of her hand. 'What have you discovered so far?'

Olivia delved into her memory to unearth the numerous bulletins she had emailed to Hollie and Matteo, surprised to find it took some effort as her brain felt like it was crammed with cotton wool. She realised that her body's defences to the onslaught of alcohol had depleted due to lack of requirement – which, of course, could only be a good thing. However, despite her wooziness, she managed to recite a couple of the missives, which caused Ying to become more serious.

'Elliot's the first guy I've dated since my divorce last year.' Ying smiled as Elliot reached across to place his palm gently on her thigh. 'I know the statistics for teenage marriages aren't good, but we ignored the advice of our families. We were nineteen and in love. Love conquers all, yes? My older sister was married, so I thought I wanted that too. We were together five years and it's only now that I understand what my parents were trying to tell me. Hattie, my sister, is divorced as well, after only three years of marriage. They have two adorable little girls, but she freely admits their relationship was not strong enough to weather the stresses children bring. She married again but that marriage too has ended – no children, thank goodness. She and Bart separated less than a year ago and they both have new partners already. Hattie is even planning a third wedding! She says she feels incomplete without a man to share her life with.'

Ying reached out for her glass of fizz and began fiddling nervously with the stem, her thoughts clearly in a different place than the buzzing, laughter-filled restaurant on Clarke Quay.

'My parents persuaded me to seek counselling and this time

I'm grateful that I took their advice. My counsellor advised me to wait two months for every year of my divorced relationship, to allow my emotions to heal and to think clearly about my future. It gave me the opportunity to find happiness as a single person, to build up my career and discover my own personality. I know this advice has helped me make better choices.'

Olivia watched as Elliot leaned over and brushed his lips across Ying's. Being witness to the exchange of affection between her friend and his girlfriend caused a perfect image of Nathan's handsome face, every contour as familiar as her own, to float across her vision as though playing on a film reel, and she experienced an overwhelming yearning to be with him so she too could lean over and brush his lips with hers and enjoy the swoop of emotion his kiss always delivered. She swallowed the last of her prosecco, pushed back her chair and stood up, her feet unsteady in her stilettos.

'Time for me to leave you both to enjoy the rest of the evening. I've got some packing to finish for the flight tomorrow night.'

'Okay, I'll see you tomorrow, Liv. I'm really looking forward to our lunchtime Tiffin accompanied by several Singapore Slings to send you on your way.'

'Me too, me too.'

She kissed Ying, hugged Elliot and tripped off towards the promenade, pushing her way through the milling couples to hail a taxi, tears dotted along her lower lashes. Once at her hotel, she scrubbed off her make-up and slipped her new dress back onto its hanger. She'd lied to Elliot – she was already packed. It hadn't taken long. She flopped onto the huge bed meant for two and stared out of the window at the vast kaleidoscope of multi-coloured lights, their twinkly presence added to by the occasional blast of fireworks.

She wasn't tired so she dragged her laptop from the top of her holdall and checked her emails, anxious to connect to a friendly missive from home. She was rewarded with a brief note from Hollie bemoaning the loss of one of her longest running criminal trials, an embarrassingly awful first round of golf for the Surrey County Ladies and demanding an update on the lessons in love.

Olivia thought of her conversation with Ying and the experiences her sister, Hattie, had encountered, and spent the next hour on the internet researching and drafting two new bulletins for Hollie and Matteo's avid consumption. What she found surprised her, and the discovery had, inevitably, jettisoned her mind back to Nathan.

Olivia Hamilton's Lessons in Love: No 11. *"Childless couples are statistically happier in their marriages than their counterparts who are parents. Marriage satisfaction levels drop as soon as a couple has children. The younger the parents and the earlier in a marriage the child arrives, the greater the impact."*

In fact, this evidence was also borne out by the relationship she had witnessed between Sarah and Graeme at Katrina's party. They had spoken to her but she had felt excluded, superfluous to their insular orbit of togetherness.

Olivia Hamilton's Lessons in Love: No 12. *"The likelihood of divorce increases with the number of previous marriages a couple has entered into."*

Olivia had pressed 'Send' before realising that neither of the two new 'lessons in love' applied to Hollie and Matteo. Neither had been married so there was still a chance the dire statistics for subsequent marriages would not apply to them, and neither had children. She slumped against the stack of plump pillows to contemplate her research. Lesson No 11 had come as a surprise. She had assumed she and Nathan would have children one day, at some vague point in the distant future, and that their arrival would enhance their marriage not increase the likelihood of its demise.

She knew one of the reasons Nathan had decided to move on was that he wanted a family before it was too late. For a fleeting second, she had the urge to email her findings to him, but she knew that was ridiculous on a number of levels.

So what, if she had at last admitted to her conscious self what her *sub*conscious self had known all along? She *did* want children, and now, as she approached her fortieth birthday, she could hear the thump of her biological clock for the first time. It was yet another sparkling nugget of newly discovered desire that would have to join the debris of her other dreams amongst the flotsam and jetsam of the wreckage of their marriage. What good would it do to admit this revelation to Nathan?

And, more to the point, what would he say if he found out she had been in Singapore for almost two weeks and had not had the decency to contact him?

Tears trickled down her cheeks as her gaze rested on her *'lessons in love: No 12'*. Any new relationship she formed had the odds stacked against it. And as she had now admitted that she did want a family, that did not bode well for her future children's stability – that was if she could even conceive a child. And then, once again, she was reminded of an earlier revelation – except this time it hit her with such intensity that she felt as though she'd been hit by a runaway rollercoaster.

Nathan had been her soulmate.

Rachel, Hollie, Henry and anyone else brave enough to express their opinion after the fact, were right. Looking down the list of bulletins, applying each one separately, it didn't take Einstein's younger sister to tell her that they had been a perfect match!

The shock was so powerful that the breath was whipped from her lungs and she finally succumbed to a deluge of sobbing before drifting into a fitful sleep – her last in South East Asia. She couldn't wait to get back to London where she could hibernate from the lonely world of her own making.

Chapter 19

The next morning Olivia woke with a blaze of determination in her heart. Her mother had always advised her to sleep on difficult decisions and, as usual, it turned out to be true.

She had decided to contact Nathan.

She intended to talk it over with Elliot when they met at the Tiffin Room at Raffles Hotel, then arrange to meet Nathan for a drink after work before she left for the airport and her overnight flight back to Heathrow – that way the meeting could not drag on because she had a plane to catch. It would force her to say everything that had been milling around in her head over the last six months, to his face and without preamble.

She stuffed the last of her toiletries into her holdall, selected the cream summer dress she'd worn for the Garzias' party in Malta, smoothed down her hair with a drop of coconut oil, and applied a slick of apricot lip gloss. To complete the ensemble, she slid her toes into her stiletto sandals, which could always be relied upon to deliver a spurt of confidence.

A surge of optimism raced through her veins. Her two-week sojourn in Singapore with Elliot had performed its magic on her floundering emotions, and the anvil-heavy weight she had carried on her shoulders since the arrival of the divorce petition at the beginning of the year had shifted, her appetite had returned with a vengeance and she no longer fought a nightly battle with the dreaded sleep monsters. Now that she had made her decision to call Nathan, she felt calm, clear-headed and optimistic.

She wondered how she would feel when she saw him again after six long months of thinking about him daily, and how he would react when he saw her. One of the many things she loved about Nathan was how his eyes lit up when he saw her, making her absolutely sure that he didn't want to be anywhere else than there by her side. She remembered the time in the first year of their marriage when he had asked her to take a week's holiday from work and he had organised a new experience for them to enjoy together for each of the nine days they were free of all the other demands on their time, free to simply reconnect and revel in each other's company. She had thought it was *the* most romantic gesture, which must have taken a great deal of planning.

They had spent one day making bespoke chocolates, another learning the Tango, and another at song-writing school, which Nathan in particular had loved. However, the day *she* had enjoyed the most was the 'throw a pot' class with echoes of *Ghost* swishing through her mind leading to a very romantic evening once they got back home. Every single activity had ended in laughter and had brought them even closer together, and at the end of the week they had made each other a solemn promise to repeat their 'date week' every year, taking it in turns to decide on the itinerary.

Sadly, it had never been repeated.

Olivia gave herself a mental slap on the arm. Today was not going to be a day of wallowing in the past, it was all about the future. She swung her handbag over her arm and caught the elevator down to the lobby where she'd arranged to meet Elliot. It wasn't far from the Pan Pacific to the iconic Raffles Hotel so when he suggested they walked, she linked her arm through his and they sauntered in the sunshine along the pristine pavements.

'So, what made you change your mind about meeting up with Nathan?'

'It's just going to be a coffee, El,' she said, smiling at the anxiety that was scrawled across his face, grateful for the gift of a supportive friend so far away from home. 'I did a lot of thinking last night when I reviewed the information I've been gathering for Rachel's project and for Hollie and Matteo's "lessons in love".'

'Ah, yes, Hollie and Matteo. The reluctant lovebirds.'

Olivia stopped in her tracks and spun round to stare at Elliot. 'What do you mean?'

'Well, when you've finished talking to Nathan about *your* relationship and you've both realised you should be together, perhaps you can work your magic on those two?'

'Those two? Elliot, you'll have to help me out here?'

'Matteo's in love with Hollie. Always has been.'

Olivia glanced at the liveried Sikh doorman guarding the entrance to Raffles, automatically smiling at his jovial greeting, but her mind was spinning with other things.

'No way! Matteo is a serial dater and Hollie's too busy waiting for Prince Charming to propose.'

'That's precisely why Matteo floats from one relationship to the next!'

Olivia stared at Elliot who simply stood there and waited for the cogs in her brain to make the necessary connections – it didn't take long.

'Oh my God, you're right! Matteo loves Hollie. And she loves him, she just doesn't realise!'

Her two best friends together? Now, if she could just talk to Nathan …

With her spirits soaring, Olivia stepped through the door into the white colonial splendour of one of the most legendary hotels in South East Asia, if not the world. The wrought-iron portico of the lobby, the crisp elegance of the marbled colonnades, everything reflected the grandeur of a romantic past. She experienced a sharp pang of loss that her escort that day was not Nathan, but it was swiftly doused by the thrill of anticipation that she would be seeing him later.

It was a momentous day indeed!

They were greeted by the uniformed maître d' and, following in the footsteps of Noël Coward, Rudyard Kipling and Somerset Maugham, were guided towards their table in the Tiffin Room. The white damask linen had been starched to the texture of card, the silver cutlery shone, and the crystal wine flutes glistened in the shards of sunlight that pierced the ceiling-height French windows.

Olivia was about to take her seat when a thunderbolt of horror struck her right between the eyes. She froze, her legs immobilised in concrete and her previously inhaled breath lodged in her throat. Elliot, bringing up the rear, bounced into her stiffened back.

'What's happened?'

Elliot followed the direction of Olivia's gaze and immediately grasped the situation. There, at a discreet corner table, sat Nathan, totally oblivious to the magnificent décor, and he hadn't noticed their arrival because all his attention was fixed on the girl sitting opposite him who could have easily been Ying's older sister – the long fringe, the lowered lashes, the Mona Lisa smile, the slender legs crossed neatly at her ankles – and it was clear to the casual observer that the couple were on a date.

Olivia felt as though a grenade had exploded in her chest and her brain had been temporarily disconnected from its modem. Then the 'fight or flight' mechanism kicked in and she opted for the 'flight' version, spinning on her heels and pushing quickly past Elliot, anxious to escape the scene before she crumbled.

'Need to leave. Now.'

Elliot whispered a few words to the confused maître d' and then followed her out of the restaurant, catching up with her on the polished teak veranda overlooking the pristine lawned gardens of Raffles Palm Court, where Olivia had collapsed onto a bench amid the frangipani trees. He quickly ordered two Singapore Slings from the over-attentive waiter just to send him away.

'I'm so sorry, Liv.'

Witnessing Elliot's genuine distress pierced Olivia's bubble of shock and liberated her bottled-up emotions into the open air, sucking the breath from her lungs and radiating pain into every crevice of her heart. She buried her head into his supportive shoulder and allowed the tears to fall unchecked as she sobbed for the loss of her husband, her marriage and her future. Their drinks arrived, along with a second and a third and, as the pink gin-infused cocktails began to numb her senses, her tears dried.

'Perhaps now you can move on too, like Nathan?'

'Can't.'

'You can. You are a beautiful and intelligent woman. And now you have a few extra pounds on your bones, well ... I haven't told you this before, but right up until you and Nathan got engaged, whenever you made the trip down to Cornwall with Hollie I told myself this time I would ask you for a date – but I always chickened out. What I'm trying to say is, there'll be loads of guys out there who would love to date you, Liv!'

'But I can't date other guys.'

The "almost" encounter with Nathan had whipped up a concoction of feelings Olivia didn't have to be a psychologist to analyse.

'Why not?'

'Because I'm still in love with Nathan.'

She smiled at Elliot, but she knew it didn't extend to her eyes. As the final sip of her Singapore Sling trickled down her throat, she realised that her visit to the Tiffin Room at the Raffles Hotel was yet another bucket-list item that had failed to live up to expectations.

'I'm sorry, Liv,' said Elliot gently, taking her hand in his.

'Thanks, El.'

'Come on, I'll ride with you to the airport.'

'No, don't. I want to take a quick trip up to Orchard Road for a few last-minute souvenirs for Rach and Hollie and then I'll catch a cab. Thanks, Elliot, I've had a wonderful time exploring Singapore with you, but all I want to do now is go home. This crazy pursuit of love has turned into a nightmare and I'm ditching the project right now.'

Chapter 20

'So I can't persuade you?'

'No, sorry.'

'Look, Liv, it's been ten weeks since you saw Nathan in Singapore – the shock of seeing him with someone else must have faded by now. As your oldest friend, it's my duty to encourage you to move on, too, and the only way to do that is by climbing back on the dating horse.'

'I'm not dating, Rachel. And I'm not going to Denmark. I've had enough air travel to last me a lifetime. For God's sake, I've flown the whole way around the world for your research project. I've covered every possible aspect – it's done.'

Olivia had not been overjoyed to discover that Rachel still expected her to continue with the project after what had happened. All she wanted to do was to hibernate until it was time to return to her dull, but predictable routine at Edwards & Co on the first of December. She only had another five weeks to wait until she could bury herself in the balm of frenetic eighteen-hour days and she literally couldn't wait. It was a few seconds before she realised that Rachel was still talking.

'No, it's not "done", and it's definitely not like you to give up halfway through a case.'

'This has got nothing to do with one of my cases!'

'It's a journey that's not yet complete.'

Olivia decided that if she were to have any chance of winning the argument she had to appeal to Rachel's academic sensibilities instead of bemoaning her personal life.

'Why Denmark, anyway? They have the highest divorce rate in the EU. I was under the impression my brief was to visit countries with the *lowest* divorce statistics – crammed to bursting with happy marriages. I've done that, even added Singapore to the list at your insistence, and you have my written findings.'

To prevent her grief over Nathan from tearing at her sanity, she had spent the whole of August and September drafting and redrafting her written report for Rachel. She had typed until her neck ached and her fingers stiffened, interspersed with bouts of melancholy, regret and not a few tears. The intensity of the pain she had felt when she had seen Nathan in Raffles had shaken her to the core.

Good grief, she hadn't cried this much when the divorce petition had been so cruelly and publicly served on her. So why was she breaking out into spurts of wailing at every opportunity now? Why was that image of fresh, new romance in the Tiffin Room still seared onto the backs of her eyelids, just waiting for her to close her eyes?

Yet, she knew the answer. The process of trawling through her copious notes, all the emails she had sent to Hollie and Matteo, and setting each of the 'lessons in love' into a coherent order for the report, had made her even more certain that Nathan had been her ideal life partner – every factor had been in their favour for a long and happy marriage.

Persuading herself it was simply an academic exercise to test her theory, she'd applied each of the principles she had discovered on her travels to their relationship, and the resulting evidence was incontrovertible.

1. **Malta** – Similar family backgrounds – *tick*. Both sets of parents still married – *tick*.

2. **Hawaii** – Married after twenty-five – *tick*. Both partners university-educated – *tick*.

3. **Singapore** – First marriage – *tick*. No children – *tick*.

How could she contemplate starting over again, weaving a new story into the tapestry of her life? In that scenario, all the factors pointed to failure so why bother? If her own research was to be believed, there was scant hope of finding another happy, stable relationship that would stand the test of time. If she hadn't been able to make a relationship work with Nathan, then there was no damn way she would achieve it with someone else.

No, she and Rachel could grow old together, like two brittle spinsters.

Then a question she had posed before shot into her mind. Even if she scratched at the deep, dark recesses of her memory, she could not unearth one instance of Rachel dating. Every single minute of her spare time was shared with her dancing gang. Why didn't Rachel date?

'Anyway, how can you lecture me from your ivory tower, Professor Denton? You *never* date. "Dance, dance, dance yourself dizzy" is all you ever do.'

More often than not, her friend Denise performed the role of dance partner. Stocky but fleet of foot, she shared Rachel's obsession with sequins and bows, sparkling rhinestones and chandelier earrings. In private, Denise sported a diamond lip stud but she chose to conceal this 'aberration of taste' from the competition judges who were consistently unable to set aside their body-jewellery prejudices.

On the one rare occasion when Olivia had sat in the audience of a dance competition, Denise had confessed her itch to get a tattoo – a fire-spouting dragon on her shoulder or a Tweety Pie winking on her quick-step-honed buttock. Apparently, Rachel had urged her to go for it, but Denise refused to risk the high probability of the deduction of marks by some of the wrinkled old prunes who frequented the judging panels of the amateur ballroom dance circuit.

'How was Manchester, by the way?' she asked when Rachel didn't answer her question.

'The show was fabulous. All the tickets sold out, which is fantastic for an amateur dance competition. Dennie got to wear her new glittery emerald shoes. Lol! You should have seen her blisters! But that didn't stop us taking silver in the Cha Cha. Then we hit Chinatown with a couple of the girls from the orchestra. I think I may still be hungover, or that could just be the sudden influx of this year's Freshers asking stupid questions. Were we so naïve in our first year at Durham, Liv?'

'Probably.' Olivia laughed.

'Another new year, though. Where does the time go?'

Then something else popped into Olivia's head; she was on a roll.

'Did you know about Matteo?'

'What about him?'

'That he's been in love with Hollie for years? Since they were teenagers, in fact?'

'Oh, that. Yes.'

'What? You knew and you never thought to say anything to me?'

'Well, it's none of my business to gossip about Hollie and Matteo. It was pretty obvious, though, don't you think?'

'No, I do not. I had no idea.'

'Okay, so why don't you weigh up the evidence, madam lawyer. They grew up together, their families were close until Matteo's mum died and his father hightailed it back to his beloved Italy like a wounded bird. He followed Hollie to London instead of joining his father and Uncle Gino at the family's vineyard or electing to stay on in Cornwall to run the family restaurant, which meant having to sell it. You know Matteo as a serial dater, right? Never more than four dates?'

'Six, that's his current record.'

'Exactly. And the *coup de grâce* in my respectful submission to my learned friend is … he's *always* hanging out at Harvey's Wine Bar with you two.'

'We *are* fabulous company.'

'I agree, but it's Hollie he's in love with, not you.'

'So, what do you think I should I do?'

'What do you mean? You do nothing.'

'Why not? Just a superficial glance at the list and you can see they fulfil the criteria for a long and happy marriage.'

'So, a trip around the world qualifies you as the undisputed Cupid of Kensington, does it?'

'No, I just don't want them to miss out on the opportunity to be happy.'

'They've spent more time together in the last year than you and Nathan who were married.'

'True. So what keeps him from moving on?'

'Well, Sherlock, that's the one thing that is conspicuous by its absence in the detailed global research you have conducted so far – *and* the reason why it's not finished yet. Plus, it's also why you can't ditch the project now.'

'What?'

'You don't know?'

'No.'

'Not even an inkling?'

'No, sorry,' she said, shaking her head and keen to move the conversation on. 'Look, Professor Denton, why don't we get back to my initial argument – why Denmark? I understand why Paris is on the list, but Copenhagen? The land of pastries and breakfast bacon and little stone mermaids?'

'Professor Andersen is a renowned expert in his field, Liv. I'm actually envious of your chance to meet such a captivating orator.

His YouTube videos have become essential viewing for many of my more erudite students. And I can't let Denise down. She hasn't said anything, but I know she was disappointed with the measly haul of one silver medal in Manchester. She had hoped for at least a bronze in the Tango as well, so I've resolved to put in whatever work is necessary to improve my performance. The standard this year is higher than ever, and the judging has become more stringent and critical. The reason, of course, can be laid firmly at the door of the "Strictly Euphoria" that's currently sweeping the nation. Has to be, because it's the first time in fifteen years that the tickets for the Finals have sold out. I owe it to Denise to strive for gold.'

'Okay, okay, you've convinced me of my selfishness.'

'You've read the recent research, Liv. Denmark tops the EU Happiness Index, with Sweden and Iceland right up there in the top five, so the Scandinavian countries must be doing something right. But as Denmark also heads the divorce statistics chart it's an anomaly that requires further digging. The question to ask is this: why, when its inhabitants are so happy with their lives, are they not staying in their marriages? Or another way of looking at it could be – why are they happier divorced?'

'I agree it's strange …'

'I have to admit that my academic interest *has* been piqued by the evidence. But not only that – and you will be particularly interested in this bit – the Danes have adopted the "no fault" divorce system. Wouldn't you like to see how this works in practice now that the UK government has seen the light after decades of lobbying by your fellow professionals and is about to introduce something similar here? The legal requirements in Denmark are a six-month separation and the divorce is finalised. *And* it only costs fifty pounds!'

'Only fifty pounds?'

'So,' continued Rachel, flicking her pumpkin earrings, a gift from Denise in honour of the approaching Hallowe'en festivities.

'Are the Danes happier because their speedy divorce process cuts down on the opportunity for hostilities, an especially cogent factor when there are children to consider? Divorce is tough on kids, so why make the legalities of ending a marriage difficult and time-stretched to prolong the agony? Protracted parental bitterness impacts on the children and is never acceptable.'

Rachel softened her voice, and her Lancashire accent became more pronounced.

'I'm sorry about you and Nathan, Liv, I truly am. And I'm sorry you had to learn of his new life in the way you did, but I think the inclusion of the experiences of Denmark will enhance the whole project. Peter Andersen has tweaked his crammed schedule to accommodate your visit and I'd be mortified if I had to cancel after the trouble he's gone to. He's had dozens of papers published on the subject of matrimonial harmony and divorce – and he even contributed to the annual World Happiness report! Not only that, I happen to think you'll like him.'

'But, Rach, I'm just so exhausted I'll probably make a mess of things,' said Olivia, twirling a strand of hair around her finger. 'I'm going up to Yorkshire to see Mum and Dad at the weekend. Can I think about the next leg and let you know on Monday?'

'Sure, don't worry, I could just about squeeze another six hours out of my eighteen-hour days at UCL to catch the Copenhagen flight myself after I've dealt with the new student intake, which is larger than ever this year, an expanded lecture schedule, the articles I've promised the Dean I'll publish, and the finals of the dance competition on Christmas Eve.'

'I …'

'Sorry, Liv, sorry, ignore me, that was uncalled for. You've done so much for me already, lots more than I could have even imagined possible. Of course you can think about it, just promise me you'll do the Paris trip on the twentieth of November so I can start collating all the documents with the final pieces of evidence from the "Capital City of Romance". I absolutely can't go to France

– there's too much going on here at the Faculty at the end of November – and Dennie would lynch me if I missed the last few rehearsals before the finals.'

'Okay, I promise I'll do Paris, and then write up my final conclusions and let you have everything by the end of November before I return to work on the first of December. But please – no interviews with esteemed French professors or ex-students. I'd prefer to just wing it in Paris, soak up the atmosphere, hunt out the nooks and crannies of love at leisure. After all, I did honeymoon there, remember?'

'Okay, it's a deal.'

What Olivia couldn't know was that Rachel had her fingers crossed behind her phone.

'Speak Monday. Tell Malcolm and Julie I said "hi".'

Chapter 21

Olivia always felt heavier after a visit to her parents' home in the Yorkshire Dales. Her mother was from the school of thought that preached happiness is a sausage casserole, or a plate of roast beef and Yorkshire puddings followed by a generous slab of treacle sponge and home-made custard, especially now that autumn was well into its stride. Julie Hamilton had taken one look at her pale, fragile daughter and scuttled off to the understairs pantry to whip up a red velvet cake, one of her childhood favourites.

She sent up a silent prayer of thanks that she hadn't undertaken the trek up to Longthorpe village six months ago when her mother would have been more than justified in resorting to the culinary route of parental love. However, as Olivia pointed her car in the direction of the motorway for her return trip to London, she felt nurtured and loved without question or reservation.

Of course her parents were upset about her divorce. They adored Nathan and had accepted him as the son they'd never had. However, they hadn't criticised or judged – that wasn't their style. When they had celebrated their fortieth wedding anniversary the previous year it was the only celebration in her bulging diary that she had made sure she would not miss by forcing herself to book three days' leave from work and organising a lift to Newby

Hall, the grand stately home near Ripon, with Rachel and Denise – there was no way her friends would entertain being late for Malcolm and Julie's special day, so that meant neither would she. And what a truly emotional, yet inspiring day it had been. In fact, thinking back, it was the last time she could remember she had spent more than twenty-four hours in Nathan's company.

On this trip, though, she was alone, and she had been weak with guilt and sadness when she had offered to join her father in the garden to drag a rake over the lawn and help him collect the first sprinkle of autumn leaves for his compost heap. Her father had chosen that moment to disclose that Nathan had continued to pop in to see them over the last year whenever his work commitments took him north. The pin on her 'Neglectful Daughter' badge stabbed painfully at her chest. Nathan's career was easily as time-sapping as hers and yet he still managed to find the time and energy for a visit to see his in-laws. Shame had spread through her veins, resulting in her devoting all her strength to tidying her parents' garden and preparing it for winter.

But as the roads heading southwards, now slick with a coating of rain, reflected the amber lights of the motorway, her overwhelming emotion was regret. Why hadn't she learned from her parents' example? Forty years as a couple and they still sat together on the ancient pink velour sofa she remembered from childhood, hands entwined, content in each other's company and sheltered from the worst of life's surprises by the umbrella of mutual love and affection.

Why had she gone jetting off around the world when all the answers for Rachel's research were on the doorstep of her own family home in Yorkshire? Her parents had been overwhelmed when she had produced the printed confirmation of the trip that she had booked for the three of them to visit Hawaii the following summer and her heart had ballooned with gratitude that she was able to do this for them.

'You should go to Copenhagen, love, it's a beautiful city. Your father and I went for the weekend six months after we were married – for an Easter break.'

Strangely, her mother had giggled and blushed, then cast a sidelong glance at her father who had returned a slow, steady smile.

'What?' asked Olivia.

'Well … why your mother is embarrassed to tell you I don't know, but you were actually conceived in a tiny B&B in Jutland. Denmark and Copenhagen have a special place in our hearts.'

Her reaction had been so strong it had whipped the words from her lips. Even now, as she concentrated on navigating the exit road from the M1 onto the M25, tears prickled at the corners of her eyes. She had not known this golden nugget of information. Why had it never occurred to her to ask her parents this most fundamental of questions?

'I didn't know that, Mum.'

'We'd love to go back, but with your dad's knees being as they are, we can't contemplate a trip at the moment. But if you could go it would be marvellous. You could take photographs, visit some of the places we went to, meet new people, new friends? I'm sure your dad will forgive me for saying that I thought the men in Denmark were very handsome.' Julie Hamilton rolled her eyes at her daughter's stiff-lipped expression at the mention of potential romance. 'Don't you think you should consider starting to date again, love? If Nathan has a new friend, and I know how hurtful seeing him like that must have been for you, then maybe that's your cue to move on too. Not courting, just a drink after work or dinner?'

'Mum, I'm just not ready to date yet,' she'd argued, despite the fact that she had penned **Olivia Hamilton's** *Lessons in Love: No 6. – 'In order to have a long-lasting relationship, you have to first of all find a date.'*

Olivia knew her mother had hoped when she had married Nathan that she had formed a partnership for life. Nathan had become an ideal son-in-law, whilst she had taken on the role of thoughtless daughter. It was time to change, time to move on to the acceptance stage of the grieving process.

'Okay, Mum, if the opportunity presents itself, I'll date. Now, I love you both and I promise to come up to Yorkshire for Christmas this year.'

That had been an easy promise to make – she had nowhere else to go. Their apartment would be sold by then and it would be her first Christmas as a newly separated woman. She harboured no illusions about how happy the happiest time of the year would be for her, and she knew she would need their comfort blanket to wrap around her shoulders.

'Have a wonderful trip, darling. Me and your dad want regular bulletins.'

Bloody bulletins! she thought as her eyes lolled and she aimed the car at the nearest Costa for a revitalising espresso before she caused an accident. However, her trip back home to Yorkshire had provided her with another valuable lesson to add to her list.

Olivia Hamilton's Lessons in Love: No 13. *"A long, stable marriage produces happiness and contentment."*

Yet the argument she had posed to Rachel still circled her brain. If that were true, then why did happiness-busting Denmark top the divorce league table? She sighed; her decision was made. She would go to Copenhagen, especially now that her mother had told her she was a product of the land of plastic building bricks and fairy tales. Perhaps Professor Andersen was even related to the famous storyteller himself.

She decided she would wait until the following morning to call Rachel and tell her the news. Anyway, Rachel was so over-burdened with work, how could she refuse when she had all the time in the world on her hands? However, despite her mother's urging, she had no intention of dating – anyone. She prayed Peter Andersen was either sixty years old or married with four children under ten. Then she smiled. What was the likelihood of the latter when his homeland was awash in broken marriages? As she collected her takeaway coffee, she made a mental note to grill Rachel on his background.

The journey from Yorkshire to Kensington was one of the longest and most tiring she could remember. Throughout the final thirty minutes, rain lashed the windscreen as she fought to concentrate on the road, the swish of the wipers lulling her mind into introspection. When the blades swung to the left, she was plunged into dark thoughts of loneliness and despair for her future; to the right, and her spirits soared with the pleasure of accomplishment. But these diametrically opposed vacillations no longer upset her – they were part of the landscape of her life now.

Eventually she arrived at her flat, tiredness dragging at her bones as she pushed open the heavy glass door into the foyer before pausing to gather a stash of envelopes from the mailbox. She shoved the bundle under her arm and made her way towards the elevator, hauling her overnight bag, *plus* an additional trolley containing a cornucopia of her mother's home-baked goodies that any contestant on the *Great British Bake Off* would have been proud to present to the discerning judges.

The apartment was silent and dark, empty and cheerless. When had it been any different? As raindrops continued to splatter on the windowpanes, she tossed her keys into a fruit bowl, which had never been blessed with a display of fresh fruit. With a heavy heart, she popped the kettle on, sloshed boiling water onto a spoonful of coffee granules and stirred. There was no milk, but what was new?

She slit open the first envelope and a short spasm of surprise shot through her body. The estate agent had received an offer for the flat! It was 10 per cent below the asking price but in the current climate they recommended acceptance. She cast her eyes around the open-plan room that served as kitchen, dining room and lounge. Clinical, impersonal and drab would have been in the sales blurb if she'd been charged with drafting the particulars. The kitchen was as pristine as the day they had moved in; the gaping stainless steel mouth of the dishwasher revealed the plastic envelope of the Bosch Instruction Manual and warranty, and the only appliances they had used were the kettle and the microwave.

It wasn't a home.

But had it ever been?

She had never had the time to lavish on interior design. It had been Nathan who had bought the sofa and the scatter rugs – even chosen the bed linen. She looked at the curtain-free windows. Which items *had* she browsed for? Or purchased to enhance their home?

None.

Clarity launched its attack with an accompanying injection of remorse. Oh God, she had been a terrible wife. Her contribution to their marriage in the last few years had been minimal and she had been totally dismissive of the need to spend time together, mooching around the cathedrals of consumerism in Central London picking out items that made them smile. She knew they would have had fun, giggling at all the kitchen gadgets they never knew existed let alone needed.

She thought of her parents' easy togetherness. Their mutual knowledge and understanding of what made each other tick made them smile, made them happy, and she groaned with self-disgust that all she'd had to offer Nathan were the crumbs of her time. The last nine months had taught her a great deal. Not only the factual information on enduring marriages and the lessons in love that formed her 'bulletins' home, but the essential *emotional* elements of a lifelong union, which she had seen with Niko's family in Malta, with her parents in Yorkshire, with Nathan's parents, and with Katrina and Will. She even understood Nathan's need to begin dating again – human beings craved attachments.

She reached for the second envelope in the pile of mail, running her finger under the flap and carefully withdrawing the formal-looking document. A jolt of shock slammed into her abdomen, sending a blast of blood to her brain. Her breath caught in her throat until tears began to trickle down her cheeks to release the pressure.

Notice of Pronouncement of Decree Nisi – Eleventh of December. It was the day before her fortieth birthday.

She had been expecting this letter at some point; she knew the process. But nothing, no insider knowledge, could prepare someone for seeing the words in black-and-white. She thought she had moved on to the final stage of her solo journey towards a new chapter – acceptance of how life was now – but she had been wrong.

Chapter 22

Olivia glanced out of the window, the dark indigo of the pre-dawn sky reflecting the image of a woman who could do with spending a little more time on her appearance, starting with a decent haircut before she went to Copenhagen. She fixed herself a black coffee and grabbed her mobile, fingering the screen for a few seconds. It was only six thirty but she knew Rachel was an early riser and would be getting ready for her commute to work.

'I'm sorry, darling, the decree nisi must have come as a huge shock. I'm sure Nathan doesn't know about it yet or he would have called you.'

'No he wouldn't, Rachel. Why would he? We're *getting divorced*. He doesn't owe me anything, not even a fleeting thought.'

'Maybe. Anyway, what better way to escape this miserable drab weather than a jaunt to Copenhagen?'

'Isn't the weather colder in Denmark than it is here?'

'Ever heard of *hygge*?'

But Olivia wasn't listening.

'Oh, and guess what I found out when I was up in Yorkshire this the weekend? Mum just casually dropped into the conversation that I was conceived in Denmark. Why did I not know that?'

'No way? Fate, destiny, call it what you will! You've got to go now, Liv! I'll call Professor Andersen to finalise the arrangements. You'll have to go to the university to meet him. His time is precious.'

'Is he married with five kids, an overweight Great Dane and a mild Manuka honey habit?'

'Actually, no. Unsurprisingly, I suppose, his Facebook page says that his current marital status is divorced. In fact—' Rachel laughed '—if you apply those bulletins of yours to yourself, I reckon he could be your perfect partner. Just saying.'

'Rachel, I absolutely—'

'Joking, only joking, but I still agree with Julie. You *should* start dating again – nothing heavy, just coffee, lunch, dinner maybe, a visit to the theatre, an art gallery, Tivoli Gardens ...'

'Rach ...'

'And who better to start a new phase of the dating game with than Peter Andersen, Professor in Family Law at the University of Copenhagen? He's intelligent, college-educated ...'

Olivia could clearly picture her friend counting off her arguments on her fingers.

'He's the same age as you, he's been married before ...'

What Rachel didn't go on to add though, was that Professor Andersen also had a reputation for being as tight as primer and paint.

'Look, Rach ...'

'He's in the same field as you ...'

Olivia sighed and decided to apply the only diversionary method she knew to change Rachel's arrow-straight track towards 'Olivia and Peter's' early engagement, their swift marriage and the delivery of three robust Danish-born kids, and then maybe a weekend pod on the Jutland shore.

'How was the competition at the weekend? Did you and Dennie win any medals?'

'We got bronze in the Viennese Waltz. Dennie was delighted, especially as she stumbled across this exquisite gold-sequinned number she wants to wear for the Christmas competition when we were trawling the shops in Brighton. Spectacular, it is. If I only had the legs! We're practising every Thursday and Sunday night at our local club, and then I'm like a hermit for the rest of the week, what with my teaching commitments and banging out the first draft of this research paper – the fourteenth of December can't come soon enough. After that, I can put all my effort into rehearsing.'

'What are you planning to do for Christmas? Are you visiting your mum in Bury?'

'I'll go for the weekend before Christmas and then again at New Year. But it's heart-breaking, Liv. She has no idea who I am now – asks me all the time why I'm visiting her. Last week, when I went up during Reading Week, she seemed genuinely frightened of me. It feels like my heart is being wrenched from my chest and wrung dry. I'm happier with Tynedale Towers, though. At least Mum hasn't been returned by the police after wandering the streets of Lancashire in her nightdress. Thank God it was August!'

Olivia swallowed down a surge of sorrow at the rapid deterioration in Rachel's beloved mother's mental health.

'So, as Mum doesn't know whether it's Christmas, Easter or Diwali, Dennie and I have decided to catch the ferry to Amsterdam to visit her dad and his new wife. We're having a traditional Dutch Christmas celebration.'

'I'm so sorry about your mum, Rach. Hey, as I'm spending Christmas with Mum and Dad in Longthorpe, why don't I pop across and visit Anne whilst I'm up there?'

'Oh, that would be fabulous, thanks.' Rachel paused for a moment to catch her breath before returning to the matter in hand. 'I'll send over your plane ticket for Copenhagen. Thanks again, Liv, did I tell you that I love you?'

'Right back at you, Rach!'

Olivia ended the call with a surge of gratitude for the

unswerving support she'd had whilst going through the trauma of her divorce. Most of her friends had been solicitous and sympathetic, dishing out those cornerstones of female solace: Chardonnay, chocolate, chatter, making sure that she didn't bury her pain under a mountain of silence where it was bound to fester and probably haunt her until she exhaled her last breath. She wasn't sure who had said 'it's good to talk', but it was certainly true, and she had taken advantage of all the listening ears that were on offer.

However, not everyone she had thought was a friend had joined the emporium of empathy. Okay, she was prepared for the fact that a few of the friends she and Nathan had gathered along the way would maybe split into his and hers – and that was fine, except it hadn't always worked out that way. One couple she had really liked had pretty much ditched her the day after the divorce petition had been served and she had no idea why.

But she didn't want to know. Knowledge wasn't power, it was pain!

What had actually upset Olivia the most, though, was the reaction of one particular long-time friend, Kate Harris, who had been horrified when she had heard that Olivia was about to become single again. Olivia had suggested they meet for a coffee, but Kate had immediately made some lacklustre excuse about having to visit her grandmother in Scotland. Olivia bought it at the time – she had no spare brain capacity to dissect the veracity of her reasons – until she saw her so-called friend sneaking into Waitrose at the appointed hour.

Kate's abandonment had hurt more than she cared to admit. What had she done to upset her? They had been friends for over fifteen years, and her baffling snub had niggled away at her for ages until she confessed her confusion to Hollie who had smiled a knowing smile and filled her in on the facts.

'It's Rick.'

'What about Rick?'

'Surely you know about his affair with his tennis coach?'

'No, I *have* had a few things on my mind recently.'

'Well, it's over now and Kate's forgiven him, but she's watching his every move, which means she's taken up tennis, joined the golf club, and is even training as an accountant so she can one day work in the same office as him.'

'A little extreme, but okay. So what's that got to do with me?'

'You're single.'

'And?'

'She's worried you might whisk him away for a night of unbridled passion.'

'Oh, God! Really? Are you seriously asking me to believe that's why she won't meet me for a coffee? That's just ridiculous!'

'Is it though? Can you blame her?'

She thought about what Hollie had said for a few moments, mulling over in her mind how *she* would have reacted if the reason she had been served with her divorce petition was that Nathan had found someone else more enthusiastic about spending time with him than she was, like the girl she had seen him having lunch with in Singapore, and her heart softened to Kate's predicament.

'No, I don't blame her, but does that mean she's abandoned *all* her single friends?'

'Yes, Sasha, Claire and Flora have received exactly the same treatment.'

'So, what will happen if, and it's only a *hypothetical* if, if I meet someone new? Will I be welcomed back into the fold to partake once again of her speciality vegan cupcakes?'

'I'm sure you'll be the first to be on the guest list to sample her beetroot and edamame bean casserole!'

Olivia's conversation with Hollie about Kate had made her think long and hard about the ripple effect of separations. When a couple split up, it wasn't only *their* lives that shot off on a new trajectory, but that of their friends and their families, too.

Everyone was forced, through no fault of their own, to accommodate the shifting dynamics, to amend, reschedule, adapt to the new landscape, treading carefully for fear of causing unnecessary offence. Hearing Kate's story had been a salutary lesson that it wasn't just those navigating their way through the minefield of divorce who were going through matrimonial mayhem and meltdown, so too were reconciling couples and couples fighting to save their marriages, and she realised that despite her own feelings of loss, she had to be there to offer her support, sympathy and solace to others.

As Olivia refilled her coffee mug and searched the frost-clogged freezer for a slice of frozen bread to drop in the toaster, a mantle of sadness enveloped her. Even though she had ditched her manic eighteen-hour days at Edwards & Co, she still struggled with the task of replenishing the fridge. What was the point, anyway? When she did decide to brave the jostle of the supermarket and fill the cupboards with healthy food, she only ended up clearing the shelves of the mouldy provisions the following week.

She carried the plate of dry toast to the sofa and plonked down with a sigh. Where would she go when the apartment was sold? And why wasn't she out there, house-hunting for her next home? She only had five weeks until she was due back at work, but lethargy ran through her veins in place of the hyperactive scuttle she was more familiar with. But there was so much to finalise she couldn't afford to indulge in this slothful behaviour – all their possessions had to be divided, wrapped, packed, and Nathan's items shipped to his parents' house. Olivia was grateful to Katrina for offering her attic space for her few boxes and was more than a little ashamed that her worldly goods would fit into just six packing cases, two suitcases and a cardboard wardrobe – with most of the space taken up by her shoe collection.

She had a new home to organise. She had the trip to Denmark to prepare for, the research paper to update, as well as the weekend visit to Paris at the end of November. She had to respect the deadline Rachel had set of the thirtieth of November for her final submission, not only to allow Rachel adequate time to collate all the evidence, but because once she was back at work there would be no time for anything else.

She hadn't seen Hollie and Matteo for over two weeks and had to admit to a feeling of awkwardness when she was in their company since Elliot had divulged Matteo's secret. She wished he hadn't told her because the last time the three of them had met at Harvey's she'd found herself surreptitiously checking out their body language, noticing how Matteo touched Hollie's hand when he was talking to her, how he laughed at her anecdotes about the astonishingly stupid exploits of her criminal clients or the time the double bass player in her orchestra had vomited over his instrument after a particularly heavy night celebrating their last performance.

Now she had been alerted to the situation, she knew Elliot was right. She had tried to get some time alone with Hollie, to guide their conversation round to discuss their relationship, but Matteo was always there and, on the one occasion when he wasn't, Hollie's flatmate Grace materialised with three standby tickets for *Mamma Mia*. Anyway, was Matteo's unrequited love any business of hers? She was hardly in a position to offer relationship advice to Hollie, was she!

A swirl of emotion began its insidious path through her body, but she shoved it away. Acceptance was the stage she was at, the prelude to moving on, and she had to focus on that, although she was still sad that she would no longer be addressed as Mrs Fitzgerald, and that she would have to tick the box marked 'divorced' on application forms and questionnaires. Why did those marketing gurus feel the need to categorise people according to their marital status, their age or their ethnicity in the twenty-first century? What on earth was with the current obsession of collecting personal data?

She popped the last bit of her dry toast in her mouth,

swallowing it down with a swig of black coffee, and decided to blast her sorrows away with a hot shower. As she padded into the bathroom, she looked over her shoulder at her unmade bed.

On second thoughts, why didn't she curl up in her duvet and read a good book?

No, it was time to stop hibernating and make a positive effort to end her habit of hiding away from the world until it was time to return to her old life. With a surge of determination, she strode into her bedroom and foraged in the bottom of her wardrobe, pulling out an old pair of leggings and hoodie, and an even older pair of trainers.

She would go for a jog; a blast of fresh air would do her good!

Chapter 23

The flight to Copenhagen was short. Well, any flight would appear short if you compared it to the global slog she had recently endured. She dragged her luggage from the conveyor belt and made her way to the exit. It felt strange that no one was jiggling a hand-scrawled welcome sign for 'Ms Olivia Hamilton' like there had been in Malta and Hawaii, and she refused to admit that a small part of her had hoped that Professor Peter Andersen would ditch the sacred halls of academia for the immaculate Arrivals plaza. However, as it was lunchtime, she suspected that the professor would probably prefer to indulge in a *smørrebrød* at his desk.

Once again, her memory's rolodex flicked back to Niko. When she had got back from Singapore, down-hearted and jet-lagged, she had politely turned down his invitation to the village *festa*. However, she hadn't had the courage to admit that the reason was that she was still in love with her soon-to-be-ex-husband.

Was she crazy?

Her marriage had ended and here was a handsome, intelligent, *fun* guy offering her a new pathway towards the future. What better balm to her aching heart than a trip to Malta, with its guarantee of cloudless skies, a warm welcome, and a sure-fire way of satisfying her mother and Rachel that she was moving on? It could be just what she needed to launch her 'new year, new me' agenda, except that it wouldn't be fair to Niko because she just didn't see him as a potential romantic partner, merely as a good friend.

She refused to acknowledge the creeping niggles her brain introduced whenever she forced herself to consider beginning the next stage of her life – how much further down the road Nathan was, whether he would be celebrating the new year with his new girlfriend, and whether he was still planning to return to London for a more settled life closer to his family as he had intended or whether he would elect to stay on in Singapore.

Despite the stern talking-to she had given herself before boarding the plane to Copenhagen, the demons of regret still managed to poke their ugly heads above the parapet as she braved her way to the unexpectedly chilly taxi rank and climbed into a waiting car. She forcibly bashed them down with a proverbial hammer and switched her thoughts to Peter Andersen and the criteria Rachel had applied to his suitability as a date.

Maybe she *should* give him a whirl whilst she was in Copenhagen?

By the time she had dumped her now-tattered holdall on the king-sized bed in the Copenhagen Plaza Hotel, she had persuaded herself to suggest dinner instead of meeting for an afternoon coffee. Denmark was the land of equality, so why not do the asking?

It only took her a few minutes to unpack her regretfully sparse luggage. It was freezing outside – *boy* was it cold – and from the contents of her bag it appeared she had packed for a summer holiday in Barbados or Ibiza. What had possessed her to do that?

She thrust the wooden hanger through her trusty scarlet shift dress and draped the white angora shrug round the shoulders. What a ridiculous choice of outfit for a visit to a northern capital at the end of October. Why had she brought it? She knew exactly why. All along she had been intending to try out this guy who, on paper at least, was an ideal partner. She had only been in Denmark for a couple of hours but she already felt a connection with the country and its people. Now that she knew she had been conceived here she did have at least a spiritual link.

As she blasted her hair dry, she inspected her face in the hotel bathroom mirror, which was superb at revealing every facial flaw. The frown lines on her forehead seemed to have deepened, which was hardly surprising as she couldn't remember the last time she had giggled uncontrollably. When did she even smile? Yet despite her lack of an answer, her 'laughter lines' around her mouth were entrenched, and the wrinkles around her eyes even more pronounced than she had expected. Her features seemed drooped; her jowls lower than she remembered. Only when she forced a smile onto her lips did her features brighten and the lines disappear.

Oh God, she was ancient. Who would want to date her?

She slammed the hairdryer into its wall bracket and tossed the sides of her hair behind her ears. Why did *anyone* bother styling their hair when a woolly hat was obligatory attire for those who did not want to freeze to death?

The hotel enjoyed an enviable location overlooking Tivoli Gardens. From the window of her guest room she had a great view of the Golden Tower ride's vertical drop and the old-fashioned wooden roller coaster. It was only two thirty and the top tourist attraction in the whole of Denmark promised an absorbing itinerary of distractions until Peter Andersen rang to arrange their meeting.

Olivia yanked on her mac and trotted down the purple-and-gold carpeted staircase to the lobby and out into the street beyond. A sharp wind curled its tongue around her exposed ears and whipped at the naked branches of the trees whilst the leaden sky pressed its weight against the gothic-inspired rooftops. Wisps of vapour trailed from her lips into the icy afternoon air as she blew on her palms for warmth. She never thought she would find herself coveting one of the knitted hats bobbing all around her on the more astute tourists' heads. And their gloves. And one of those woolly scarves. She ducked into one of the souvenir shops to kit herself out in essential Scandinavian knitwear.

With her purse well and truly punished for her lack of forward planning in the luggage department, Olivia made her way to the Tivoli Gardens' renaissance-inspired entrance of tall vertical columns and a central dome, which, to her mind, was reminiscent of the entrance to Walt Disney World in Florida. Again, her Danish Krone took a hammering as she forked out the exorbitant entrance fee.

But it was worth every penny. Scattered liberally amongst the immaculate gardens of weeping willow and chestnut trees were more pumpkins than she had ever seen in one place. Whole cascades of the basketball-sized fruit tumbled from wooden carts, bedecked scarecrow heads and surrounded the myriad fountains; there was even an enormous pumpkin atop the white Moorish-style dome of the Nimb Building.

Oh God, how had she forgotten?

It was Hallowe'en at the end of the week and the celebrations were in full swing! Witches, ghosts and ghouls roamed the gardens and haunted the rides, happy couples sauntered arm-in-arm clutching candyfloss, hot dogs and, strangely, ice cream cones, and the aroma of burnt sugar mingled with cloves and fried onions sent Olivia's stomach rumbling. She lingered at one of the many stalls dotted around the park selling local crafts, then meandered along the pristine pathways until she reached the Pleanen, a large open-air stage, where she paused to watch a show of dancing zombies, monsters and vampires performing their very best 'Thriller' moves.

Moving on, she found herself in front of a Japanese-style pagoda, its tiered eaves twinkling with fairy lights in the fading afternoon light. The fragrance of pan-Asian spices floated on the icy air, reminding her of her visit to Singapore, but she suppressed her hunger pangs, anxious not to spoil her anticipated dinner with Peter Andersen.

To round off her visit, despite feeling a little ridiculous, she tossed an imaginary coin and decided to climb aboard the carousel instead of the Ferris Wheel – heights had never been her thing and the tiny cars on the wheel were open to the elements. There was no way she would have voluntarily ridden the Star Flyer – a sky-high carousel of swings, or the Golden Tower – a vertical drop ride from the top of which you could apparently see Sweden!

The old-fashioned ride blew away all thoughts of discomfort, although she wasn't sure whether she would ever feel her fingers again. As she alighted from the brightly painted white horse and made her way through the crowds towards the exit, nostalgia spread a warm glow through her veins. Riding the carousel had reminded her of the times her parents had taken her to the annual travelling fair in Leeds; every year she had returned home with a goldfish in a bag, a cuddly toy, and a toffee apple clutched in her sticky palm.

By now, dusk had transformed the gardens into a magical fantasyland lit by thousands, if not millions, of electric light bulbs that lined the contours of the buildings, the branches of the trees and the sweep of the fountains. However, the most spectacular sight by far was the white carved façade of the Nimb Building, its Arabian-style minarets illuminated like candles on a birthday cake. Families strolled through the fairy-tale scenery, following in the footsteps of the master storyteller himself – Hans Christian Andersen – who had adored Tivoli Gardens. Together they were collecting those golden coins of happiness – or *hygge* as the Danes called it – that their country was so renowned for providing in bucketloads.

It was only as she strode back through the oak-panelled lobby of the hotel that Olivia realised she had forgotten to take her mobile phone with her. When she arrived in her room, she discarded her hat and gloves and quickly scrolled down the screen – three missed calls. She didn't recognise the number, so she settled against the mountain of pillows and dialled the disappointed caller back.

'Hello, it's Olivia Hamilton.'

'Ah yes, Ms Hamilton. Welcome to Copenhagen.'

A pleasant swirl of interest meandered through Olivia's chest as the deep melodious tones of Peter Andersen's voice met her ears.

'Thank you, it's good to be here.'

'Okay, I've received Professor Denton's emails and I have to say that I appreciate her generous offer to pick up the tab for dinner. I have a heavy schedule this week; this evening is the best time for me. Would you mind if we ate in a restaurant adjacent to the university to cut down on my travelling time?'

Despite the directness of his words, Olivia loved his accent – that faint trace of an American twang that occurred when a person learned English from an American teacher. She even persuaded herself that the timbre of his voice held a hint of George Clooney's dulcet tones – and that it didn't matter at all that he had appeared over-anxious to ensure she would be picking up the cheque. She experienced an instant thrill of excitement to be meeting him for dinner and not for coffee.

'Dinner tonight is great. Just give me the name of the restaurant and I'll meet you there.'

'Good. Shall we say 8 p.m. at Restaurant Maven on Nikolaj Plads? Until then.' And without further preamble, he ended their conversation.

Olivia jumped in the shower, taking her time to scrub away the day's grime from her whirl round Tivoli Gardens before stepping into her short scarlet dress, noticing for the first time that she actually struggled with the zipper. Completing her outfit with a pair of black stiletto knee-high boots, she began to muse through the 'lessons in love' she had gathered that were now so familiar to her.

How would she feel about Peter Andersen when she met him? Would she find a friend, like Niko, with whom she could talk for hours and in whose company she could revel in, but minus the sexual attraction? Or would their encounter be similar to the one she'd had with Steve in Hawaii? Plenty of sensual vibes, but a total absence of sparky conversation because they had nothing at all in common? She knew it was most likely to be the former than the latter, but what about if there was both?

As she skipped down the stairs, tightening the belt of her coat against the onslaught of the bitter temperature, she experienced an uptick in her mood. She felt attractive and young in her short dress and heels and enjoyed the loose swing of her shoulder-length hair. She was reminded of something Alani had said, that she loved being free to date whenever and whomsoever she wished.

Maybe she should take a leaf out of Alani's dating book and go for it!

When she emerged from the hotel, a nervous anticipation tingled at her extremities – or it could have been the bitingly cold air nibbling at her fingertips. Whichever it was, she was really looking forward to meeting Professor Peter Andersen. They had so much in common irrespective of the number of ticks he scored on the 'love board'.

The city streets around the nineteenth-century university teemed with tourists and students in search of a meal that would not require a mortgage. Even the fixed-price menus displayed outside the cafés and bars offered exorbitant prices – no wonder Peter had made sure Rachel was paying. The traffic-free, cobbled squares of the Latin Quarter were lined with second-hand book-shops, which she would have loved to spend time browsing through, but she didn't want to be late – to Olivia, tardiness was next to rudeness because it meant that the latecomer felt their time was more important than their dinner guest's time.

The circular sign depicting a cyclist grasping a penny-farthing announced she had arrived at the Maven Restaurant and Vinbar. Housed in a converted red brick chapel, Olivia adored the gothic arched windows and the silver candelabra, but most of all the enticing fragrance of baked bread and the blast of warmth.

Good God, this country was cold!

A waiter led her to a corner table, but there was no sign of Professor Andersen's smiling greeting.

'Can I offer you a drink, madam?'

'A glass of prosecco rosé, please.'

She grabbed the menu from the young waiter so as not to feel conspicuous by the absence of her dinner date. She checked her watch. Eight fifteen. Had she been stood up?

Chapter 24

At eight thirty, Olivia squeezed the last dribble from her glass of prosecco – which in Copenhagen cost more than a whole bottle would in London – and gathered up the fake Gucci handbag she had bought in Singapore. She had never been stood up before and she struggled to know how to react. Then she checked herself. This was not a date, it was a business meeting, and she'd had many colleagues and clients cancel their appointments with her for a variety of reasons over the years.

As she raised her buttocks from her chair, a hassled-looking, sandy-haired guy with a full ginger beard rushed into the restaurant. Her lips twitched at the corners as she took in his mustard-coloured corduroy trousers, open-necked burgundy shirt displaying a sprout of red chest hair and, horror of horrors, open-toed leather sandals. In October! She had to battle every instinct to wrench her eyes from the overlong nails.

Of course, it was her table he headed for.

'I apologise for my tardiness, Olivia. I so easily become distracted by my work. Time is our enemy, is it not?'

She heard those same chocolate-coated tones, so apparent during their telephone call, but so out of kilter with the physical incarnation standing in front of her.

'Oh, it's no problem, Professor Andersen,' she assured him whilst shaking his proffered hand and checking out his chewed fingernails and the gunk collected around the nose pads of his gold-rimmed spectacles. A faint whiff of stale tobacco floated to her nostrils when he draped his tweed sports jacket over the back of the chair opposite her and sat down.

'The food here is superb,' he said as he passed the leather-bound wine menu back to the sommelier without consulting her. 'We'll have a bottle of the Bordeaux.'

Fortunately, the wine arrived swiftly.

'Skål, Olivia. And "cheers" to our dinner's benefactor – Professor Rachel Denton!'

Without performing the ritual of sniffing and tasting, Peter chucked the whole contents of his glass down his throat and smacked his lips noisily. Olivia watched in nauseated fascination as minuscule, blood-red globules of the wine dangled from the end of his beard. She just about managed to prevent a retch by averting her eyes to thank the waiter and enquire as to his recommendations from the menu. Despite recognising her shallow behaviour of judging her dinner companion on his appearance, Olivia couldn't resist mentally composing a swift bulletin to add to Hollie and Matteo's list.

Olivia Hamilton's Lessons in Love: No 14. *"No matter what it says on paper, or the extensively researched Happiness Index, without the spark of physical attraction or emotional chemistry, there's no chance of love blossoming in the wild."*

But, if she restricted the frequency of her glances in the direction of his food-splattered beard and his curling toenails, their evening turned out to be perfectly pleasant. Olivia tried not to think of Peter's regular absences from their table to replenish his nicotine levels and the waft of cigarette smoke that clung to his clothes when he returned. Luckily, they shared a wide breadth of subjects in common as well as an easy eloquence with which to express their opinions. Peter was superbly adept at holding an audience's avid attention and, after their initial awkwardness, the conversation flowed.

'What surprises me as well as Rachel is that, despite topping the recent World Happiness Index, Denmark has one of the highest divorce rates in the EU. How do you account for that?'

Peter swirled the contents of his third glass of wine around the goblet, running his tongue over his lower lip then poking its tip into the corners of his mouth to extract a last morsel of the lemon-infused bread that had accompanied his seafood soup. Olivia disguised her grimace by taking a gulp of her Perrier. Yet Peter was right – the food was heavenly. The aroma of her crab croquette was tantalising and rewarded her taste buds with an abundance of flavour. When their main courses arrived, Peter confirmed that his rib-eye steak had been prepared to perfection and she had to admit that her grilled lobster was the best she'd had, including Elliot's feted Cornish Lobster.

'We Danes top the Happiness Index due to several factors, Olivia. Whilst the old adage says money cannot buy happiness, sadly its accumulation is the means of achieving a comfortable standard of living. Denmark is blessed with low unemployment. We are also bestowed with higher-than-average salaries despite having the shortest working week in the EU. An increasing percentage of our population are college-educated, which contributes to economic stability and prosperity just as much as our North Sea oil. We also boast strong technological and creative industries. We have Bang and Olufsen, and don't ignore one of our best design exports – Lego! And I have no doubt you will be aware of the recent upsurge of interest in Danish design, literature and TV dramas.'

'Oh, yes, I am. My friend, Hollie Shaw, is a criminal defence advocate. She loves Nordic Noir. One of her favourite novels is *Murder in the Dark* by Dan Turèll. I've never heard her beg before but that's exactly what she did when Rachel told her she had tickets to the Q&A the book's translator gave via video-link at UCL,' said Olivia with a laugh.

'Well, the novel is set right here in Copenhagen, but it is not the city you will encounter whilst you're here, I hope,' said Peter, his expression morphing into earnestness as he continued his explanation for his fellow Danes' happiness. 'As a nation we tend to be rule-followers. There is also a strong sense of community here. We are a small country with a respect for collective civic responsibility. We trust our government and boast a high level of participation in the political process. Did you know that over 90 per cent of Danish citizens exercise their right to vote? I believe the figure is closer to 65 per cent in the UK. We have a progressive welfare system, good healthcare and childcare provision and, as I have said, a superb education system. But on an individual level, we also support each other. We can rely on our neighbours and colleagues, even our employers, for their support in times of need. We also have one of the oldest monarchies in the world and our royal family is popular with its subjects.'

The waiter arrived with their desserts. Olivia hardly noticed the chocolate mousse served with brown-butter ice cream and melted white chocolate. She now understood completely why Professor Peter Andersen was so popular as a lecturer and public speaker. His voice had the knack of drawing in its listener and holding on to their interest with a tenacious grip – and he certainly took full advantage of the effects because Olivia couldn't get a word in edgeways.

'Denmark, too, has an abundance of natural beauty. We enjoy outdoor pursuits despite the cold. We protect our environment and 15 per cent of our energy comes from renewable sources. Our streets are safe and the crime rate is low. The air we breathe is clean and the water we drink is of superior quality. Our life expectancy is high and here in Denmark we have one of the smallest gaps between rich and poor in the world.'

Peter leaned forward, his soft brown gaze resting on Olivia's enamoured silver eyes. This time she could not, did not want to, tear her eyes away. What Peter had to say was not only fascinating but he possessed the ability of ensuring relevance in every sentence he spoke. She chastised herself for not bringing a notepad or voice recorder – his contribution to Rachel's research project would enhance not only its breadth but also its credibility – and she was relieved she'd eschewed the temptation of alcohol.

'But, Olivia, you are here for my personal synopsis, are you not? So this is it. The Danes are a very level-headed people. We do not strive for brash exuberance or the peaks of exhilarating joy. Therefore, we do not experience the rush of intense happiness before suffering the inevitable crush of the anti-climax. In my view, the modern-day "constant craving" for "happiness" can be likened to an addiction; that ruthless quest for a vibrant upsurge of hormones and the subsequent delivery of euphoria, necessitating its constant repeat. Instead, Danish people are satisfied with a steady, longer-lasting contentment – what I like to call "an amiable cosiness". We keep our expectations grounded in the real world. None of the euphoria, no, but none of the crash and burn, either.'

Peter's eyes lingered on Olivia as she dug her teaspoon into the rich chocolate mousse.

'Nor do we gorge ourselves on high-fat, sugar-laden, commercially produced fast food. We prefer our food in its natural state, eaten simply, taking pleasure in its flavour, its aroma, and in the presence of family or good friends not on a tray slumped in front of the computer monitor or the television. We do not understand the concept of yo-yo dieting and have cultivated a more stable, healthy relationship with our food. These are some of the reasons Denmark has topped the Happiness league table.'

Olivia had forgotten her amusement at Peter's attire and rug-like beard. The tone of his voice was hypnotic. She was riveted by his research and no longer had to quell the urge to run screaming from the horror of his discoloured toenails.

'So, why the high divorce rate when Danish couples are so happy? It doesn't make any sense.'

'There are many factors that can explain the anomaly. But the one in which I believe you personally are interested, Olivia—' his eyes twinkled behind his glasses '—is that the legal process of divorce has been made easier and swifter. Only six months' separation is required and we apply a low court fee. We have a "no blame" divorce system, too. I hope to be able to email you a useful paper, which one of my students has recently completed, comparing the different systems for the dissolution of marriage around the European Union.'

'Thank you, that's very …'

'But there are other reasons, of course. The system of ending a marriage only applies after the fact, yes? I have told you Denmark has the shortest working week. We also are blessed with a higher than average number of public holidays. It means we see a lot of our spouses and family. We have high female employment and equality of salary. Mothers do not depend on their partners for child support, and we have a generous state welfare system, which contributes to childcare costs for working families. Did you know we have allowances for children up to the age of twenty-four, if they are still pursuing their education?'

Peter absently scratched at his beard and Olivia recalled his own personal circumstances.

'Many couples agree their child custody and contact arrangements on a fifty-fifty basis and it's not uncommon for separated families to still holiday together or to spend Christmas and birthdays in each other's company. It makes for happier, better-adjusted children. I myself will be spending the holidays with my former spouse and children. Another very important point is that because divorce is widespread there is no stigma attached – it's no big deal, unlike in some nations. Danes refuse to remain in relationships that have failed.'

Professor Andersen was right. *Wasn't he always?* thought Olivia.

Time *was* the enemy of the absorbed listener, because she had failed to notice that the waiters were starting to clear the tables around them.

'I think we are preventing these good people from pursuing their social lives. That will not make them happy!' Peter laughed as he rose to help Olivia with her coat.

'Thank you for your time this evening, Professor Andersen. I promise I'll try my best to do justice to your input into Rachel's research.'

'Most welcome, Olivia.' And he leaned forward to plant a wet kiss on her cheek. Olivia stifled a giggle as his bristles stabbed her skin.

Once back at the hotel, wrapped in a warm fluffy dressing gown, she paused to think a while before banging out her promised missives to Hollie and Matteo. What she had learned from Professor Andersen was not as straightforward as a list of lessons on how to find enduring love. On the contrary, Denmark's experience had provided evidence that disproved the contention that enduring relationships led to lifelong happiness. Their conversation, though, had turned out to be one of the most expensive discussions she had ever had, recalling Peter's urgent escape to the restroom when the bill arrived. Thank God for credit cards and Rachel's generosity.

After careful consideration of everything she had heard that evening, she plumped for a deviation from her usual 'lessons in love' to 'mindful missives'.

Olivia Hamilton's Mindful Missives: No 15. *"Acceptance of the validity of all lifestyles, not just the institution of marriage, ensures societal contentment and cohesion."*

Olivia Hamilton's Mindful Missives: No 16. *"Calm contentment, rather than joyous jubilation, produces a happier lifestyle."*

And then she added an extra one purely as a reminder to herself.

Olivia Hamilton's Mindful Missives: No 17. *"Never, ever, ever* *judge a book by its cover. Beneath the tangled ginger beard there may be a sparkling intellect and a heart of gold."*

Olivia slid between the smooth cotton sheets and dragged the duvet up to her chin. The exhilarating jog back to the hotel through the streets of hip boutiques and vintage bazaars had lubricated her mental cogs just enough for her to succumb to a bout of self-recrimination followed by self-pity.

Firstly, she was disgusted at how shallow she had become. Despite not possessing the hoped-for dating material, Prof Andersen had been a charming dinner companion. What did his attention to pedicures matter when the conversation was so absorbing? She chastised her prejudices and resolved to eradicate them, but what upset her most about the evening's revelations was the realisation that if the happiest country in the world couldn't make marriage work, what hope was there for the everyone else who chose that institution as a way to declare their love for each other?

Would she ever find love again? And if she *was* lucky enough to stumble across a guy who was a non-smoker with a pristine mani-pedi and a rigorous skin care routine, *and* who sent ripples of unbridled desire through her icy veins, when she applied the current list of her lessons in love to any future relationship, what was the likelihood their partnership would last? Too many of the risk factors were present and instead of counting sheep, she decided to count them:

One: It would be her second marriage – a proven increased risk.

Two: If college-educated couples remained together this would reduce the pool of eligibility of those with similar educational backgrounds from which to select.

Three: Any future partner was likely to have had a previous long-term relationship, possibly children. The advent of step-families was not something she had concentrated on in her travels, but she bet her aunt Mary's silver teapot their existence did not *reduce* the risk of failure.

Four: At her age – and this hurt more than she had anticipated – she was unlikely to have children, so that was something a potential partner may consider disadvantageous.

She saw her life stretching away into a wilderness of loneliness and abstinence and her head began to spin despite her recent achievement of having almost conquered her reliance on the insidious effects of alcohol.

Yet, sadly, she wasn't the only one. Look at Rachel – still single at forty. Why hadn't she settled down? A question to broach when the time was right. Was this how Rachel counted her own sheep?

Guilt at not considering her oldest friend's predicament gnawed at her conscience. When she returned to work in December – only a month away now – she was adamant she would not resume her neglectful behaviour towards her family and friends. If Rachel could chastise her about her dating itinerary then it worked both ways – and she intended to include Denise in that lecture, too. When had *she* last had a date?

Then there was Hollie and Matteo. Over twenty years they had known each other and now Elliot had told her that Matteo had loved Hollie for all that time but was too scared of losing her friendship to reveal his true feelings. Why? No, her head would explode if she tumbled down that rabbit hole.

Tears gathered along Olivia's lashes in the exorbitantly priced Copenhagen hotel room. Unlike her parents, Katrina and Will, Henry and Jean, even Hollie and Matteo, and Rachel and Denise to a certain extent, she had no one to share her life with. No one to care for her when she was sick or support her when she was sad. Her future would be childless, which meant no grandchildren to dote on when she grew old and infirm.

She was immensely grateful for the welcome embrace delivered by the oblivion of sleep.

Chapter 25

Olivia woke, not to the alarm on her bedside table, but to the incessant buzz of her mobile phone. She groaned, reaching out to grab it and to see who was calling her at … She peeled her eyes open to peer at the screen. What? One o'clock in the morning? No way! Who on earth would be ringing her at one o'clock in the morning? Then she saw Katrina's name flash up and her stomach gave an uncomfortable twist.

'Hi, Katrina, is everything okay?'

'I'm not sure.'

'What do you mean? Where are you?'

'I'm in the office.'

'But it's one o'clock in the morning … on a Saturday night!'

'It's only midnight here, and I needed to finalise a few things before I start my maternity leave.'

'Kat, that's really not …'

'Don't you start, I've already had the lecture from Will and I've promised him faithfully that this will be the last time I work late or on a weekend. Bless him, he's spent the whole day with the tribe at the swimming baths and then treating them to a feast at the local pizzeria – I'll tell you who's the most exhausted.'

Olivia pushed herself up to a sitting position and switched on the bedside lamp, ready to add her own gentle reprimand to Will's. Katrina's baby was due in less than six weeks and the last time she had seen her, her belly was huge, and she had confided to Olivia that she was struggling to commute from home to the office on the overcrowded Tube. As Christmas approached, the crush was only getting worse and rarely did London's travellers or tourists give up their precious seats for a heavily pregnant woman, citing equality of entitlement. However, donating a Saturday to the Edwards & Co coffers wasn't going to do her any good either, although Olivia completely understood how time spent in the office could easily disappear into a vortex of obscurity.

'So, Kat, is there a reason you called? Has something happened?'

'Yes, no, yes, oh, Livvie, I'm sorry ... I ... I shouldn't have called you.'

Olivia's sluggishness from sleep vanished immediately when she heard the distress in her friend's voice. Of course something had happened, Katrina wouldn't be ringing her from the office at midnight unless something was seriously wrong. A coil of dread began to tighten its hold in her stomach and, call it premonition, call it a sixth sense, but she suddenly knew.

'Oh, God, it's Miles, isn't it? What's he done now?'

'I ... I don't know where to start.'

Whilst Olivia was desperate to know what her nemesis had done now, she was more concerned about Katrina's well-being. An eight-month-pregnant woman should not be sitting in the office of a law firm at midnight on a Saturday night because she was worried about her work. In fact, no one should, and that realisation hit her like a thunderbolt, but she would have to save the scrutiny of its meaning for later.

'Kat, are you okay? Maybe you should call a taxi and go home. Get some sleep and call me in the morning. Whatever it is can wait.'

'No it can't, it really can't.'

This time the bottom of Olivia's stomach fell to her toes. She knew from Katrina that many of her former clients had hated the vicious diatribe of correspondence issued by Miles on their behalf and had demanded their files to be transferred elsewhere, but there were also others that had come knocking on their doors, appreciating his hard-line tactics. Those new clients relished the veiled threats of '*agree to our demands for financial settlements or we will issue exorbitant, protracted court proceedings*'. It was a risk not many but the most wealthy or reckless were prepared to take, and, as Miles had hoped, his opponents often crumbled under the pressure, reluctantly agreeing to less advantageous terms of settlement.

These hostile tactics were exactly the sort of thing Olivia loathed, but what had upset her the most was the email she had received from the Chair of the professional association she was a member of, which advocated a conciliatory and non-confrontational approach to divorce negotiations, threatening their firm's expulsion because of their 'recent departure from the Code of Practice'.

However, the biggest shock had been Henry's reaction when she had called him to express her indignation that the whole ethos of Edwards & Co's family department had changed beyond recognition and that it would take her a long time to rectify the damage when she got back to work. To her surprise, Henry had informed her of his relief that Miles had seized the reins in the nick of time and that he supported the way he conducted his caseload, pointing out that she only had to take a cursory glance at the company's accounts to see that the paying clients liked what they got.

An 8 per cent increase in fees! How could she argue with the figures? She suspected the increase was more to do with the recent upturn in the country's economic fortunes than anything Miles had done, but when she returned, she knew she would have a fight on her hands, not just with Miles, but with Henry and probably Lewis, too, who had an expensive house and an ex-wife to keep happy. At least she would have James on her side.

'Come on, Kat. Tell me what's happened. I can take it.'

She heard Katrina sigh and groan a little as she settled herself into one of the office chairs. Oh, God, it looked like this this was going to be a long conversation.

'Well, I'd finished everything I needed to do here at five, and I was about to set the alarm when I heard the phone ringing in reception.'

'You didn't answer it, did you? Five o'clock on a Saturday night?'

'Says the woman who is often sitting at her desk at ten!'

'Okay, so who was it?'

'Gordon Kenwood.'

'Ah, yes, the CEO of that tech company. What did he want?'

'Well, when I answered the phone he was a little … well, not just a little, a lot, angry. Apparently, he'd been trying to get hold of Miles for over two weeks and was going on about how disgraceful the service was. I offered to take his number, to ask Miles to call him on Monday morning, but he said he'd already left seven messages and had lost count of how many emails he'd sent.'

'Oh, God, I knew this would happen.'

'He started talking about how he was considering reporting the firm to the OSS for negligence, especially after he'd received an exorbitant invoice for work he was sure wasn't being carried out because at those rates he'd expect a response to every query he raised within the hour. I think those were his words.'

'I'm sorry you had to deal with that, Kat.'

'Oh, that wasn't all he said. Now he had someone on the phone, he needed answers and he wasn't going to hang up until he got them.'

'What do you mean?'

'He wanted me to check his file to make sure that Miles had

sent a letter to his wife's "dragon-faced solicitor" like he'd promised. Then he apologised for his tone and explained that he had just been subjected to a torrent of vitriol from his soon-to-be ex-spouse about the incompetent and unacceptable delay of his lawyers, and whilst he made it a religion never to agree with anything his ex-wife said, on this occasion he suspected she could be right.'

'Why didn't you tell him to wait until Monday? You could have gone straight to Henry about it. Gordon Kenwood is a multi-millionaire; the financial negotiations are complex and delicate and his wife's solicitor is none other than Ralph Carlton! Miles will be way out of his league.'

'I know I should have done that, but to be honest, my curiosity was aroused. I said I'd pull out his file and call him back but he said he wasn't falling for that old chestnut, which did make me smile, so I left him hanging on the line in reception whilst I went back up to Miles's room. You know, Livvie, I totally understand how you get sucked into spending so much time in the office.'

'Hearing you say that makes me feel awful. You should be at home, Kat, with your family. Are you sure we can't finish this off in the morning?'

'I'm sure. So, I waddled my way down to where Miles hides out and when I opened the door of his office and switched on the light, the chaos hit me right between the eyes. It was complete pandemonium, worse even that the girls' bedroom after they've had one of their teddy bear tea parties! The whole place is strewn with half-drafted documents and random correspondence, there's piles and piles of books and briefs and lever-arch files, not to mention the mouldy coffee cups he couldn't be bothered to return to the kitchen. I had to pick my way through the discarded files on the floor just to get to his filing cabinets.'

Olivia rolled her eyes. She knew Miles viewed filing paperwork as an administrative task and therefore beneath him, but because he was so arrogant and superior in the way he spoke to his assistant Geraldine she refused to help him. She wondered fleetingly if Henry ever ventured down to that end of their offices, but she knew the answer. Henry operated a strict 'clear desk' policy, and it sounded like the directive had not been implemented by Miles for months – nine probably.

'I couldn't find Gordon Kenwood's file under "K" so I started to search his desk, then the windowsill, and finally I spotted it shoved on the third shelf of the bookcase. I pulled out the correspondence clip and started to flick through the pages, trying to find the letter Mr Kenwood was talking about so I could read it out to him over the phone, then lock the door and go home where I hoped to find a home-made lasagne waiting for me.'

'But you're still there, so what happened?'

'Well, there was a whole jumble of loose letters from Margaret Kenwood's lawyers – yes, you're right, it is Ralph Carlton – as well as printed emails from Gordon Kenwood demanding updates. There was also a bunch of court documents advising of a hearing date for the Issues Resolutions Hearing, which is due to take place next week. No wonder Mr Kenwood was irate – if he's instructed Miles to submit an offer of financial settlement, it's going to be a highly relevant issue when the apportionment of costs is discussed.'

'So what did the letter say?'

'That's the point, I couldn't find a letter.'

'No letter?' A niggle of panic tickled at Olivia's chest.

'But then I thought, knowing Miles's dislike for admin tasks, I bet he'd just forgotten to print a copy out for the file. So I booted up his computer, searched for the Kenwood folder, and quickly scanned all the outgoing correspondence.'

'And?'

'Nothing.'

'Oh, God.'

'You know, Liv, I don't like Miles very much, but I didn't think he was anything other than a competent solicitor. For God's sake, he's learned his trade from a highly sought-after expert in the field with over fifteen years of experience! But looking at that screen, I realised for the first time that he'd been pulling the wool over our eyes – well, not yours.'

'We're going to have to report this to Henry, but what did you say to Gordon Kenwood?'

'Well …'

Olivia heard it in her friend's tone and the cramp in her stomach tightened.

'What? There's more? What else?'

'So, I was about to close down Miles's computer when I thought I'd take a quick peek at Gordon Charles Kenwood's account ledger and I nearly had the baby there and then.'

'Why?'

'No wonder he'd made that comment about expecting his solicitor to be available twenty-four-seven. When I saw his last invoice, I had to check twice to make sure there hadn't been a mistake because it was over a third higher than any of the monthly invoices we send out.'

'A third higher?'

Was Miles overcharging their clients, too? Suspicion snaked through her mind. It was absolutely unforgivable, never mind illegal, to inflate an invoice, and it would wreck a firm's reputation in an instant if such practices were proven. Many clients complained about the cost of their divorce – it was an expensive business, made worse if a couple decided to dispute their granny's silver salt and pepper pots, or the contact arrangements for their pet poodle. But Edwards & Co had always been meticulous in maintaining accurate time-recording records with which to assure their clients that the fees they were charged were justified.

'Do you think … do you think Miles is overcharging …'

'That's exactly what I thought too, so I checked his time-recording for the Kenwood file and it all looks above board. The last invoice can be substantiated by the time spent.'

'Then why were his legal fees so high?'

'I've not had time to look into that because …'

Katrina's hesitation sent alarm bells ringing and Olivia's heart began to hammer out a concerto of panic. Surely there was nothing else?

'Kat?'

'I was about to go back to reception to apologise to Mr Kenwood, to tell him that I couldn't find his file and to promise to get Henry himself to call first thing on Monday morning, and I think it was tiredness after spending the whole day at the office, but when I went to stand up, my knee caught on the protruding handle of Miles's desk drawer.'

'Oh, Kat, you really should—'

'I tried to kick the drawer shut but it wouldn't budge, so I yanked it open and saw there was a thick buff-coloured folder wedged inside. I pulled it out, placed it carefully on top of all the other files scattered across his desk and I was about to leave when I realised if I left it there Miles would know I've been snooping in his office – I couldn't stand another row, so I went back, grabbed the file and …'

'And what?'

'I got a bit of a … a bit of a twinge.'

'Oh, Kat …'

'I'm fine, I'm fine, but it made me drop the file and all the papers spewed out, so I had to lower myself to the floor – I'm not kidding you, it was like a comedy sketch – and try to shuffle everything back in and that's when I saw it.'

'Saw what?'

'I recognised it straight away.'

Suddenly, Olivia got the weirdest feeling that she was floating on a cloud and looking down on the drama that was being played out below her. She'd had a few glasses of wine, a lot of rich food and an evening of thought-provoking conversation, and now she was listening to her friend recite something that was getting curiouser and curiouser by the minute.

Was this in fact a dream?

But when Katrina uttered her next words, she knew it was the complete opposite – it was a nightmare.

'It was a letter, a letter from the Office for the Supervision of Solicitors.'

'Oh, my God, no! Did you read it? What did it say?'

'Apparently, our esteemed colleague, Moronic Miles, has been summoned to a tribunal hearing to answer a litany of malpractice complaints filed by three of our wealthiest and most important clients.'

'Noooo …'

Olivia's mind whipped back to the excruciating rumours that had been swirling around the corridors of the legal profession since she had started her sabbatical, every one of them instigated by Miles, about her supposedly fragile mental health. As was the way with these things, the gossip had inevitably morphed from her taking a short break into her being unable to leave her flat, and one contemporary had even been told that Olivia had been detained in the local psychiatric clinic.

'What do you think we should do?' asked Olivia, her brain in complete turmoil.

'Oh, I'm already onto it. I've spent the last four hours trawling through Miles's cabinets, scrutinising his files and … hang on.'

'What? What's happened? Katrina?'

'Just another twinge, oh, and now there's the door!'

'Don't answer it!'

'It's okay, it's Will. Hi, Will.'

'This is absolutely ridiculous, Kat. Why are you still here and why has your phone been engaged for so long? I thought, I thought … look, get your coat, we're going home, and I won't take no for an answer. And you are not coming into the office on Monday either, even if I have to barricade you in the bathroom with your favourite bubbles and a scented candle!'

Hearing Will's voice made Olivia smile with relief.

'Sorry, Liv, got to go. I'll call you later, okay?'

'Okay.'

It was only when Olivia was checking out the next morning that she wondered whether Gordon Kenwood was *still* holding on the phone waiting for his questions to be answered.

Chapter 26

Harvey's Wine Bar was buzzing.

'So, are you planning to take Jessica home to Italy for Christmas? Introduce her to your dad?' asked Hollie, pouring all three of them a glass of the Italian fizz they knew and loved. 'What was it last night? Eighth date? Must be serious?'

Olivia watched from the corner of her eye to see if Hollie's expression revealed any indication of jealousy, but she saw nothing, only a gentle tease. Poor Matteo, her heart ached for him, but he was an expert at deflecting questions about his relationships.

'Don't really know where home is, Hols. Can't really call Italy my home. Sure, Dad's there, and all his family, but I've never lived there. And there's no one left from Mum's side of the family down in Cornwall.'

'Hey, why don't you come to Newquay with me, then? Elliot will be home from Singapore and it'll be just like old times. We can race along the cliffs, go crabbing, go rock-pooling, build a few sandcastles, even go surfing.'

Hollie tossed a playful glance in Olivia's direction as she flicked her ginger curls away from her face. In her joy at recalling her childhood, she looked much younger than her thirty-five years.

'Mum and Dad would love to have you to stay, and not just for the discounted wine!'

This time Olivia scoured Matteo's face for his reaction. Sure enough, it delivered her the confirmation that Elliot was spot on with his detective deductions. Matteo's eyes seem to light up from his very soul at the offer to spend the Christmas holidays in Cornwall with Hollie and her family.

'I'd love to, Hols, but it'll just be me.'

'Why?'

'Jess and I broke up.' Matteo averted his eyes from Hollie's enquiry and instead caught Olivia's before swiftly looking towards the bar, his cheeks reddening as he grabbed his wine glass and drew in a mouthful of the effervescent bubbles before muttering, 'She was getting a bit too possessive. Not really my bag.'

'Oh, for God's sake, Matteo, what on earth is wrong with you?' cried Hollie, rolling her eyes at him, but her smile was wide and friendly. 'Once the chase is over you give up. She's the sixth girl you've dated this year. You've got to start to think about settling down at some point.'

Olivia's senses were on high alert. She scrutinised Matteo's body language and realised, for the first time, that he wasn't laughing at Hollie's banter or joining in with the criticism of his dating practices like he usually did. The splash of joy had swiftly changed to a haunting sadness lodged deep in his mahogany eyes and his feelings were blatantly obvious to her, so why weren't they obvious to Hollie?

She eased back from the conversation, sipping at the prosecco Matteo had recommended, and watched the two best friends spar, the corners of her lips curled upwards knowingly. Matteo laughed at something Hollie said, and swung his raised eyebrows to Olivia for her contribution, and in that instant he realised she knew. He flashed her a warning sign via a microscopic headshake, but Olivia resolved to speak to him before he went down to Cornwall for the Christmas holidays.

It was time for Matteo to let Hollie know how he felt about her.

She drained her glass, welcoming the warm glow that the sweet nectar delivered as it trickled down her throat and into her chest. However, the blush of pleasure she could feel suffusing her cheeks could not be attributed to her third glass of fizz, which in her new regime of abstinence had caused her head to swim a little, but at the thought of her two friends getting together to celebrate the festivities. She allowed Matteo to replenish her glass without objection, smiling her thanks before returning to the folds of the plump sofa to continue her contemplation.

Applying Olivia Hamilton's Lessons in Love, she concluded that:

One: Hollie and Matteo had known each other, and their respective families, since childhood. Both families had a great deal in common – a love of Cornwall and of the great outdoors – and both of them had backgrounds in the restaurant trade. That ticked the 'shared history' box.

Two: Both had graduated from university and had gone on to establish satisfying and financially stable careers. That ticked the 'college-educated' box.

Three: Neither of them had been married before. Another tick.

Four: Both were well past their teenage years. They had experience of the world and were mature enough to know themselves and each other.

The list of positives was stacking up nicely. But the *coup de grâce* was that communication and friendship had never been an issue. They were best friends!

However, there was one question she had to ask which might just spoil the whole scenario. Did Hollie possess the same workaholic gene she herself possessed? Would *she* allow her addiction to helping others through the most traumatic times of their lives, impact negatively on the most important relationship in her life?

Whilst on her global pursuit of love, regular calls, texts and emails had nurtured her friendship with Hollie who had continued with her gruelling schedule of police station call-outs for the whole nine months Olivia had been away from her own office. On top of that, she had rehearsed every Wednesday evening for the Christmas concert her orchestra were putting on in aid of the local hospice, and then every weekend she shot down to the golf club for lessons from Nathan's brother and an afternoon round of golf.

So, if they did get together, would Hollie and Matteo be destined to emulate her and Nathan? And if that was right, was it worth destroying their current relationship? They had a fabulous friendship – a closeness, a deep knowledge of each other's hearts and souls. They had shared the ups and downs of life for almost three decades. Hollie had been particularly supportive when Matteo's mother had passed away, taking a month's unpaid leave to return to Cornwall and share in the family's grief, and help to man the restaurant tables until Matteo and Antonio decided what to do with the pizzeria. The pair also shared a sense of fun, and Hollie had never stood Matteo up when he arranged tickets to clarinet recitals or the open-mike comedy shows he loved, unlike Olivia had done with Nathan. Maybe it *would* work.

'Olivia? Earth to Olivia?'

'Sorry, just thinking about …'

Olivia placed her empty wine glass on the table and smiled at her two closest friends. It would be amazing if they got together, and she was oblivious to the fact that her overindulgence of wine had plastered a rictus grin on her face.

Hollie traded an eye-roll with Matteo. 'I was asking about Kat. How's the baby?'

'Gorgeous, just gorgeous. Matteo, do you think I can get a Perrier, plenty ice and lemon? My head is starting to spin and there's something serious I need to get your advice on.'

'Sure.'

Matteo cast a worried look at Olivia before trotting obediently to the bar.

'What've they called her?' asked Hollie, who, despite being on her second bottle of wine, displayed no adverse effects because unlike Olivia, her tolerance levels were still being well fuelled.

'Charlotte Eliza Windwood. But she's called Lottie. Oh, thanks, Matteo.'

Olivia swallowed half the ice-filled glass of sparkling water before ploughing into the story Katrina had shared with her on Saturday night, and then added to three days later whilst Olivia had cuddled the sleeping Lottie in the Windwood's cosy conservatory.

'The day before Lottie arrived, Kat went into the office to tie up a few loose ends on a couple of cases she was dealing with. Guess what she found?'

Hollie and Matteo listened in gobsmacked silence as she recounted the details of Miles's incompetence and extensive negligence. Neither of them commented when she told them of the involvement of the OSS, and that Miles had been summoned to attend a disciplinary hearing, a fact he had sought to conceal from Henry, Lewis and James.

What she didn't share with them was the tears she had shed when Henry had eventually called her after hearing the full story from Katrina, and instead of welcoming her back into the fold with open arms, he had told her that he and Lewis were considering their options, with closing down the matrimonial department altogether one of them. Her whole body had heaved with emotion, with agony and regret, but also mingled in with the melee of misery was a generous dose of loneliness and futility.

If she didn't have a career to go back to, what was she going to do? What had all those hours she'd spent slaving away at her desk, late at night, early in the mornings, weekends when she should have been out socialising with Nathan and her friends, been for? Had losing the person she loved most in the world all been for nothing? Or could she salvage at least something from the lessons she'd learned over the last few months?

'I'm proud of you, Liv.'

'You are? Why?'

'If I'd been in your shoes, I'd have stormed into Edwards & Co and had it out with Miles in front of the whole office. That man is a traitorous slimeball. God, we slag off Ralph Carlton but at least he's upfront about his rottweiler tactics, *and* he really knows his stuff. Miles, on the other hand, is a bungling, blithering idiot not fit to lick Ralph's shoes. I'm surprised about Henry and Lewis's reaction though.'

'I suppose …'

And then it hit her like a sledgehammer. It was clear that if Hollie was hearing the story for the first time, then the rest of the legal profession would also have no knowledge of Miles's treachery, and the reason for that had to be that they were intending to brush his actions under the carpet. 'Damage limitation' they would call it, and if they were prepared to put cash-flow before integrity and truth, then irrespective of whether they decided to close the department or not, there was no way she could continue to work alongside them as her trusted professional partners.

Matteo got it before Hollie.

'What's the point of storming into the office when what he's done has been sanctioned by the senior partners? In fact, any unpleasant scene would play right into Miles's court as evidence that Olivia is mentally deranged.'

'Ah, yes, okay, I get it,' murmured Hollie, eying Olivia closely before making a determined effort to change the subject to safer ground. 'So, Paris on Friday? The capital city of love and romance? Are you excited?'

'I might have been if I wasn't travelling alone – and don't forget, it's where Nathan and I spent our honeymoon. Oh, Hols, after everything that's happened, I really don't want to go, but equally I don't want to let Rachel down. I actually don't think Paris is one of the essential trips in her project, and I've already written up all my notes and drafted my findings for her research paper, but she keeps on reminding me that I did promise her that I would go. Actually, she was rather shirty with me when I tried to wriggle out of it last night.'

'Really, that's not like Rachel. I hope she's okay.'

'I think it's the stress of the NABD qualifiers in two weeks' time. She and Denise are rehearsing four times a week at the moment, *and* she's lecturing an additional subject this semester, *and* if she doesn't finalise her research paper on time the grant monies have to be returned. So I did get her point when she snapped that she would love to slip into my stilettos and grab a flight to Paris for the weekend.'

Olivia decided not to mention to Hollie that it had been the first time in over twenty years of friendship that Rachel had spoken harshly to her and she had quickly apologised for her insensitivity.

'So, I've pulled on my big girl pants and agreed to fly over to Paris with no more complaints. Okay, so my life is a complete explosion of rotten manure, but it could be a lot worse, and I'm not the only one struggling with what life throws at the unsuspecting traveller by any means. However, I intend to steer clear of all those romantic little cafés and bistros Nathan and I frequented on our last trip.'

'Has Rachel set up any meetings for you like she did at your other ports of call?'

'Only a quick drink with one of her old college friends on the Saturday night, which she's refused to cancel, but it shouldn't be a problem. I intend to spend the rest of the weekend getting lost in the labyrinths of the Louvre and studiously avoiding the treasures of Sacre Coeur, Notre Dame and Les Invalides.'

But most of all she intended to avoid the Pont des Arts where she and Nathan had attached an engraved padlock to the railings before throwing the key into the River Seine. She had been saddened to read that the Parisian authorities had removed some of the ironwork laden with the symbols of everlasting love because the bridge was crumbling under their weight.

What a metaphor for the veracity of everlasting love! Maybe true enduring love wasn't all it was cracked up to be – simply a lottery that only the lucky few got to win. Clearly those who had commissioned Rachel's research had been astute in their initial instructions when they had asked her to look into the causes of divorce and not the positive aspects of maintaining a loving union. No one would secure a grant to undertake the ridiculous wild goose she had spent the last nine months hunting down.

Almost a whole year of chasing love – what a waste.

But was it?

She had to accept that *some* positives had come from her sojourn with the residents of the real world. She now ate more healthily, had conquered her battle with insomnia, and had all but eradicated her reliance on excessive alcohol intake to soothe away the day's stresses. On an emotional level, since that fateful day in January, she had gained a great deal of insight into the way she had been living her life and now understood it was time to make a few changes, the main one being to devote more time to the people she loved.

For a start, she was going to spend the holidays with her parents in Yorkshire this year. She had allowed too many Christmases to slide by without a nod to the magic and joy the annual celebration brings, and this time she would *not* sit at the dinner table, counting down the hours until she could get back to the office so she could have the place to herself and catch up on her backlog of paperwork. She intended to embrace the festivities and had even splurged on a hamper from Fortnum & Mason as a treat for her mother.

And she wanted to make much more of an effort to support her oldest friend. She hadn't told Rachel yet, but she had secured a highly sought-after ticket to be in the audience of the Amateur Ballroom Dance Finals on Christmas Eve – a first for her, despite the fact Rachel and Denise had been dancing for over ten years.

And she still had the invitation from Niko to visit his family in the New Year to celebrate the twelfth night feast on the sixth of January. He was the only guy she had met that year who she had really felt a connection with and she was giving his invitation some thought. She thought of Alani and the chatty email updates she still sent gushing about her blossoming romance with Brett, conveniently forgetting her vehement assertions that she intended to play the field for as long as possible.

And last but not least, her time in the legal wilderness had given her the space to come to terms with the breakdown of her marriage and accept that she and Nathan were no longer a couple. She still loved him, she knew she always would, but it was time to move on, and admitting that gave her some solace. She had to focus on the future now.

Hollie's laughter pierced her introspection and she smiled. It was obvious to her now, and any casual observer, that her two friends didn't just enjoy each other's company, but they were in love with each other. She knew they didn't need her there. Had they even missed her when she was away on her global jaunt? In fact, had *any* of the other home-fearing professionals gathered in Harvey's wondered where Olivia Hamilton had disappeared to? She was tired, but it wasn't the bone-crunching exhaustion of before. She was a healthier weight, her complexion was less ashen and more rose-tinted, and, tonight excepted, she could say no to another white wine spritzer.

Yes, her sabbatical had taught her a lot and she now possessed a deeper knowledge of herself and the impact her chosen lifestyle had on her relationships. The lessons learned, although hard, would ensure she never again put her career before her family and friends, and she had a new bulletin to add to her list.

Olivia Hamilton's Lessons in Love: No 18. "*All relationships, no matter what form they take, are equally valid and their stability brings happiness.*"

Glancing again at Matteo and Hollie who were still arguing about something, she added:

Olivia Hamilton's Lessons in Love: No 19. "*Communication is everything. The ability to listen carefully, and to respond appropriately, is of crucial importance for nourishing an enduring relationship.*"

'Don't suppose there's a space in your holdall for me?' said Hollie, attempting to drag Olivia back into the conversation when Matteo returned to the bar. 'City of Romance, when do people have time for that?'

Olivia smiled at her friend as she accepted an empty champagne flute from Matteo. She watched him hand two more to Hollie and twist the cork on the bottle before pouring three glasses and then raising his to the girls before taking a mouthful.

'Hey, I know it's not Paris, Hols, but what about a trip to Rome?' Matteo set down the wine cooler with the bottle protruding from its rim. 'I'm flying out to meet a wine producer my Uncle Gino has recommended at the weekend. Why don't you tag along?'

Matteo, aware of Olivia's scrutiny, studiously avoided looking in her direction, sipping his wine to conceal the fervent hope in his eyes. She wasn't fooled, but it seemed Hollie was oblivious. Olivia held her breath and, with every molecule in her body, she willed Hollie to agree, whilst fearing her rejection and the effect of its impact on Matteo.

'You know, why not? Stuart's on call this weekend. I've done the last five so I reckon I deserve a break. And the orchestra have been granted a rare hiatus from rehearsals as we'll be playing back-to-back concerts from now until Christmas and everyone needs to get their Christmas shopping done.'

'Great!'

Hollie shuffled her buttocks to the edge of the sofa, tossed her hair behind her ears and met Matteo's gaze.

'Can we do all the cheesy tourist stuff, though, Matt? The Colosseum, the Trevi Fountain, the Spanish Steps?'

'Sure we can.'

Matteo's handsome features remained calm, but Olivia didn't miss the flash of exhilaration written in his chocolate-brown eyes. She smiled and resolved to call Matteo the next day to urge him to come clean about his feelings whilst they were together in Rome. What better venue was there to declare his love for his best friend's sister than overlooking the Trevi Fountain?

'Sounds like a fabulous trip!'

'Well, why don't you come to Rome with us instead of Paris?' declared Hollie.

'Oh God, no! Rachel would kill me if I don't finalise her mission of madness.'

Not to mention Matteo, she thought as she quelled the urge to giggle at the relief that was scrawled across his expression.

Chapter 27

It still surprised Olivia how long it took to get from landing on the tarmac at Charles de Gaulle airport to stepping into the oak-panelled lobby of her Parisian hotel. Longer than the whole flight from Heathrow to Paris.

The hotel that Rachel had booked for her was located down a narrow avenue a short distance from the Champs-Élysées – far enough away from the Ritz in the Place Vendôme to prevent her from taking a detour for old times' sake. She loved the quirkiness of this old, typically Parisian hotel with its tall, shuttered windows and Juliet balconies fashioned from lacy ironwork, and its revolving front entrance and honey-veined marble foyer that glistening under a parade of huge, teardrop chandeliers.

There was no offer to escort her or her luggage to her room, so she went in search of the elevator to the fourth floor and was delighted with her pretty room overlooking the internal courtyard – an oasis of calm with its black granite fish fountain and a selection of wrought-iron bistro sets. She slung her holdall on the bed, elegantly upholstered in duck-egg blue and cream with accents of burnt orange. There was even a pair of Louis XIV-inspired chairs cosying up to a little table by the window.

The bathroom was minuscule – she almost had to climb in the bath to get into the shower cubicle – but it was clean.

After freshening up, she dragged out her hand-knit Aran jumper and the matching bobble hat, scarf and gloves she had bought in Copenhagen, and struck out along the Rue du Faubourg Saint-Honoré in search of dinner. The air was cold enough to send stringy spurts of breath into the descending twilight, and she rubbed her palms together and stamped her boots to encourage warmth.

Tonight was all hers.

She intended to meander along the wide boulevards bedecked with twinkling precursors of Christmas, select a local French bistro and order anything that took her fancy from the menu. When Rachel had disclosed the choice of dining location for the following evening, she had expelled a very unladylike snort. What was Rachel's college friend thinking when he'd selected the Jules Verne – the expensive restaurant at the top of the Eiffel Tower? Okay, it was a romantic setting and a place where many, many couples proposed, but why did they have to meet there? They were strangers. It was embarrassing.

All the more reason to indulge this Friday evening, she decided.

Her promenade took her to an inauspicious café on a side street just off Rue de Rivoli. She was guided through the cosy throng of locals to a seat at the back by a disinterested waiter who simply pointed to that day's menu scrawled on a blackboard and left her to it. The delicious aroma of roast chicken, warm red wine and toasted caramel enveloped her senses, and her stomach demanded immediate attention. She unwound her scarf and discarded the bulky jumper over the back of her wooden chair before scrabbling in her handbag for the security of her phone, surprised at the awkwardness she felt at having to dine alone.

Five texts from Hollie and two from Matteo. She read them with increasing excitement. Next, she crossed over to Hollie's

Instagram page where there were a myriad of photograph. featuring every Roman monument and tourist attraction, all beneath a clear azure sky, with the pair of them grinning for selfies in T-shirts and sandals. There wasn't a thick woollen sweater in sight.

Matteo hadn't said anything yet, that was obvious, thought Olivia. When she had called him to wish him luck, Matteo had confessed how he felt about Hollie immediately and promised Olivia he would grasp this ideal opportunity to broach the subject. Olivia had begun to explain how great they were for each other but had only managed to get to the first of the lessons on her list before Matteo had interrupted her.

'You can spout science and statistics at me all you want, Liv, but what ensures couples stay together is one thing and one thing only.'

'What's that, then?' she had asked, scrunching up her nose in confusion.

'Love, Olivia darling! You've heard of that, surely? The unadulterated harmony of passion, desire and affection, of never wanting to be away from the other person's side? It's that desperate craving to be in the other person's company every second of every day, the need to hear their opinions on every mundane detail, of the unerring need to spend your whole life together and even that would not be long enough, as my beloved father has proved. Love, Olivia! Only love!'

Love!

She couldn't believe it. How could she have omitted its overriding influence in her research? Snapshots of her brief encounters of potential romance swirled through her mind – the heart-stopping moments in the vineyard with Niko, the knee-buckling desire on the beach in Waikiki as Steve demonstrated his surfing technique and six-pack, the way Elliot caught Ying's eye across the table at the restaurant on Clarke Quay, the comfortable affection shared by her parents, the overwhelming joy she

...aw on Katrina and Will's face when they held their new-born daughter.

Her conversation with Matteo, although brief and intended by Olivia to make *him* think about his relationship with Hollie, had forced her to consider his words very carefully. It was only then that she had had her light-bulb moment. Her epiphany. She couldn't believe she had overlooked the obvious!

Was Matteo an oracle? Of course not. It was her – she was stupid and blinkered! Love was what made relationships tick and what maintained their growth. All the miles she had travelled that year and she had completely missed, or subconsciously avoided, the most important lesson of all. Never mind the elephant in the far-flung hotel rooms where she had rested her head, this was a Tyrannosaurus Rex of an omission.

Wake up, Olivia!

And she knew then what the final item on her list had to be: **Olivia Hamilton's Lessons in Love: No 20.** "*Love is all you need.*"

Love, in all its various manifestations, was the glue that held relationships together. Love was the answer to Rachel's research question; nothing else mattered. Without it, all the previous nineteen lessons meant nothing. Love could overcome every one of the risk factors; with your soulmate by your side, any storm could be weathered. The deep emotional bond between two people could defy any scientific formula, any calculated attempt by the academics to shoehorn the answer to lasting happiness into a particular box and label it with the amalgamated elements.

But, as with all living things, love had to be nurtured to survive. That meant investing in the partnership, treating it and each other with respect, understanding, support, trust, togetherness, attraction, desire, intimacy – all of which required the application of *time*.

It was too late for her and Nathan.

But, as she greedily guzzled a plate of steaming *pochouse*, she knew she had loved Nathan, and still loved Nathan with all her heart and soul. Even after the shock of seeing him start again with someone new, she knew she adored him. Unlike her, Nathan had always found time to lavish on their relationship – to purchase tickets for the theatre, to scrounge a reservation at a sought-after restaurant or bring home a carefully considered piece of artwork to break up the clinical coldness of their apartment walls, gestures that had mostly gone unnoticed.

Well, she could either stay miserable for the rest of her life, pining for the relationship she had tossed away on the altar of her career, or she could deliver herself a metaphorical kick up the backside and get on with moving on. What was done was done, and when she eventually managed to pin Nathan down for a conversation instead of pinging emails backwards and forwards, she would acknowledge her mistakes and apologise to him, then she would thank him for all the wonderful things he had done throughout their marriage to keep it alive.

As she sauntered back to the hotel, her stomach stuffed to bursting with a generous portion of crêpes smothered in chocolate spread, her spirits lifted like a helium balloon. Every shop, restaurant, café or tabac was gearing up for Christmas – exactly one month away – although the French did not go in for the same explosion of overt consumerism as the UK. She loved their style, their individuality and creativity. Even the colourful windows of their patisseries were works of culinary art that looked more like high-end jewellery shops than bakeries.

She experienced a spasm of regret for not returning to Paris sooner, as Nathan had planned, but she shoved it away. Another lesson she had learned that year was that regret was a useless, negative emotion. She had a great deal to ponder on over the coming months – her job, her career, her choice of home now that the apartment had an offer on it, dating – although probably not men sporting open-toed sandals and full-on carpet beards.

All her decisions from now on would be made based on positive influences.

She touched the back of her hand to the tip of her nose. Freezing. Time to return to the welcome warmth of a brandy at the hotel bar and an early night. She had a crammed agenda the following day, then the evening dinner to get through, after which the rest of her time in the French capital – 'the City of Light' – was her own. She intended to take a trip on the train out to Versailles on Sunday morning, something else that had been on her bucket list for years.

The hotel bar was full of Japanese tourists toasting each other's health with copious amounts of cognac, so Olivia decided to raid the minibar in her room for her nightcap and settled back against the pillows, swirling the amber liquid in her palm. She hadn't recognised the name when Rachel had told her the details of the college friend that she wanted Olivia to have dinner with, which had surprised her because she and Rachel had been inseparable for the whole three years they were at Durham University. Apparently, Charles was a lawyer too, now practising in Paris.

Lucky guy, Olivia thought.

Rachel had assured her the two of them would have plenty in common and urged her to discuss his opinions on the divorce process in France, as well as his views on what contributed to the longevity of French relationships. She doubted Rachel's friend's work schedule was as manic as his London counterparts' though, especially with the French people's love of long leisurely lunches and elegant, laid-back lifestyle.

She clicked off the Louis XIV lamp and the brandy ensured an excellent night's sleep.

Chapter 28

After an early morning caffeine boost from a double espresso, and a warm, flaky *pain au chocolat*, Olivia set out to walk the length of the Champs-Élysées from the gridlocked L'Arc de Triomphe all the way down to the Place de la Concorde. Every metre of the famous boulevard thronged with couples, young and old, linking arms and laughing, happy to be in one of the most beautiful cities in the world. The more astute traveller, who took the time to raise their eyes skyward, was gifted with an impressive view of magnificent Parisian architecture, but Olivia wasn't interested in the buildings that lined the streets; she was on a mission. She hadn't actually admitted it to herself, but there was only one place her purposeful stride was taking her.

The Pont des Arts.

The bridge with thousands and thousands of locks in every shape, colour and size hung from the metal railings, every one of them inscribed with just two names, their keys tossed into the glittering River Seine below, along with a kiss and a wish for an enduring relationship.

What would she find there now? Had the authorities really removed all the locks, including her own silver, heart-shaped lock that had been engraved with their names and the date of their wedding? The answer was an emphatic yes and a wave of sadness swept over her.

But the new improved Olivia refused to succumb to tears. She simply spun on her heels and headed for the Louvre, snapping photos on her phone to send to Hollie and Matteo in their contest of one-upmanship for the best photographic record of a long weekend in two of the most visited capitals of Europe. The last photo from Matteo was of the two of them climbing the crumbling steps to the top of the Colosseum. Next on their itinerary, he had told her, was an afternoon visit to the Trevi Fountain – a sculpture that had taken Olivia's breath away when she had visited with Nathan before they were married. She hoped its splendour would provide the perfect backdrop for Matteo's confession.

At last, the Arc de Triomphe du Carrousel, a smaller version of the one at the other end of the Champs-Élysées, appeared in front of her with the magnificent Louvre Palace beyond. She adored I. M. Pei's controversial glass pyramid, plonked in the central courtyard like an alien landing craft that had been added under the direction of François Mitterrand. Some loved it; others did not. But wasn't the juxtaposition of modern against ancient what the world-renowned museum was all about?

The Louvre was one of the largest and most visited museums in the world so she decided to concentrate on one wing only – the Richelieu Wing. She walked beneath the light-filled atrium through to the marbled entrance foyer, then descended to the lower ground floor where the walls reverberated with the building's chequered past as a fort and then as a royal residence. She spent the remainder of the morning drinking in the exquisite Oriental antiquities before standing motionless in Room 3 in front of 'The Hammurabi Code', a black basalt-carved document from the Babylonian civilisation recording over two hundred laws beneath reliefs of the King and the Sun God. As one of the most ancient collection of laws in the history of humankind, the exhibit held a certain resonance for Olivia.

Next, she moved to the first floor of the Cour Carrée's north wing to the Department of Decorative Arts' much-anticipated reconstruction of an eighteenth-century Louis XIV suite of period rooms. Olivia could do nothing but marvel in silence at the exquisite design skills of the French artisans and cabinetmakers of the time. She allowed her eyes to feast on the gilt-painted wall carvings, luxurious gold and silver Rococo mirrors, intricately sculptured cornices, stately fireplaces, richly detailed tapestries and woven rugs, porcelain and ceramics. She particularly admired the black and gold clocks standing like sentries on two elaborately decorated pedestals.

Finally, she fought her way through the throng of clicking cameras for a glimpse of the 'Mona Lisa', protected by a floor-to-ceiling sheet of security glass, a wooden barrier, a roped-off section for wheelchair users and two menacing-looking security guards. The world-famous portrait surprised Olivia – it was so much smaller and insignificant in the flesh, and there were hundreds of other paintings, sculptures, furnishings and artefacts in the Louvre she preferred. Now, if someone offered her one of those Louis XIV clocks for her mantelpiece …

Despite selecting her ballet pumps that morning, her feet screamed to be rested. Blisters threatened at her heels so she decided to ride the Metro back to the hotel. She calculated that she would have at least an hour of relaxation before she had to dress for dinner at the Jules Verne at eight.

The bathroom was windowless and claustrophobic, but she soaked her aching calf muscles for as long as possible. She had packed her favourite Stella McCartney dress for the restaurant, not wanting to appear as having made no effort, but the elegant outfit demanded heels, which meant taking a taxi over the river to the Eiffel Tower instead of walking across at the Pont de l'Alma.

She blasted her hair with the hotel hairdryer before deciding for the first time that it was long enough to sweep into a chic up-do as favoured by Hollie. She studied the effect in the dressing

..able mirror until, in a flash of defiance, she flung the red dress back onto her bed. Instead, she dragged on a pair of black, wide-legged dress pants, a Phillip Lim Chinese silk top and finished the ensemble off with a long string of imitation pearls that Ruby, Katrina's eldest, had made for her last birthday. As she left her room, she pulled her Aran sweater over her head, shoved her heels into her bag and slipped on her comfortable, patent leather ballet pumps for the walk.

Saturday evening had brought out the Parisians in crowds. All along the quaint cobbled avenues glamorous couples strolled, the collars on their heavy wool overcoats turned up against the cold. She was happy that she could now watch them hug and kiss without the harsh stab of regret and envy; the passage of time had begun to erase the sharp edges of her pain and all that remained was the dull ache of sadness loitering in the harder-to-reach crevices of her heart.

She trotted down Avenue George V towards the river. Every luxury hotel, fashion designer's emporium and restaurant's façade had been illuminated to show off its best architectural features and Paris took on a golden shimmer, which warmed the heart if not the fingertips. Her spirits were notched up even further when giant flakes of soft feathery snow began to descend, spreading a blanket of silence and magic.

Beneath the gargantuan iron-frame legs of the Eiffel Tower, children spun the souvenir carousels of mini plastic replicas of the iconic monument with wide-eyed hope of a keepsake of the visit, their faces filled with the joy the weeks leading up to Christmas inspired. Families, bundled into duffel coats and goose-down jackets to ward off the icy temperatures, ate roasted chestnuts from paper cones and freshly made crêpes dusted in sugar. It might not be the dining experience of the Michelin-starred restaurant halfway to the top of the Eiffel Tower, but to Olivia enjoying a Saturday night in each other's company nibbling on sweet treats was equally, if not more, enjoyable.

As she had come to learn over the last few months, love required nothing else but time together making memories, just as Matteo and Hollie were doing, and her thoughts flipped over to her two best friends partying the weekend away in Rome. Since six o'clock, there had been a complete communications blackout: no posts to Facebook, no photographs uploaded to Instagram, no cheeky texts. Nothing. She had sent a couple of texts and even an email but had received no reply. She hoped all was well and resolved to call one of them just as soon as she could escape from her dinner companion.

Under the skeletal branches of the white-frosted trees, Olivia waited in line for the North elevator, which would deliver her directly to the Jules Verne restaurant. Her mind zoomed back over her last year. She had to admit that if she had taken the time to think about it, she had known the secret to a long and happy marriage all along. She had loved Nathan when they began their relationship and adored him with all her heart on their wedding day and whenever the image of him in the Tiffin Room at Raffles floated across her mind's eye, her heart gave a nip of pain.

And she *still* loved him.

She loved the way his blond hair curled against his collar, the way he scratched at his chin when he was thinking of something complicated, the way he made perfect poached eggs for her on Sunday mornings, the lemony aroma of his favourite cologne. She adored his sense of humour, his friendly personality, his love and acceptance of her family and their circle of friends. She loved how she had always felt a sense of comfort, trust and security in the time they had spent together. Strands of ribbon bearing Nathan's name ran deep within her soul, which she knew would never truly fade despite their separation and the passage of time – they had occupied the same wavelength, just as she had seen in Hollie and Matteo.

Yet Nathan had loved her more; so much more that he had wanted to move their relationship on to the next phase – to have a family with her, to extend and share their love with their children and she was sad that she hadn't been able to see that until this moment.

Nathan knew all about love; it had taken her longer to catch up, but now she got it.

Better late than never.

She sighed as the lift sped up to the Second Level, offering a spectacular night-time view over the City of Light. As soon as the door opened, she darted straight to the restrooms to discard her maiden-aunt sweater, replace her pumps with her stilettos, and fix her make-up and hair until the effect was sort of passable for the type of restaurant she would be dining in. That was another thing she had learned along the way – beauty was only skin deep; what was the point of a smooth, polished exterior when just below the surface were ragged raging waters? Anyway, she wasn't there to impress the guy, just to have a friendly chat about Rachel and the French legal profession – the only two things they had in common.

She checked her watch. Ten minutes past eight. Yet she couldn't resist taking a few extra moments to check her texts again. As she scrolled through the list, relief spread through her veins. One from Hollie and one from Rachel. She selected Hollie's first, anxious to reassure herself that all was well in the warm streets of Rome.

OMG! Matteo loves me! And guess what? I love him too! Why had I never realised? And it's all thanks to you, Liv, and your lessons in love. I'll share all the details tomorrow. Tonight is for the celebration of passionate Italian lerve! Good luck to you!

Olivia's heart sang. Tears threatened to burst their banks, but she refused to meet a stranger at one of the most elegant restaurants in Paris with puffy, red-veined eyes. And what did Hollie mean 'Good luck to you!'?

She was obviously delirious with desire, thought Olivia with a smile, before selecting Rachel's message.

Where are you? He says you're late???

Olivia smiled and texted back.

Okay, okay, bully! I'm just in the ladies at the Jules Verne fixing my lipstick so I'll be out in a minute. But you'll be pleased to know that I've had the epiphany, Rach. "Love" is the answer! "Love" is the reason that marriages endure. Stick that in your paper and nothing else!

Thank God for that! And thank God you've arrived. Now go!

Olivia beamed as a sense of wellbeing flooded through her veins. She twirled a tendril of escaped hair at the side of each cheek, touched up her pink-frosted lip gloss and pushed open the door. The view through the windows was mesmerising. Every hour the initially-intended-to-be-temporary structure of the Eiffel Tower glistened with millions of sparkling fairy lights; a beacon of Parisian evidence that even the temporary, if enough love is lavished upon it, can last a lifetime.

And what a romantic setting for those intending to propose that night? She straightened her shoulders and when the maître d' greeted her and asked her to follow him, she resolved to thoroughly enjoy the evening ahead

Except when he indicated her table next to the window, her whole world tilted on its axis.

Chapter 29

Olivia was rarely lost for words but gobsmacked just about covered it. Her first thought was that her eyes were playing tricks on her, that he couldn't be standing there next to the table overlooking the whole of Paris, staring back at her with that smile, that wonderful, amazing, happy smile that had stayed with her every minute of every day since the moment they had met.

As the shock abated, she realised the maître d' was waiting to help her into her seat and, on trembling legs, with her heart hammering out a symphony of disbelief and confusion, she closed the space between them and slid into the chair opposite him. She opened her mouth to say something, but nothing came out; she had so much to say she didn't know where to start, so instead she simply feasted her eyes on the man sitting in front of her, drinking in his soft grey eyes, the curl of his hair against his collar, but most of all the way he was looking at her, just as he always had – as though she were the only girl in the world.

'Hi, Liv.'

Nathan reached across the table to take her hand, the slight tremor in his fingers belying his nerves as he scoured her face, taking in every detail as if he'd forgotten what she looked like.

She suddenly felt self-conscious, a feeling she had never experienced when she was in Nathan's company. She knew she had changed significantly over the last ten months; her hair was longer, softer, looser, the dark smudges under her eyes had gone, her frown lines had melted away, but the most seismic change of all was that she was a completely different person.

'Hi, Nathan.'

Her voice sounded strange, like it belonged to someone else, and to calm her swirling emotions she took a quick sip of the iced water the waiter had poured for them after handing out the menus. Why was he here? What was he going to say to her? Would it be something that made her heart sing or sent her screaming for the door? And where was Rachel's friend Charles?

She began to feel light-headed at the enormity of the situation, that this might be her one and only chance to hear the answers to the kaleidoscope of questions that had ricocheted around her brain for months, each one leading to another and another and another. But she just couldn't bring herself to be the first to break the magical spell that had transported Nathan to that restaurant in the sky.

What if she looked away, glanced at the menu, asked him what was going on, and he disappeared in a puff of smoke? What if this was some kind of mirage brought on by the culmination of ten long months of intense stress and she was actually staring at the increasingly perplexed face of Rachel's Parisian lawyer friend?

No, that was ridiculous; she wasn't crazy, just shocked.

However, she was inordinately grateful when she heard Nathan inhale a deep breath – after all, he'd had time to prepare for this conversation, time to rehearse what he was going to say when they next saw each other. Nevertheless, she still detected a slight twitch of anxiety at the corner of his lips, a fact that caused her heart to squeeze.

'Thank you for coming, Liv, and I'm sorry about the deception.'

'That's ... that's okay.'

'It wasn't my idea, but I couldn't risk you not turning up.'

Olivia knew Nathan was telling the truth, because for as long as she had known him, he had preferred to take the open, more direct approach to every difficult situation, adamant that clear, honest communication meant less risk of misunderstandings and distrust. Was he right, though? Would she have avoided this meeting? Maybe. Maybe not.

'Would you believe I've called Rachel more times in the last twenty-four hours than the whole of last year? And when eight o'clock came and went and you hadn't shown up, I sent her so many panicky texts that I think she was about to call in the men in white coats.'

'She told me I was meeting a Parisian lawyer friend of hers.'

'I know.'

'Called Charles.'

'I know.'

And then it hit her – Nathan Charles Fitzgerald – the man she had married.

'Ahhh ...'

'Rachel has been amazing, a true friend and an astute counsellor. From the moment that divorce petition was served, I regretted it with every fibre of my body. I wanted to call you, to talk to you, to meet up with you, to ask you to forgive me, but when I called Rachel to ask for her advice, to ask if she would mediate for me, she told me you'd left for Malta and that I had to give you some time to come to terms with life away from Edwards & Co. I argued, I was desperate to hear your voice, frantic to explain, and you've no idea how difficult it was to let your calls go to voicemail – it was one of the hardest things I've ever had to do.'

Nathan scratched at the stubble on his cheeks, his eyes fixed earnestly on hers.

'But Rachel stuck to her guns. She listened to me for hours

pouring my heart out, but she just kept saying the same thing: that it was important for you to complete your journey – both physical and emotional – and only then would she agree to orchestrate a meeting, which of course she's done with her customary precision and timing.'

As the waiter set down their exquisitely presented meals, Olivia took a moment to glance at the other diners in the Jules Verne, all of whom had their own agenda for choosing such a restaurant on that Saturday night in Paris, and all totally oblivious to their neighbour's unfolding story.

'I was in Singapore, you know.'

'Yes, Rachel told me – but only after you'd left. The girl you saw me with at Raffles was Jasmine Wong; she's a commercial property lawyer for one of the big law firms over there and she picked the venue, which I have to say completely threw me. I'd been under the impression that Jasmine and I were there for a business meeting, but when she suggested we extend our discussions at her apartment, I realised that I had made a huge mistake. She's attractive, intelligent, good company, but she's not you, Liv. I'd expected my inaugural drink at the most iconic hotel in the city to be in the Writers' Bar where you and I would drink Singapore Slings whilst chucking peanut shells on the floor and discussing the books of all the famous authors who'd knocked back those cocktails before us!'

Olivia smiled when she remembered them adding that experience to their bucket list.

'Elliot made sure I did all the tourist things.'

'Singapore's an amazing city, but I didn't do a lot of sightseeing.'

'Why not?'

'Because everywhere I went, everything I did, I wanted to share it with you. I loved my job over there, and the people I met were hospitable and welcoming, but all I could think about was what you were doing, where you might be on that crazy round-the-world trip Rachel had sent you on, whether I should just ignore her advice and just give you a call.'

'I wish you had,' whispered Olivia, her voice strained with emotion.

If only she had known how Nathan was feeling, she wouldn't have had to go through the trauma, the searing pain of the loss of their relationship. All those times she had tried to call him, and he had sat and watched his phone ring, then listened to her voicemail. If it hadn't been for Rachel, they could have been having this conversation months ago!

But when she thought about it, she hadn't been ready to talk to Nathan. Rachel was right; she had been on an emotional journey that had led her along a path of self-discovery, of self-knowledge, a journey that had given her an invaluable insight into the person she had become and how it had affected the people who loved her, and then she had been given the priceless gift of learning how to change, to become a better friend, a better daughter, a better partner.

'When my secondment was up, I couldn't wait to get back to the grey, overcast skies of London. I'm not ashamed to admit that I was homesick, and the day I landed at Heathrow airport, I rushed round to the apartment and nearly had a heart attack when I saw the "Sold" board outside. I couldn't stop myself, I hammered on the door, but there was no reply and when I called Rachel she told me you were in Copenhagen – but that was when she told me that she had organised this trip to Paris.'

'She really is devious, our friend.' Olivia smiled, her heart soaring with gratitude that she had someone as wonderful as Rachel fighting her corner, knowing exactly when the time was right to release her from her crazy pursuit of love so she could put what she had learned into practice.

'I made the biggest mistake of my life when I sent you that divorce petition, Liv. At the time, I thought it was the only way I'd be able to have a fulfilling life, a happy home, a family, but

252

these last few months have been complete hell – much worse than last year when we hardly set eyes on each other. I love you, Liv, always have, always will, and if I have to settle for a few crumbs of your time, then I know it will be better than the excruciating pain of missing you every hour of every day.'

'You still love me?'

Nathan nodded; his eyes filled with uncertainty as he waited for her response.

A surge of emotion whooshed into her chest, sending delicious sparkles of joy out to her fingertips. She smiled, which turned into a grin when she understood what Rachel had done for her and Nathan, for her oldest friend's enduring love for them both, and for her determination to ensure that they realised their love for each other too. She had so much to tell him, so many stories to recite of the places she had been, the people she had met, and what she had discovered on her global trek to gather her lessons in love.

But all that could wait, because there was one thing, and one thing only, she wanted him to know right then as their glasses of champagne were replenished by the waiter.

'I love you, too. Nathan. Always have, always will.'

And when Nathan leaned forward to brush his lips against hers, with the same expression on his handsome face as she had carried in her mind's eye all the way around the world and back again, her battered, ragged heart ballooned with happiness.

Chapter 30

Six months later

'*We are gathered here today to witness our friends, Hollie Helen Shaw and Matteo Luigi Cristiani make a solemn commitment to each other ...*'

The congregation had gathered in a tiny, whitewashed hotel overlooking the beach and the eternal expanse of the Atlantic Ocean. It was a perfect setting for a perfect couple, and, in Olivia's opinion, the view from the full-width French windows rivalled any of the spectacular scenery she had enjoyed on her travels around the world the previous year. *Of course* the sun was shining – it was Hollie and Matteo's wedding day!

'*... and you may kiss the bride!*'

When the two best friends kissed, every single one of their guests whistled and whooped and cheered; even little Lottie joined in with a piercing shriek of pleasure as Katrina jiggled the newest addition to their family, resplendent in an ivory silk bridesmaid dress, on her lap. Elliot was first to step forward and congratulate the newly married couple, hugging his sister, and then offering his palm to Matteo before pulling him in for an affectionate shoulder bump.

To Olivia, the look on Matteo's face spoke volumes. Love was worth waiting for. He had, at last, got all he had ever wanted and wished for – those golden coins of happiness had rained down on his life and delivered Hollie as his bride. She had noticed Matteo's father, Antonio, had spent the whole of the short ceremony wiping away tears having confided earlier in the day that he hoped with all his heart that his beloved son and Hollie would have even a fraction of the enduring love he and his wife had enjoyed.

The wedding party filed from the room, pausing to congratulate the ecstatic couple, wishing them well on their life's journey and on their honeymoon along the Amalfi Coast, before they took part in a second wedding celebration organised by Matteo's family in Italy.

'Well, that was a beautiful ceremony, Liv,' declared Rachel, patting her eyes with the huge cotton handkerchief Denise had given her and then tucking her plum-and-apricot-streaked hair behind her ears to display a pair of silver earrings in the shape of horseshoes, which she'd commissioned especially for the June wedding. 'You are a complete natural. I'm sure your services will be in great demand, so I was wondering if I could book you …'

'Not in too much demand, I hope.' Nathan laughed, appearing at Olivia's side, hooking his arm around her shoulder and dropping a kiss on her cheek. 'We've moved down here for a quieter life, although I'm not sure how long *that* will last.'

Nathan gave Olivia a knowing smile and she beamed back at him, her heart bursting with love for the man who made her heart soar. Life was about to get more complicated, but this time it was going to be in a good way, in the best way, and she couldn't wait! They had decided not to announce their news until the following day as they didn't want to steal any of the limelight from Hollie and Matteo, but she had already got her eye on a Moses basket and a little pink elephant in a shop in St Ives, their new hometown where they had invested the money from the sale of their London apartment in a cute stone cottage with a picket fence and honeysuckle growing round the eaves.

As soon as she had got back from Paris, she had resigned from Edwards & Co, and Nathan had arranged to job-share, with most of his work being home-based; his foreign trips were greatly curtailed as his colleague jumped at the chance to spend the company's expenses in a far-flung country.

Life couldn't get any better. It had been an amazing day seeing two of her best friends in the world commit their lives to each other, a celebration that was filled with joy and laughter and all the people she loved the most – even her parents had made the trip from Yorkshire to Cornwall to witness their beloved daughter's first ceremony.

'Thank you, Liv. You are the best friend anyone could ask for.'

Hollie flung her arms around Olivia's neck, radiant and laughing, her white, flapper-style wedding dress perfect for the Cornish summer ceremony. She bent down to hand her freesia-filled bridal bouquet to a delighted Ruby and then linked her arms through Matteo's and Nathan's, indicating for Rachel and Denise to join them, and then calling Elliot and Ying over too. When the whole gang were assembled, Hollie cleared her throat theatrically and, in her best advocate's voice, made her announcement.

'Ladies and gentlemen! Can I have three cheers for Olivia? Hip hip!'

'Hooray!'

'Hip hip!'

'Hooray!'

'Hip hip!'

'Hooray!'

'One wedding ceremony down, only four hundred and ninety-nine to go!'

And the whole wedding party laughed and clapped and cheered again.

For Olivia had taken the first step towards rebalancing the karma of love. From that day forward, she had become the proud owner of a licence to conduct not only her best friend's wedding ceremony but everyone else's, too; anyone who wanted to declare their union to the world with the assistance of the newest Wedding Registrar in the county of Cornwall – Mrs Olivia Jane Fitzgerald.

Acknowledgements

A book is never the product of only one person, so I'd like to extend my grateful thanks to my fabulous editor Charlotte Mursell who helped to make Livvie's story sparkle, and to Anna Sikorska who designed the most fabulous, smile-inducing cover.

Dear Reader,

Thank you so much for taking the time to read this book – we hope you enjoyed it! If you did, we'd be so appreciative if you left a review.

Here at HQ Digital we are dedicated to publishing fiction that will keep you turning the pages into the early hours. We publish a variety of genres, from heartwarming romance, to thrilling crime and sweeping historical fiction.

To find out more about our books, enter competitions and discover exclusive content, please join our community of readers by following us at:

@HQDigitalUK

facebook.com/HQDigitalUK

Are you a budding writer?
We're also looking for authors to join the HQ Digital family!
Please submit your manuscript to:

HQDigital@harpercollins.co.uk.

Hope to hear from you soon!